Lust

A FORBIDDEN AGE GAP ROMANCE

SKYLER MASON

Editing by Heidi Shoham

Cover Design by Cover Couture

www.bookcovercouture.com

For Sierra Simone, who wrote the book that gave me the courage to write this one.

And for making men of the cloth sexy.

Chapter One

B randon

Mariana pulls her hair into a knot at the top of her head, revealing her long neck. I don't remember admiring a woman's neck before, but hers is so delicate and graceful. I'll bet that pretty skin is as velvety soft as a flower petal.

Fuck. Why am I sitting here gawking at my best friend's youngest daughter in the middle of a family barbecue?

I never should have started courting her older sister. It felt wrong the moment Hector asked me to do it. Beautiful as Sofia is, I haven't felt that special spark with her, and she's too young for me.

Mariana is much, much too young for me.

My damn celibacy vow must be fucking with my head after three years of not touching a woman. I should have known waiting until marriage was taking it too far. It's not like I believe sex outside of marriage is wrong. My goal was to eliminate distractions and narrow my focus on building my church, and I'd only have to wait until I found a wife, after all.

I assumed I'd have found her by now.

"Brandon," Hector says, breaking me out of my reverie. He draws his brows together. "I need to talk to you about something."

I frown, shifting in my chair. Does he sense the direction of my thoughts? I hope he didn't catch me staring at Mariana after she just stripped down to her bikini.

"Do we need to go somewhere private?" I ask.

He shakes his head, his gaze drifting to Sofia. She's standing in the middle of the pool, a small child in her arms. She's always playing with one of her nieces or nephews at these family events. Dread clamps around my chest. She's so good with children. It's her dream to be a mother. She told me on one of our first dates.

It was a clear message.

"I wouldn't be here right now if my intentions weren't serious."

"How are things going with the two of you?" Hector asks, his voice dropping to a whisper.

I take a sip of my Corona, giving myself a chance to think of a reply that won't sound half-hearted. "I'm taking it slow. I still feel like she's too young."

He huffs out a laugh, patting my back. "You don't think you're a little too old to be single, brother?"

Brother. What he means is "brother in Christ," but the word holds so much more warmth coming from him. Hector has been like an older brother ever since he brought me to God four years ago. Now that I'm leading what's become one of the biggest churches in Santa Barbara, every Christian in my acquaintance seems to be in too much awe of me for real friendship. Aside from my younger brother, Hector is the only true confidant I have, which is why I did him this favor. I started "courting" his daughter, as he calls it, against my better judgment.

I set down my beer, leaning back in my chair. "I just don't

want to rush into anything. I know she's serious about settling down and starting a family."

Hector nods. "You're damn right she is. She'll be thirty in September."

I exhale a deep breath. Ever since Sofia's broken engagement three years ago, Hector's been eager to see her married. In a world where women often get married in their early twenties, it must be hard for Sofia to be constantly reminded of her singlehood.

"That's still eight years younger than me."

He waves a hand. "Age differences don't mean anything after thirty. I think it's time for you to settle down too." His lips quirk. "A forty-year-old single pastor. You're like an exotic bird."

I snort before taking a sip of my beer. "I'm thirty-eight, but thanks for aging me up. The church needs to adapt to the times. People shouldn't get married if they don't want to."

Hector chuckles, shaking his head. "A liberal pastor. Even more exotic. But I agree with you to some extent. Marriage isn't for everyone."

"Exactly," I say, relieved by his concession. Hector still attends the evangelical church where I met him, which is much more conservative than the one I lead now. He and I don't always see eye to eye on issues, but at least he tries to be open-minded.

"Being a pastor's wife isn't for everyone either," I say. "I have to be even more careful now than ever."

"You don't think Sofia would make a good pastor's wife?"

"I certainly haven't asked her."

Hector's gaze finds Sofia as she lifts her baby niece into the air and gently tosses her in the pool. "Look at her with little Ava," he says. "She was born to be a mother. She was like that with Mari when she was a baby, even though she was a little girl herself."

I let out a long sigh. There's no convincing him when he gets into these moods. Like many Christian fathers, Hector seems to focus most of his parental anxiety on his daughters. He's much more relaxed with his oldest son. He's worried that Sofia's biological clock is ticking, that she's going to miss her dream of becoming a mother. No encouragement on my part—no deepening of my voice to sound like an authoritative pastor and telling him to trust in God's timing—has made a difference.

He treats me without reverence, which is one of the things I love most about him.

My gaze is drawn to Mariana's bikini-clad form as she makes her way from the pool. She's gotten thinner since I last saw her, and she was already lean. Maybe the stress of finishing college has taken a toll on her?

I quickly avert my gaze as she heads toward us, hoping she didn't notice me staring.

"Mari," Hector scolds. "Get a towel. You're half naked in front of your pastor."

Mari steps into my view as she grabs a towel from one of the patio chairs. She shoots me a cheeky smile. "Am I causing you to stumble in your faith, Pastor?"

My gut clenches, and liquid heat pulses through my veins. I try to force a smile. Hector is now scolding her, but his words are muffled in my head, as if coming from far away.

How is it possible that I'm getting hard? She's a full-grown woman, yes, but she's Mariana. I met her when she was twenty years old. I'm old enough to be her damn father.

"I would never blame a woman's body for the state of my faith." I'm surprised how even my voice sounds.

Mariana's eyes light up. She's so expressive. Every little thought and emotion plays out in those dark, sparkling eyes. "See, Dad. This is why you need to start going to New Morning Church. Pastor Brandon isn't sexist."

Hector scowls at her. "I don't like you implying that my pastor *is* sexist. And I'm not going to a church pastored by a man I've seen drunk as a skunk and stripped down to his boxers." Hector pats me hard on the back, and I snort. He loves bringing up embarrassing stories from before I committed my life to God, back when he was trying to minister to me.

Mariana's dark gaze meets mine before falling to my chest. "I'll bet that was quite a sight."

My whole body grows hot.

"Mari!" Hector scolds.

I take a breath to gather myself, hoping that my face doesn't look as flushed as it feels. This is what Mariana does. I know this. She's the baby of the family through and through. She often says mildly shocking things just to get a rise out of her dad.

Brazenly flirting with me is one of her favorite pastimes. It's never fazed me. She always seemed like a rebellious teenager, even as a twenty-four-year-old woman.

Today, she actually feels like the woman she is.

I don't like it.

Mariana pats my shoulder, and electricity shoots down my arm. "He knows I'm teasing."

Of course she's teasing.

So why is it suddenly getting to me? Why am I now imagining a seductive lilt to that husky voice of hers?

Hector's wife, Ana, makes her way to the patio, a frown marring her face. She grabs Mariana's arm and pulls her through the slider door to the kitchen. "No more sparkling wine for Mariana," she says, and though her tone is light, I know she's about to scold her youngest. They all still seem to see Mariana as much younger than she is, a consequence of her being the baby.

I thought I saw her that way, too.

When did that change?

Hector chuckles as he turns to me. "That's our Mari. You can never predict what she's going to say." His voice grows hushed. "She's going to be a powerhouse when she finally comes back to the Lord. She's going to use that passion to do great things."

I look away so that he can't read my feelings on my face. I can't give him words of encouragement because they would ring hollow. For as long as I've known him, he's been praying for Mariana to come back to God.

The truth is that I don't think all of us were meant to be Christians.

"What if you... I don't know." Hector scratches the back of his head. "Do you think you could talk to her?"

I don't have to ask what he means. This isn't the first time he's asked me to give Mariana pastoral counseling.

"I'm not sure what more I can say. She comes to New Morning sometimes. She hears my messages."

He shakes his head sharply. "She's a Sunday morning Christian. She only goes to church for show. To please me and Ana." His jaw tightens. "She's not on fire for God."

Because she's an atheist. I want to tell him, but I can't. Mariana swore me to secrecy when she told me several months ago. We were on a walk at an outdoor party—the sound of the ocean made it impossible for anyone to overhear us—and yet she lowered her voice when she said "atheist," like it was a dirty word.

To people in our world, it is, and it made my heart ache that she trusted me enough to tell me. I promised myself I would never betray that trust.

"I'll let her know she can talk to me about her struggles, but I'm not going to push her."

He smirks, his gaze drifting back to Sofia. "Because you might be her brother-in-law someday. You want to make a good impression."

I grit my teeth, shooting him what I hope is a playful eye roll. He smiles back, and I resist the urge to let out a groan.

My pulse is only beginning to slow to a steady beat, and it's not because of the woman I'm courting.

Chapter Two

M ariana

Brandon's voice is lower and huskier during Saturday evening service. I can't be the only one in the congregation who imagines lying naked with him in the middle of the night.

Not during sex. This is the voice he would use just after. He'd be lying there with his tatted forearms bent, resting his head in his palms. The white sheet would just barely cover his muscular hips. Those warm, dark eyes would probe into mine, welcoming me to tell him all of my secrets.

I would too. He's so warm and inviting and nonjudgmental. I can only imagine how much kinder he'd be after I showed him with my tongue how much I—

Heat washes over me when those dark eyes of his meet mine in real time. I shift in my seat, my heart racing. Why do I always feel like he can read my mind?

I can't let him see that he's unsettled me.

When I smile slowly, his eyes widen minutely, and he licks his lips before looking away.

I glance over at my sister, and thankfully her attention is fixed on the Bible on her lap as she highlights a verse.

God, I'm so childish. Here I am trying to taunt Brandon right in the middle of church when I've been doing everything in my power to reconcile my relationship with Sofia. Why does rebellion always rise within me whenever I'm near him?

Not that Sofia minds when I flirt with Brandon. She knows he's not into her, even though Dad is pushing for them to be together. Brandon treats both me and Sofi like little kids. She was shocked when he asked her out, but she went along with it anyway. She's too pragmatic about her current situation to care why he really did it.

He pities her. Just like everyone else in this damn community. All because of her broken engagement. She's been so hurt over it for so long that she's now almost thirty and still single—an old maid in the evangelical community.

"As we close today," Pastor Brandon says, those big arms gripping the pulpit, "let's remember that our faith calls us to actively care for the poor in our communities. This week, I challenge us all to step out of our comfort zones. Let's be walking examples of Christ's love in a world that desperately needs hope and compassion." He smiles. "Amen."

Applause breaks out, and I repress a smile as I glance around the congregation. I don't remember my childhood pastor getting this kind of a reaction after a sermon. How funny humans are, unable to separate physical beauty from something that is supposed to be spiritual and not of this earth.

Sofia smiles at me. "Let's go see what he needs us to do."

I grit my teeth as she walks proudly toward him. There's possessiveness in that walk of hers. She knows Brandon's not into her, but she's not above showing off to the world that she landed the "hot pastor." It wouldn't annoy me if I didn't know the real reason behind it.

8

She wants her ex-fiancé, Finn, to find out they're courting. She wants him to learn through the Christian gossip chain that on Saturday nights, she acts like the pastor's wife in a church led by a man who looks like an Avenger.

She wants Finn to regret abandoning her.

As we make our way through the crowd, Brandon steps down from the stage and is instantly surrounded by a group of young people—mostly pretty women—and I can't fight the smile rising to my lips.

How could he not enjoy this? Dad constantly teases him about his near celebrity status in this town. New Morning didn't become one of the largest churches in Santa Barbara within two years because of Brandon's preaching abilities. Yet, he always responds stoically to dad's jibes, like it's never even occurred to him that he's gorgeous.

Nothing on this earth is more annoying than a pastor with false humility.

Maybe that's how I've justified flirting with him all these years when I know how much it flusters him.

As soon as we get close, Brandon turns toward Sofia and smiles. He walks over to her and presses a light kiss against her cheek. His lips are stiff—almost tucked in—but if Sofia notices, she doesn't show it.

"What do you need us to do?" she asks him.

"Why don't you start by making sure we haven't run out of coffee and cookies?"

She smiles before walking away, and Brandon's gaze drifts to me. A tingle runs down my spine. I must be vain for thinking he's as affected by my presence as I am by his, but sometimes he gives me an intense look that cuts right into my belly.

He smiles. "Mariana."

My full name. Always my full name, and the undulating syllables are like music on his lips.

"My favorite atheist," he says, and a flush rises to my cheeks.

My eyes dart toward the coffee station at the back of the auditorium, and I release a breath when I see Sofia arranging napkins.

"Oh, I'm sorry," Brandon says, following my gaze to Sofia. "Did I say that too loud?"

"No." I tuck a strand of hair behind my ear. "I'm just paranoid."

"It's okay." His eyes hold a smile. "I'm still your pastor, even if you're a...you-know-what. You can be paranoid around me."

The tension leaves my shoulders. It's moments like these when I wish he weren't a pastor. He's so damn warm and kind. I'd probably have a serious crush if I weren't convinced he wants to fix me. Just like the rest of my family does.

"I shouldn't have brought it up in public," he says. "You told me in confidence."

Ah, yes. I told him on the beach at Livvy's engagement party, when those beautiful dark eyes were turning my head to mush. I would have told him anything.

"It's okay." I wave a hand. "I'm sure my mom and dad already know, even if they're in denial. It's Sofia I'm really worried about."

Brandon frowns. "'I find that surprising."

"She's more sensitive than everyone else, and she and I... We haven't been as close since she and Finn broke up." I shoot him a knowing look. "I never liked him."

Brandon smiles faintly. "I think maybe you were onto something with that guy."

I huff out a laugh, glancing at the back of the auditorium to make sure Sofia is out of earshot. "Yeah, when he cheated on her a month before their wedding, I thought something might be a little off."

He sets his hand on my shoulder, and a pleasant shiver rolls over my skin. He's so close I can smell his musky cologne. "Sometimes we blame the person who saw it coming. We superstitiously feel like they caused it. But Sofia's a reasonable person. She'll let it go when the hurt wears off."

"When?" In my frustration, my voice is louder than I intended. "It's been almost three years. And I know what he did was absolutely devastating—leaving her and having a baby with someone else—but why is she still pining for him?" I shake my head. "I would have seduced one of his best friends, or maybe his dad, and then sent Finn the bill for all the lost wedding deposits."

Brandon bursts into laughter, shaking his head. "I can't believe you just said that in the house of God."

I smile sheepishly, as he continues to laugh. Fuck, it feels so good when he looks at me this way. His austerely handsome face is so gentle when he's delighted.

And his delight does strange things to my insides.

As his smile fades, his gaze lingers on my face. "Even if your relationship is strained, you're still here with her." His voice is hushed. "You're here almost every week, even though you don't believe in God. That's real sisterly love."

My throat grows tight. I wish she saw it that way, but to her, attending church should be a given for anyone. It isn't a sign that I love her, that I'd do anything to make things right between us.

"Coming to this church isn't that bad," I say. "I love hearing you talk about the ancient world. It's fascinating, and compared to other pastors, you don't pretend like the Bible was written for a twenty-first century audience."

"Thank you. That means a lot, especially coming from someone with a history degree. Our conversations are always...interesting, Mariana."

My heart pounds in my chest. Oh, when he says my name with that hushed, pastor voice...

"Thank you," I say. "I find them interesting too."

And I find you delicious.

He steps closer to me, his eyes boring into mine. "You weren't asking for guidance, but I know your lack of faith is a struggle, if only because of the awkward position it puts you in with your family. I'm always here if you need someone to talk to. About anything."

11

My stomach drops like a rock. Here we are again.

Dad must have talked to him.

Ministry. It's always about ministry. No one in the church community has any genuine interest in me or what I have to say. It's all about fixing my broken pieces even when I've always felt whole just as I am.

"Do you need me to take vacuum duty tonight?" Sofia asks from behind me, making me jump.

"I think we're fine," Brandon says. "Let's just get the chairs stacked and call it a night. I'll make sure the vacuuming gets done after second service tomorrow."

Sofia sets her hands on her hips, pretending to frown. "We are absolutely not leaving here tonight without vacuuming."

Brandon frowns. "I don't want to put you out. You both already do so much."

A look flashes in Sofia's eyes so quickly that it would be indiscernible to anyone else. But this is my big sister, and I know her better than even our own parents.

She hates that he lumped me in the same category as her, as if I help as much as she does.

Because even though she won't admit it to herself, she knows I'm not really a Christian, and someone who doesn't believe in God doesn't deserve the honor of being the Mary to her Martha.

"The whole reason I'm here is to help you with the things that don't normally get done," Sofia says. "As a matter of fact, I wanted to ask if you need any PA help this week. I have Wednesday off, and I'd be happy to fill in."

Brandon shuts his eyes and runs a palm over his forehead. "That's very kind of you, but to be honest, I'm not sure." He smiles sheepishly. "Not having a PA means I'm also in charge of scheduling, and I haven't made a schedule for the volunteers yet." He chuckles. "You'd never think I once owned a business with the mess I am right now."

I frown. "What happened to your PA?"

"She's on maternity leave," Sofia says, smiling. "And Pastor Brandon thinks he can do it all."

He shakes his head. "I miscalculated. The problem with volunteers is it's a hassle to arrange and schedule everything. It becomes a job of its own. And Daisy normally does so much more than typical PA tasks. She has a bachelor's in church history, so she helps me with sermons. I didn't realize how much I needed her until she went on leave."

Sofia's eyes grow wide. "Mari has a history degree."

Heat creeps into my neck. Where is she going with this?

Brandon licks his lip. "Yeah, I know."

"And she's been looking for some kind of volunteer or internship position before she starts graduate school." Sofia looks at me. "This is perfect. You can fill in for Daisy's last few months off. Mom and Dad would be ecstatic."

My mouth falls open. Why the hell does she want me to do this? She knows I'm not suited for...

Oh my God. She planned this.

My gaze rushes over Brandon's face, but he looks just as baffled as I am. Maybe he's not in on her scheme.

But Dad is. Maybe even Mom too.

And how can I say no? In the two months since I graduated, Mom and Dad have been paying my portion of the rent on the apartment Sofia and I share, which they said they wouldn't do unless I found an internship or was volunteering somewhere. Not to mention the fact that they had to fund an extra two years of college after I changed my major, which my dad loves to remind me of whenever he wants something from me.

"I'd love to help," I say, my voice strained.

Something strange and unreadable flashes in Brandon's eyes. He clears his throat. "I don't want to put you out. It's a lot of hours to work without getting paid."

"It'll look great on my resume." I force a smile. "We'll call it an internship. Make sure you throw in some theology education, Pastor."

SKYLER MASON

His gaze drops to my mouth, and my stomach flutters. I wasn't even trying to flirt with him, though I usually only call him Pastor as a tease when I want to fluster him.

"Well..." He swallows. "I guess it's the perfect situation."

Sofia grins. "Yay! Mom and Dad will be overjoyed when they find out."

My stomach plummets. I'm playing right into their plans to "fix" me.

Which means they're all bound for yet another disappointment.

"When can she start?" Sofia asks.

"Well..." Brandon swallows. "We have volunteers for the position this week, but I suppose I could tell them they aren't needed anymore. Would you be able to come in Monday?"

Was it just my imagination, or did his voice quiver a little bit? I smile. "I'll be here."

As we walk to the car, I turn to Sofia. "Did Mom and Dad ask you to volunteer me?"

She shrugs without looking my way, "So what if they did? It's a good opportunity for you to learn some church history."

Since she refuses to meet my eyes, I take the opportunity to roll them as dramatically as I can. This is always how it is with my family. Being the youngest means they shamelessly try to take control of my life whenever they see fit. None of them have any clue what qualifies as a good internship for my concentration, and now I'm locked into one I don't really need.

But at least I'll be seeing Pastor Brandon every day.

14

Chapter Three

B randon

Why am I uneasy?

This is a perfect situation for what Hector asked of me. I'll have plenty of alone time with Mariana to talk about her struggles.

Alone time.

Fuck. I'm not actually afraid of being alone with my best friend's daughter, am I? Even if my body seems to be reacting to her against my will, that's only because I've been celibate for too long. Celibacy won't make me a slave to my lust. I'm not in danger of mauling her and bending her over my office desk.

And I won't imagine it, either.

When I pull up into my driveway, the balcony light is on. Warmth washes over me, easing my frayed nerves. Ethan is here. He must be studying on the balcony.

I won't be coming home to a big empty house.

I step inside my front door, and I'm greeted by the sterile scent of the tile cleaner. The housekeeper must have come by this morning. Damn it. How does this house still smell like it was just built and freshly painted when I've lived here for ten years?

This is the problem with buying the big house before you start a family. It feels so empty while I'm waiting to fill it. I thought at the ripe age of thirty-eight I'd be coming home to the sound of children's voices and a wife to kiss.

I lived a different life when I bought this house. I owned a business. I made more money in a month than I do in a year now. Starting a family was the next logical step.

Too bad I was a selfish hedonist who sought constant new partners. I never had any relationships that lasted longer than a few months. It turned out that wanting to start a family and actually doing the work to build one were two different things.

"Hey, bro," I say after walking through the slider door.

Ethan looks up from his laptop, his eyes sleepy. "Hey." His voice is raspy, as if from disuse.

I grab a beer from the patio bar. "Pulling all-nighters or what?"

He groans. "I've barely slept at all the last two days. All my midterms landed on this week. And we have the Sierra game on Friday. I'm going to be sleepwalking."

I smile. "More like sleep route running."

"Exactly." He shakes his head. "It's going to be a nightmare."

I pat his back. "You'll get through it. You always do."

Ethan leans back into his chair, running a hand through his already somewhat disheveled hair. "I think I need to nap for a couple hours before I pull my all-nighter. Can you wake me up before you go to bed?"

I take a sip of my beer. "Sure thing. I put those blackout shades in the guest room just for you."

He smiles faintly, and I can't help but read a little pity in his expression. He's caught on to my loneliness these past few weeks.

16

Just as he makes it to the slider door, he turns to me. "Was Sofia at church tonight?

I plant a smile on my face. "She was."

Ethan shakes his head. "I can't believe you still haven't even kissed her. She's a bombshell."

My smile threatens to falter. I can't believe I don't have the desire to kiss her pretty mouth either. He's right that she's a beautiful woman, and she has that naïve sweetness that would have called to the wickedness within me years ago. By now, I would have faked warmth and sincerity, using my velvety voice to coax her into my bed ten times over. I'd be ready to find my next conquest.

I was a bastard before God transformed me.

"I'm just being careful," I say. "The Hernandezes are too important to me to be flippant about this. If I hurt her, it could get ugly."

He smirks. "Hector would kill you."

I grunt. "Yes, he would."

And I would lose the only family I have other than Ethan.

He leans up against the glass door, his eyes narrowing. "Do you think maybe you want to get married so badly because you want to have what Hector has? The big family barbecues and the kids running around."

I take a sip of my beer. "Who says I want to get married *badly*?"

He shoots me a skeptical look that makes my face heat.

"If I were going to get serious with Sofia," I say, "which Hector seems to want, I need to give her time. She's still hung up on her ex-fiancé. Well...Mariana implied it tonight after the service."

His eyes widen. "Mari was at church?"

I nod. "She comes sometimes. With Sofia and or her friend Livvy."

He smiles, shaking his head. "She's who I would go after. Sofia is obviously gorgeous, but Mari... She's something else."

Heat washes over my skin, and my teeth clench of their own will. Where is this irritation with Ethan coming from? Sure, I'm protective of both Mariana and Sofia. But this is my little brother. He's not a threat.

Fuck.

God, please say lust isn't fucking with my head again.

"She's going to start working at the church," I say. "Sofia volunteered her to fill in for Daisy."

Ethan frowns. "Mari? Why would she do that? She doesn't seem like she's that into church."

"I think Hector might have asked Sofia to volunteer her. It all felt a little staged when she brought it up tonight."

He shakes his head. "Why are they so pushy with her? When Hector was trying to minister to you, he went out to the bars with you. He was around when you were getting drunk and taking women home. He met you where you were. He wasn't pushy at all."

I shrug. "I'm not his daughter. It's different when fear is involved. He even asked me to talk to her."

"Well, you're good at that. You could actually make her see how good God is."

"No," I say sharply. "I don't want to do that. Christianity isn't for everyone."

Ethan stays quiet for a while. He doesn't agree with me on this topic, I know, but he's too much in awe of my position in the church and my education to argue with me.

"What are you going to do?" he eventually asks.

I shrug. "I'm going to use the time to talk to her, but I won't try to convert her. I'll let her vent."

He chuckles. "That'll be entertaining. She's fun when she gets all fired up."

Damn right she is. Those dark eyes of hers sparkle, and she gets that cute little mischievous smile. Then she calls me "pastor" in that low, sultry voice.

Fuck.

I can't think this way. Not if I'm going to help her.

God, help me to see her as I did before. Give me back those protective instincts that weren't even slightly carnal.

I can't lust for her. Not if I'm going to act as her pastor.

Chapter Four

M ariana

"The pencil skirt will be less comfortable," Livvy says, "but you look like a badass CEO, and I feel like you'll be more confident than if you wear something looser."

"I want to look professional." I narrow my eyes at myself in the mirror and lower my chin, trying my best to look like a badass. "He might be my future brother-in-law."

Livvy snorts. "It's so weird that he actually listened to your dad and asked her out. Anyone with eyes can see he's attracted to you."

I shoot her a skeptical look in the mirror. Livvy and her sister, Vanessa, have been telling me for months that they think Brandon has a crush on me, which is utterly ridiculous. He treats me like a little kid.

Livvy grins. "How much do you want to bet he's going to do a double take when he sees you in this outfit?

I flutter my eyelids as I pull my hair into a tight bun at the back of my neck. "He'd be so grossed out if he heard you say that. He thinks he's my second dad. And not my daddy in a hot way, though I would love it if he spanked me."

Livvy giggles. "He's so hot it's obscene. Sometimes I look at him up at the pulpit and can't believe he's my pastor." Her smile fades. "But I disagree with you about the dad thing. He's friends with my dad, too. He definitely doesn't look at Vanessa or me the way he looks at you."

"Or Sofia, which is strange. Since he's, you know, dating her."

Livvy's dark eyes probe into mine through the mirror. "She's stalking Finn on Instagram right now. I could see it over her shoulder when I came in."

A weight pulls at the center of my chest. There's no mistaking the concern in Livvy's voice.

"I think it's normal." My voice is not quite steady. "She hasn't dated at all since Finn. We tend to stay hung up on the last person we were in a relationship with."

Livvy frowns. "She's in a relationship with Brandon."

"They're *courting*," I correct. "That's what Mom and Dad call it, at least. And Sofi."

Her nose wrinkles. "It's so weird how she's still caught up in purity culture. She seems too levelheaded for it."

"She doesn't question things the same way we do. Plus, she's impatient to get married, and purity culture speeds up the process. Saving yourself until marriage means a quick engagement."

"Not with Brandon, if that's what she's hoping for. He doesn't even believe sex outside of marriage is wrong."

A naughty smile tugs at my lips. "What a bummer for her that *she* thinks it's wrong. Can you imagine what sex with Brandon would be like? He was kinky before he became a pastor. I'm certain of it."

Livvy slaps her palm over her face, and her chest shakes with repressed laughter. "Oh, Mari. You're his intern now. What's more kinky than that?"

I put one finger over my lips and gesture with my head at my open bedroom door. "If Sofi hears us, she'll tell my dad. I need them to think I'm serious about this job."

Livvy wrinkles her nose. "It was so shady that they did this to you. It feels like an ambush."

I rub the bit of gloss I applied around my lips. "It'll look good on my resume."

Livvy frowns. "You could have found something much more relevant to your concentration."

I shrug. "But I haven't yet, and I'm starting school in a couple months. At least this'll keep my parents happy."

She's quiet for a moment. "I feel like you do that a lot. Things you don't feel like doing but keep your parents happy."

My throat grows tight, and I look away from Livvy. Her voice is so gentle. Her words are free of accusation. She's genuinely concerned.

"Alright," I say to change the subject. "Let's see what Sofi thinks of my outfit."

Livvy smiles sadly, because she knows me well. She knows I'm not in the mood to discuss my fraught relationship with my family. As we walk into the kitchen, Sofia slams her phone on the table.

Ah, she wants to hide that she was looking at Finn's Instagram.

"How do I look?" I ask her.

Her expression is dull as she runs her gaze from the neck of my button-up shirt to the hem of my pencil skirt. "That skirt is too tight. Remember you're working for a church."

She says "church" with so much emphasis, I have to clench my teeth to keep myself from snarling at her.

This is just how it's been between us lately. She's utterly dismissive and sometimes just straight up mean.

I run my palms down the fabric on my thighs. "It's not like I have any curves to speak of."

Livvy glares at Sofia, and my heart clenches. My bestie always has my back. She's been more upset at Sofia's treatment of me than I have these past several months.

"New Morning isn't like the church we grew up in," Livvy says, her voice gentle but with a hint of steel in it.

Sofia keeps her eyes fixed on her spoon. "I still think it's too tight."

Livvy shoots me an irritated look, and I turn away to roll my eyes without Sofia seeing.

"Well, there's nothing I can do about it now. I'll be late if I change."

"You better get going then," Sofia says. "It's really important to Mom and Dad that you do well today."

I inhale a steady breath to calm my pulse. What bullshit that they all orchestrated this behind my back and have absolutely no remorse.

I hate being the baby of the family.

"I'll make sure I do you all proud," I say, unable to keep the sarcasm out of my voice. "Livvy, want to walk me out?"

Livvy's expression tells me she's moments away from giving Sofia a piece of her mind, and I can't have that. Not when I want Sofia to be proud of me, even though I know that I should have more dignity and expect her to meet me halfway as we bridge the chasm between us.

But she doesn't feel the depth of it, and that's the problem. She doesn't need me like I need her.

It sucks.

Brandon

I had an epiphany this morning.

This sudden lust for Mariana is nothing extraordinary. It's embedded in my genes. This must be exactly what it's like for my dad. This is why he's now had three wives and countless affairs.

He's hit with lust and then immediately succumbs to it. As with all intense emotions, it fades quickly, and he's on to the next conquest.

As much as I'm loath to admit it, I have a part of him within me.

Unlike him though, I won't succumb to lust. I may have been a slave to my desires before I found God, just like my worthless father, but now I have a higher purpose. I have a guiding light to pull me from my darker impulses. Having fleeting thoughts about Mariana is beyond my control, but they won't guide my actions.

I need time, though.

I can't start ministering to her alone in my office until this lust starts to lose its potency, which given my old habits and need for novelty, will probably be any day.

Until then, I need to keep my distance from her as much as I can. She's a sharp, watchful girl. Socially intuitive. I can't give her the opportunity to pick up on the direction of my thoughts, not if I want her to feel comfortable opening up to me.

There's a vacant office at the other end of the church. Sure, it might seem odd to put my personal assistant that far away from me, but I can give Mariana research-related tasks. It's the perfect solution.

She'll get the internship she needs for her resume, and I'll have the space to let whatever this is fade. I won't be constantly surrounded by her dancing eyes and naughty smile.

Fuck. I don't like thinking of her this way.

I'm startled when my receptionist, Harper, peeks into my office and smiles. "Mari just arrived."

I nod. "Send her in."

A moment later, Mariana steps inside my office, and my gut clenches. Her hair is swept up, revealing her swanlike neck. She's wearing a formfitting skirt that hugs the flare of her hips and those toned thighs.

I've seen her in tight clothes before, damn it. I've seen her in a bikini. Why is my body reacting this way now?

"I have some things for you to fill out before you get started," I say, hating how husky my voice sounds.

She smiles as she walks over to my desk, stopping only a few feet away. She smells so damn good.

Why have I never noticed the way she smells before?

"Since it's a volunteer position," I say, "there isn't a whole lot to fill out. Just this form right here, and then—" I flip the page over "—sign and date on the back."

"Got it." She smiles as she grabs the paper from my hand. She glances at the two couches at the front of my office, and it's only when she perches her hip on the edge of my desk that I realize my mistake.

Damn it. I forgot to get her a clipboard, so now she's forced to stay at my desk to sign the papers. She's so fucking close. I can almost feel the heat radiating from her body.

"I have to go check on something," I say. "I'll be back in a few minutes."

She frowns before nodding, and I rush out of the office, my heart pounding in my chest. When I make it outside, I run my cold hands over my hot face.

What is wrong with me? This is Mariana. I'm around her all the time. I've never been this aware of her before today.

I'm psyching myself out. That's what this is. I'm not used to thinking about her this way, and it's making me self-conscious when I shouldn't be. It's not like I'm going to lose control and maul her, pin her up against my bookshelf and pound myself inside her.

Fuck. Now I'm picturing it.

After a few minutes, I muster up the courage to walk back into the office. I clear my throat. "I have an office set up for you. Right this way."

Mariana follows me through the hallway, and her scent washes over me yet again.

I wish I had never made that celibacy vow. Why couldn't I have promised God I'd be celibate for a year? That would have been plenty of time to focus on my new role as a pastor. There was no need to wait until I find the woman I want to marry, especially when that might never happen for all I know.

I need a woman soon. A woman who's not Mariana to purge me of these unwanted thoughts.

Maybe I need to spend some time in prayer about what I should do about that celibacy vow.

"Where is this office?" Mariana asks, her voice full of surprise.

It must seem odd to her that I'm putting her, my temporary personal assistant, this far away from me.

"It's our old media coordinator's office, and it's one of the biggest in the building." It's not a lie, but I wish I could have said it with more conviction.

"Here it is," I say, gesturing through the doorway. Mariana walks inside and looks around the area.

"You should have plenty of room," I say.

She frowns. "There's more than enough room, but..." Those piercing dark eyes meet mine. "Why don't I have Daisy's office?"

I avert my eyes from hers. "I wanted to give you a good experience as an...intern. You said you wanted to learn theology."

"You think I'll learn theology from you better all the way over here?"

It sounds so ridiculous when she puts it that way, and I wish I had thought of a better excuse. "I figured you wouldn't be bothered so much with the noise. You can read articles and do research for my sermons."

She nods slowly, but I sense that she's still perplexed.

"Well," I start, needing to get the hell out of here. "Daisy put everything you need to know in here." I hand Mariana a three-ring plastic binder. "You should be set for the next few hours. Do you need help with that?" I gesture at the computer.

Mariana glances at the computer, then back at me. "Do I need help...turning it on?"

I smile to hide the real reason for the question. That

computer is an old piece of shit, and she actually might need help turning it on. But fuck, I can't tell her that.

Then she'll know I put her in here for no good reason.

Those big eyes grow heavy-lidded. "I think I've got it covered, *Pastor*." She says "Pastor" with that irreverent cheekiness that's always amused me.

Not anymore. Now it resurrects dangerous memories of my wicked past. I want to use my authoritative pastor voice to command her onto her knees.

Fuck, I need to get out of here.

With effort, I smile. "Let me know if you need anything. Harper can help you too if I'm busy."

Just as I make it to the door, her voice halts me. "Oh, no."

My stomach sinks. "What happened?"

"The computer just shut off."

Why didn't I anticipate this? "Yeah, it gets overheated pretty easily. Hold the power button down for several seconds."

She follows my instruction, and nothing happens.

"You kind of have to...jam your finger in there."

Still nothing.

"This thing is a little...old." I walk over to the desk. She scoots her chair aside to make room for me, but she's not nearly far enough away for comfort. I lean down to press the monitor button, jamming my finger in hard and counting to ten. But as her scent washes over me, the numbers in my mind fade into the abyss.

She smells like something tropical. Beach spray, I think an old girlfriend called it. The smell of tanning oil and orchids. It makes me wish we were lying on a tropical beach, and I was running my hand along her oiled-down skin.

Oh, Jesus. What would Hector think if he knew I imagined these things about his baby daughter, the one he wants me to guide spiritually?

I let go of the power button, and the screen flickers, which is a good sign. "It'll take forever to start up, and you should shut down every program that pops up or else it will overheat."

She smiles primly. "Got it."

I nod. "Need anything else?"

"I was wondering..." She licks her bottom lip. "Never mind."

"What?"

"Dad's always teasing you about your tattoo sleeves, and I was thinking..." Her little brow knits as her gaze shifts to my left biceps. "What does that one mean?"

Fuck, I love that adorable, inquisitive frown on her face as she stares at my stupid tattoo. The one I've had since college that stands out like a sore thumb compared to all the others. I've had a good laugh about it with friends over the years.

"It's a Lakers tattoo," I say.

Her cute little nose wrinkles, and I can't help but chuckle.

She licks her lips as she stares at my arm, making my stomach clench.

"It's very dramatic looking for a Lakers tattoo."

"I thought I was going to play for them someday. In fact, I was certain of it."

Her eyes grow wide. "Were you that good?"

"Nope. Not even close."

She laughs. "That's a bummer."

I shrug. "I was pretty good. I got a scholarship in college, but nowhere near NBA good."

She smiles sweetly. "We do have quite the audacity as teenagers, don't we?"

Warmth rushes through my veins. "We do."

"When I was fifteen, I truly thought I was going to be married to Harry Styles by now. There wasn't a doubt in my mind."

I let out a laugh. "That wasn't even that long ago."

When her smile fades, I wince. "I don't mean to sound patronizing."

She lifts a brow. "You're over a decade younger than my dad. You do realize that, right?"

"I do. It doesn't feel like it though."

She crosses her arms over her chest. "It's because you're men. Age is only a big deal with women because men are obsessed with our ages. We're not obsessed with yours. I'm a grown woman. You're a grown man. It doesn't matter that I'm your friend's daughter. I'm your peer, too."

Warmth fills my chest. I love how direct she is. How those dark brows dance up and down her forehead. How those bright, expressive eyes flash when she's passionate about something. Hector is right. She is a powerhouse.

"I'm sorry if I treat you like a kid. I promise I don't mean to do it. I know you're a grown woman."

It's only when her gaze lowers that I realize that I've moved so close to her that my thigh is nearly touching hers. I jerk back. "Well..." I scratch the back of my head. "The computer fans have stopped roaring, which is a good sign. Let me know if it gives you any more trouble."

"I will," she says, her voice raspy.

I rush out of that room as if I'm on fire.

God help me. I know she's a grown woman, but I don't want to see her that way.

I want this desire for her to go away.

Chapter Five

M ariana

I've been trying my hardest to concentrate on my work. I've been banished to the abandoned hallway.

It's not my imagination. He's uncomfortable around me.

Why?

Maybe he doesn't want me to fill in for Daisy. Maybe he thinks I'm too irresponsible. I know my dad constantly vents to him about what he perceives as my wild, party-girl ways, but I thought Brandon was too progressive to take those worries seriously. I party probably less than most college students, and I've always been safe when it comes to sex. I told Brandon as much the last time my dad asked him to talk to me.

Fuck Brandon for listening to my dad, if that's what this really is. I got into one of the best history master's programs in the whole country. He's lucky to have me in this lowly volunteer position.

And I refuse to stay in my office of shame, especially if he's trying to hide me from the rest of his staff. I need to get myself some coffee, and if I run into anyone on the way, I'll be sure to strike up a watercooler conversation with them.

I march out of my office and into the lobby. The thermal coffee carafe is gone, but I know I saw it earlier. Damn it. Where is Harper? She looks near my age and would be the perfect person to chat with.

I walk to Brandon's office and peek my head through the doorway. "Do you know if there's any more coffee?"

He looks up from his computer, those piercing dark eyes locking onto mine. "I'm not sure. Harper usually handles that."

He sounds annoyed, and I fight the urge to sneer. He's no longer the CEO of a big gym franchise. This is the church, damn it, and he's technically my pastor. He can be a little nicer.

I shift my weight. "Oh. Okay. I'll just go ask her."

Just as I start to turn around, he stands up from his desk. "I can make you some. I make it much stronger than Harper."

His smile is warm, and it makes my head grow a little fuzzy. He's so fucking gorgeous.

All this beauty wasted on a pastor.

No. I can't think that way. It's not fair to judge him when he's truly good at what he does. I'm frustrated with my own family when it comes to religion, and I can't let myself take it out on him.

He gestures for me to come into his office before disappearing, and I take the opportunity to scan his bookshelf. A huge stack of books and files sit at the corner. What is this?

I glance over my shoulder before reaching out and grabbing a book from the top of the stack. Damn. I think this is either Greek or Hebrew, probably ancient too. I knew he was educated, but I had no idea he could read the Bible in its original language.

"What are you reading?"

My cheeks warm, and I snap the book shut. When I look up, Brandon is standing next to me with two mugs in hand.

"I wasn't actually." I smile. "I don't read Greek. Or Hebrew. I'm not sure which this is."

His lips quirk as he hands me my coffee. "How did you know it was one of the two?"

I shrug, taking a sip. "I don't. I was just guessing. I know the Bible was written in both. And some in Aramaic."

He takes a sip of his own coffee. "You sure do know your history. It's Greek, by the way."

My head jerks up. "You can read Greek?"

He nods. "I have a master's in divinity. Most programs teach Greek and Hebrew."

I grin. "I'd love to learn another language. I mean, obviously you've heard me speak Spanish, but I've known that since birth. I would love to learn new languages throughout my lifetime. I feel like it would expand my mind and make me see the world differently."

He grins. "You think language works that way?"

"I do. We think in words, so there's no way it wouldn't in some way shape the way we see the world. The world as we know it is basically just made up of our thoughts."

His eyes are warm, crinkling at the edges. This is how he looked at me that night on the beach, and it made my stomach tie into knots then. It does the same now.

"It doesn't surprise me that you became an atheist," he says. "Your dad told me you drove him crazy growing up with all your questions."

I force a smile, even as a coldness settles in my chest. I'm sure my dad seemed lighthearted when he told Brandon that, but had I been there, I would have picked up on that edge of irritation in his voice. He wouldn't have had the warm smile that Brandon is giving me now. Maybe that's why Brandon is such a good pastor. He's not afraid of people who question God, which makes him a safe place.

"I sure did," I say. "Enough that they eventually didn't want to even try to answer them anymore. I spent a lot of time in our old pastor's office."

Brandon's smile fades, and I brace myself for his pity. "Was your pastor able to answer your questions?"

I grin. "It was Pastor Dave from First Covenant."

"Oh, that's right." He flinches ever so slightly, clearly not needing any more explanation. Dave was once his pastor too.

"Even as a kid, I knew his answers were bullshit. I once asked him to prove to me that God exists, and he said, 'Just look around you. Could all this beauty exist without God?'" I grimace. "What kind of answer is that?"

Brandon's gaze is intense and assessing, and my cheeks grow warm. With effort, I shoot him a cheeky smile. "What would you say? If a kid asked you that question, I mean."

He's quiet for a moment. "I'd say I can't prove that God exists."

I roll my eyes. "That's too easy."

"It's the truth."

"Then why do you believe in something with no evidence?" I gesture at the stack of books. "You're an educated person. Doesn't it bother you?"

His lips quirk. "Not really."

"Why?"

"Because I'm much happier now than before I became a Christian. I don't mind being wrong if it makes my life better."

I scowl. "How? I don't understand it. Livvy says the exact same thing. How can people be happy that way?" I shake my head. "And why has it never worked for me?"

"I don't know."

"Am I just a big know-it-all, and I have to be right all the time, even when it doesn't matter?"

His eyes alight, and he looks like he's repressing a smile. "I don't know."

My stomach flutters. It's the look again. As if he's amused with me.

No, delighted.

Fuck, I love talking to him about this stuff. I've never known a Christian who could debate with me philosophically without letting emotions get in the way. My dad can't even do it, and he's a damn lawyer. When I was a kid, he was a criminal defense attorney, and yet he seemed afraid of my questions. Fear seems to override reason with a certain type of Christian.

I love that Brandon is fearless. I love that he's giving me this warm, beautiful smile that makes my stomach flutter.

I hope my giddiness isn't written on my face. I don't want to seem like a silly little girl. I want him to see how competent I am at this job.

"What's with this big pile of books?" I ask, grasping for a change of subject.

Brandon's eyes follow my gaze, clouding when they land on the stack. "Textbooks. Articles. Information I gathered in graduate school and after. I refer to them sometimes when I write my sermons. They used to be in my home office, but I spend so much more time here, so it didn't make sense to keep them there anymore."

I nod as my gaze roves over the stack. It must be nearly four feet tall. "It can't be easy to find what you need..."

"It isn't. I've been meaning to organize it for weeks now. Instead, I just shift the piles around when I need something."

"Why don't I organize it for you?"

His expression shutters." There's no need."

"It sounds like there is."

"I don't want to make you do something so tedious."

"It wouldn't be tedious at all. I'll get to browse through the books while I figure out an organization system. For a history major, that's like Christmas morning."

When I grin, his jaw stiffens. Why does he seem irritated that I want to help out?

Ah. He thinks I won't be able to do the job well.

"I'll be right in front of you," I say. "If I mess anything up, you'll see it."

His expression grows even grimmer.

"I won't, though," I add quickly. "But if I do, let me know. I don't get my feelings hurt easily."

He stares at me for a full five seconds before speaking. "Alright."

Brandon

How did I not see myself walking right into that one?

She caught me off guard with her vulnerability about her struggles growing up. I found myself wanting to take her in my arms and comfort her.

That alone should have set off alarm bells in my mind. When have I ever had the desire to physically comfort her when she's confided in me, or any other church member?

Never.

Now I'm trapped with her in my office for the foreseeable future. Her limber body moving around me, stretching to reach high shelves... Her scent washing over me when she brushes past me to grab a book...

Fucking fuck.

Where did this desire for her come from, and why is it only getting worse?

"Is everything okay?" she asks, her voice softer than before.

Heat rises to my cheeks. "Yeah, I'm fine. Just zoning out."

She stares at me for a moment, biting that full bottom lip. The sight of it sends electricity into my gut.

"Do you need me to come back and work on this later?" she asks.

"No."

I can do this. My end of day prayer meditation can be rescheduled to right the fuck now.

That way I can tune her out.

I grab my prayer request list from the top drawer of my desk and search for the last item I left off on. Ah, Nolan James. The troubled youth. His mom told me he's an atheist, and she's utterly beside herself.

Lord, I pray you'll reach out to Nolan and find him if you will it. If not, please help soothe the bumps in their relationship. Help him to not feel rejected by his family the way I sense Mariana feels rejected by hers...

She's examining a book right now. That long neck of hers is curved. I sense that sadness even now. That sense of otherness. Rejection.

I wish I could hold her.

Our eyes meet, and she smiles dreamily. *Do you want me?* The words drift over me, echoing in my head and tightening my groin. Holy fuck. Did she really say that?

"I'm sorry, what?" My words are sharp.

She jerks back. "I didn't mean to interrupt you."

"What did you say?"

"I asked if you wanted me to create a master list?"

I blink. "A what?"

She frowns. "It's like a key for all your texts. I can put the subject and author and where to find them on your shelf." She gestures with that long, beautiful arm.

I stand up quickly. "I need to go make a phone call."

The widening of her eyes makes heat wash over my skin. I'm acting like a crazy person. But I have to get out of here. Now.

Chapter Six

M ariana

His sigh is so heavy it's almost a groan. I discreetly peek over my shoulder to see him staring at his laptop with a clenched jaw.

I'm annoying him. Badly.

It's not like I'm constantly asking him questions and distracting him from his work. I'm a pro at organizing books and articles. Any questions I've asked have been to make the process of researching easy for him.

I'm intruding on his space. That must be it. Or maybe he wanted to organize the books himself. I would much prefer to do my own organizing if I were in his shoes. But then why did he let it go for so long? Why did he make it sound like such a burden?

He lets out another loud sigh before standing up from his desk. It's probably the tenth time he's gotten up to leave during the last two hours I've been organizing.

"Do you want coffee?" he asks.

I do want coffee, but he sounds like the last thing in the world he wants to do right now is get it for me.

"No, I'm fine."

He's gone for a long time, so I do my best to stay focused on my work. But as his absence extends, the more I find myself struggling to concentrate.

If he really didn't want me to organize these books, he should have said so. I never took him for passive aggressive. He's always so open and assertive with my family. He's even scolded me on occasion. Like on Fourth of July a few years ago when I stood too close to the cone fountain firework. Brandon yanked me away and took the stick lighter from my hand. "I'm revoking your pyrotechnician privileges," he said in a deep, stern voice that tied my stomach into knots.

I wish he would have spanked me.

Fuck, I need to keep my imagination in check. I can't be horny for Brandon during work hours if I want him to see how good I am at my job.

I glance at the book in my hand, determined to keep focused on my task. Based on the title, it seems to be an introductory text on pastoral counseling. I bet he rarely uses this. He's already skilled at counseling. It should probably go on one of the top shelves. I glance up to the open space on the far-left corner.

I can't reach that, even if I go on my tiptoes and stretch my arm. Brandon is probably the only person here tall enough to reach that far...

I won't be asking the grump to help me. I'll find a stepladder before I do that.

When I peek out into the lobby, Harper is nowhere to be found. After looking around Brandon's office, I make a quick decision. I grab the ottoman near the couches and roll it in front of the bookshelf. I step up onto it and stretch my arm as high as I can.

I'm still not high enough. Maybe I could—

"Mariana!" A deep voice booms.

I whip my head around, and the ottoman rolls underneath my feet. As I flail backward, time seems to slow. I brace for the impact, but it never comes.

Instead, I find myself wrapped in Brandon's strong arms, his chest cushioning my fall. The textbook plops in front of me.

Our eyes meet, and for a moment, neither of us can look away. His eyes are almost black.

"Are you alright?" he asks breathlessly.

I nod, unable to speak, my cheeks burning. How did I let that happen? A rolling ottoman of all things. Of course I was going to fall.

"You're sure you're not hurt?" His big hand comes up and cradles the back of my head. "It looked like you clipped the desk."

"No." I swallow, shaking my head. "You caught me in time."

His eyes narrow. "Barely."

"Barely was perfect in this case. I didn't hit my head."

"But you could have." His voice is biting, and it makes heat pool in my belly.

Oh God, I love being scolded by him with that stern daddy voice and those dark eyes cutting into me. This is the way he looked that night with the fireworks.

Except his huge arms weren't wrapped around me. He wasn't cradling me in his lap while his breath brushed against my skin.

Right now, we're close enough to kiss.

"I thought I had better balance than that." My voice is husky. "I'm a hiker. I've stood on wobbly boulders before."

Brandon's face is flushed. His gaze roves to my mouth. "I didn't know you liked to hike."

"I love it."

His lips move a little closer.

Oh, fuck.

Is he going to kiss me?

Of their own will, my lips part. His nostrils flare, and a moment later, I'm being lifted into the air and set down on my feet.

"Just because you *can* stand on unstable surfaces, doesn't mean you should when you have other options. Next time you need help, come find me."

I wave a hand. "I still climb my parents' oak tree when I need to get a ball off the roof for my nieces and nephews."

His eyes flash. "Do your parents know you do that?"

My tummy flutters. I love it when he acts like a daddy.

But I can't let him see how much I love it.

I shoot him a cheeky smile. "Why don't you tell them, Pastor? Get me grounded."

He narrows his eyes as his lips quirk. "Watch it, young lady."

I let out a laugh even as pressure builds in my belly. I'll bet he says things like this to his sexual partners.

No, I'm certain of it.

Goddamn it, I'll never know him that way, and in the moment, that feels like a tragedy.

His smile fades. "You should probably go get your things. It's well past five."

"Oh." I jerk back and tuck a strand of hair behind my ears. "I didn't realize that."

His gaze lingers on my face. What is he thinking? Why are those dark eyes so...

Intense?

Brandon

What a disaster.

That's what I get for avoiding her intentionally. If only I had kept myself under control, she wouldn't have been without me when she needed my help.

She could have been seriously hurt. Her head was a hair away from slamming on the corner of my desk. My pulse was pounding like a hammer when I saw her fall.

And it kept hammering.

It's pounding still.

"Well, I'm heading out."

Her husky voice curls through my insides, clenching my gut. With effort, I keep my head down for a beat, not wanting her to see my inner turmoil on my face. I form what I hope is a polite smile before looking up. "You did great today."

She snorts. "I know you're lying. You've been annoyed with me all day. I'm sorry I invaded your space."

My head jerks back. Is that really what she thinks? "Mariana, I haven't been annoyed with you at all."

She stares at me skeptically, making my face warm. God, I must have really been transparent today, though she misinterpreted the reason. How could I have allowed myself to be so cold to her?

"I mean it," I say. "I've been very stressed today about...something else, and I'm realizing now that I must have taken it out on you. For that, I'm very sorry."

She expels a breath through pursed lips. "I didn't even think of that. I'm sorry if I took it personally."

I shake my head sharply. "Don't apologize. It was your first day. You're helping me out of a bind. And here I was rude to you. I am very sorry."

She smiles sweetly, and something loosens in my chest.

Oh God, this isn't good. This pent-up lust is swaying into tender territory, and I can't feel tenderness for this woman.

Not this kind of tenderness, at least. It's not at all familial.

It's the kind that makes me want to pull her onto my lap and nuzzle my face against hers. I want to call her *my* Mariana.

Clearly, aiming for distance from her didn't do me a lick of good.

God, please show me the way. Help me through this.

Chapter Seven

M ariana

With one hand on the steering wheel, I use the other to knead my shoulders, sending tingles down my spine. God, what a day.

I don't need to tell Sofia about how curt Brandon was with me all day—that he seems to think I'm just as irresponsible as the rest of my family does. She certainly doesn't need to know about the ottoman incident.

I'll have to think of something good to tell her. He did assign me an important organizing task, though I had to practically beg him to let me do it. But it allowed me to browse through all kinds of Biblical history books, which will probably sound impressive to her.

As I walk into our apartment, the scent of warm cookies hits my nose. A smile tugs at my lips. Baking was our thing growing up. Something just Sofia and I shared. My mom was too precious about her culinary processes to let me participate in cooking or baking, but Sofia always did, from the moment she was old enough to do it herself.

There's a skip in my step as I walk through the living room, but as soon as I enter the kitchen, my stomach plummets.

Sofia and her best friend, Danielle, are both smiling over a bowl of batter. Dani pours a bag of chocolate chips while Sofia stirs. They make such a pretty picture.

You've been replaced, Mari.

What a childish thought, yet I can't reason this ache in my chest away. Sofia was *mine*. My big sister. She used to go out of her way to arrange girls' nights for just the two of us, with cookie baking and Netflix binges.

Until Finn came into the picture. I didn't like him, and that meant Sofia pushed me into the periphery of her life.

When I set my work bag on a kitchen chair and walk to the counter, Sofia's smile falters, but I don't let it deter me. "Hey, Dani," I say.

"How was your first day?" Sofia asks without looking my way.

"Great," I say, infusing cheerfulness into my voice.

"How was Brandon?"

"Grumpy." I find myself unable to muster the energy to do a song and dance for her. She might as well just hear the truth.

Sofia frowns as she scoops a ball of dough from the bowl. "I can't imagine him grumpy. Maybe a little stern...but not grumpy."

"He can't be grumpy with you," I say. "He's dating you."

"Courting," Sofia corrects.

Dani giggles. "I still can't believe it. Pastor Brandon is courting you. I mean, I know he's like...part of your family, almost. But to me, he's like a celebrity."

Sofia smiles to herself, and I strain my face to keep my eyes from rolling. I'm as vain as the next person, so I shouldn't fault her for loving the attention her situation with Brandon gives her.

But I know where that smile comes from, and it's not Brandon.

"I know it's not Christlike to say this..." Dani's expression grows prim. "But Finn is going to lose his mind when he finds out, if he hasn't already."

I let out a breathless laugh, unable to help myself. Dani must have read my mind.

If Sofia noticed my laughter, she doesn't show it. Her triumphant smile grows. "Brandon and I get coffee right by Finn's work. He's probably seen us."

"Can you imagine?" Dani's tone is giddy. "He's probably..."

I force myself to retreat into my head as I march out of the kitchen and into my room. I can't listen anymore.

Under any other circumstances, I would only be mildly irritated with Sofia for her pettiness.

Now, it's like a tight fist is clenching around my heart.

She doesn't even care about my feelings anymore. She doesn't care that the distance between us hurts so much it's hard to take a breath sometimes. The Sofia who gave me the honor of running the hand mixer even though I splashed the cookie dough all over the counter never would have let a man come between us, especially when I did nothing wrong other than dislike him. I was her baby sister, and she adored me.

Or so I thought.

* * *

"Mari, before we start our hunt, you have to tell us all about your first day working for Pastor Brandon," Vanessa says as we walk into the bridal boutique.

Livvy's eyes spark. "I think she has something juicy to tell us. I see it on her face."

I repress a smile. "Juicy? About my sister's boyfriend?"

Livvy rolls her eyes. "We both know that's not a real thing."

"Tell that to my family," I say.

Vanessa shakes her head. "I can't believe they want him with Sofia when he's constantly flirting with you."

I wave a hand. "I'm the one who flirts with him. What you think is flirting on his part is just him getting annoyed with me." A smile rises to my lips when his stern face flashes in my mind.

"Watch it, young lady."

What would he think if he knew how much it turned me on when he teased me yesterday?

"I actually do have one juicy thing to tell you," I say, "and it's so epically embarrassing, you'll probably think I'm making it up."

"What?" Vanessa and Livvy ask in unison.

I pretend to examine the fabric of a satin dress I know Livvy would hate, my cheeks warming at the memory of Brandon's huge arms around me. "I may or may not have fallen off an ottoman when I was trying to put a book on a high shelf." I pause for effect. "And Pastor Brandon may or may not have caught me."

Vanessa's mouth drops open. "How did that happen?"

I roll my eyes at my own stupidity. "I don't know what I was thinking. I was too embarrassed to ask Brandon for a stepladder."

Livvy's expression is incredulous. "You're never embarrassed."

I shrug. "I could tell he was annoyed with me for asking too many questions."

Vanessa's brows shoot up. "That doesn't sound like the Pastor Brandon I know. Especially not with *you*."

I roll my eyes dramatically, trying to ignore the fluttering in my stomach at her insinuation. Even if he were as horny for me as I am for him, what difference would it make?

He's celibate, damn it. He's not going to have sex with anyone but his future wife.

A tragedy, really.

I pull at the hem of a lacey blue dress to give me a better view of it. "He said he was just stressed out."

"Maybe he was stressed out because you got him all worked up," Livvy says. "And he had no way to release the...tension, if you know what I mean."

I giggle, but my laughter quickly fades when a sparkle at the corner of the shop draws my attention. Electricity skates across my skin when I get a full view of the mermaid dress.

I can see Livvy in that dress. On a beach at sunset. With Cole smiling down at her with adoring eyes.

"Livvy," I mutter. "I think I might have found the dress. And I do mean *the* dress."

She frowns, her eyes following my gaze. "You mean *my* dress?"

"Yes."

"No, no. I can't look at wedding dresses. My mom would murder me. Ness and I promised her today would only be bridesmaid shopping."

Despite her denial, we all make our way over to the dress as if drawn to it by an invisible force. As we get closer, the sunlight sparkles over the delicate beading.

"Ness, what do you think?" I ask.

"Oh, Livvy," she says in a hushed voice. "You have to try it on."

I shoot Livvy a stern look. "The shape of it is perfect for your curves."

She bites her lip. "I can't try it on. I'll just take a picture of it for next time."

"No." Vanessa's eyes twinkle with mischief. She walks over to the dress and pulls it off the rack. "You're trying it on today. We won't tell Mom. We'll stage something with her if we have to."

Livvy groans. "That's so deceitful, Ness."

I purse my lips to hide my smile. Sometimes my bestie is so earnestly sweet I want to laugh.

"We've been dress shopping with her at least five times already," Vanessa says. "It's her fault you haven't found anything you love yet. She's too critical, and she gets into your head."

"And if it's not here the next time you look for dresses?" I ask. "You'll always wonder."

Livvy's eyes widen minutely, and I know I've won. Vanessa shoots me a sly smile, and a moment later, we're standing in the large dressing room helping Livvy into the dress. After I've hooked the last button, Livvy turns around, and both Vanessa and I gasp.

"Oh, Livvy," Vanessa says.

"This is the one," I mutter, my throat growing tight.

How is it possible that my childhood best friend is going to be a wife in two months?

"Oh, wow." Livvy's voice is just above a whisper as she stares at herself in the mirror, her big doe eyes roving up and down the dress. "Am I cheesy for wanting to cry?"

"Are you kidding me?" My voice is shaky. "I'm already crying."

"Me too," Vanessa squeaks. She rushes to her sister and wraps her arms around her. "I can't believe you're getting married, and you're going to have babies soon."

Livvy giggles even as a tear falls down her cheek. "It's surreal, huh? Like I'm only pretending. Like when we made veils out of paper when we were little. Remember that, Mari?"

My throat grows tight. "Yes," I say, but that's not the memory playing in my mind.

I'm pulled back in time. I see a beautiful face hovering over me while I sit on the hard lid of the toilet. As her deft fingers move, featherlight strokes brush over my eyelids.

"Who are you going to marry today?" Sofia asks.

"Papi," I answer, and her laughter drifts through me like music.

Is that how it really happened, or has the memory grown warmer and softer over the years, as if it were touched by gentle morning sunlight? Loss seems to do that to memory.

The Sofia from that day is gone. That version of me is gone, too.

They'll never come back.

Chapter Eight

B randon

I have a new plan for today.

Mariana's confession that I was rude to her weighed on my conscience. I can't inadvertently punish her for something she's not even intending to do. My lust is my responsibility.

It's not her fault she has those dancing eyes and that mischievous smile. It's not her fault she has those delicate curves I can't keep my eyes from roaming. I'm being selfish keeping her locked away at the back of the church just because I can't keep my horny thoughts in check.

Before I went to bed last night, I prayed that God would help me get through this month of being constantly around Mariana. This morning, I woke up with a message from God.

You were meant to do this.

From the moment the words echoed in my heart, I knew what they meant. Hector's request for me to talk to Mariana wasn't a fluke. Right now, she needs me. I felt it yesterday when she talked about growing up questioning God in a family of devout Christians. It wasn't a coincidence that she told me specifically.

I'm her pastor, even if she doesn't believe. I'm the one called by God to help her. For the first time, I truly believe I can.

I'll show her that she's perfect just the way she is. If God wanted her to believe, he would have called her. There wouldn't be so many beliefs in the world if God expected us all to be of one mind.

I can minister to her in a way that respects her lack of faith.

Ministering to her will help me as well. Our spiritual connection will transcend the lust I feel. Even if twinges of it remain, my heart will be too full of compassion for them to trouble me.

There's a soft knock before Mariana's lovely face appears in my office doorway. I'm not even bothered by the fact that I want to bite that full bottom lip of hers. I'm human, and I can't control my thoughts, but I don't have to let them rule me.

"Harper is at lunch, so I'm filling in for her," she says. "Nolan and his mom are here."

I nod. "Ask his mom if she wouldn't mind waiting in the lobby or the prayer room. I'd prefer to speak to Nolan alone."

She nods and disappears. Shortly after, she guides Nolan into my office. He holds a slight smirk, and my shoulders tense.

Jesus, help me. I know he's just a kid, and at one time, I had a cocky attitude just like his.

Maybe that's why he annoys me so much.

"Can I get you coffee, Nolan?" Mariana asks.

He grins at her. "Can you put some tequila in it?"

"I don't know." Mariana turns to me with a questioning frown. "Are we allowed to give minors alcohol, Pastor?"

Warmth seeps through my veins, and I'm relieved anew at my change of heart. She's exactly where she's supposed to be. I shouldn't be wishing her away because of my own human frailty.

I smile. "I'm afraid not."

She winces dramatically. "Sorry, Nolan. Only plain coffee for you. But I can load it up with lots of French vanilla creamer."

Nolan smiles at her, but this time, his eyes are much warmer.

Damn. She's good at this, but why am I surprised? She has that playful personality—the ability to put people at ease by just being herself.

As soon as Mariana leaves the room, the spell is broken, and Nolan's cocky smile returns.

I inhale deeply. "So your mom tells me you've been getting into a lot of arguments with her and your dad lately. Do you want to talk about it?"

That smirk doesn't waver. "Nope."

I sigh. "I'm not going to force you to talk, but your mom took the time to set up this appointment and bring you here. We have to fill the next forty-five minutes somehow."

He cocks a brow, and my jaw clenches. God help me with this kid. I don't want to talk any more than he does.

"I think your tattoo is stupid," he says, looking at the purple and gold abomination on my left biceps.

I force a smile. "When I was your age, I thought I'd play for the Lakers."

Nolan snorts. "You're like six foot nothing."

"We're not always wise when we're young."

"Oh my God." Nolan runs his fingers through the long strands of his blond hair. "I can't. I seriously just can't right now. You're the last person I want to talk to. I don't even believe in God."

I grit my teeth. This is going to be difficult.

A moment later, a soft knock reverberates on the door, and Mariana enters with a paper coffee cup in one hand. She smiles at Nolan. "I put five creamers in here. Your coffee is practically white."

Just like before, Nolan's whole expression softens, and an idea sprouts. Keeping my gaze locked on Nolan, I gesture at Mariana. "She's an atheist, too." I grimace when I recall her self-consciousness at church a few days ago. "I hope you don't mind that I shared that, Mariana."

She smiles, relieving the tension in my shoulders. "Not at all."
As if reading my mind, she plops down on the couch across from
Nolan. "So you're a heathen too?"

Nolan laughs. "Yep. And proud of it. Organized religion is so
stupid. Bunch of sheep."

Mariana narrows her eyes thoughtfully. "I used to think that
too. It made me really mad that no one could prove to me that
God was real."

"Exactly." Nolan's eyes light up. "The way they try to prove
it's real is by using scriptures from the Bible. I'm always like, 'Bro,
I don't believe in the Bible. Show me science.'"

Mariana nods thoughtfully. "I completely agree with you,
which is why I stopped asking those questions. They're never
going to be able to give us satisfying answers. And the only reason
that makes us mad is because we're still trying to hold on to our
faith."

Nolan scoffs. "I am not trying to hold on to my faith."

Mariana lowers her chin. "Then why do you ask those
questions?"

"Because my mom and dad force me to go to church."

"Bring headphones and listen to podcasts during church."

Nolan rolls his eyes. "They'd never let me do that."

Mariana shrugs. "Our parents make us do a lot of boring
things when we're teenagers."

"Yeah, but this is different."

"How is it different?"

He raises both hands in the air. "It's fucked up to teach kids if
they don't believe a certain thing, they're going to hell. And yet
almost every single person in my life thinks it's totally normal. I
watch this philosopher guy on YouTube, and he thinks it's child
abuse. Literally."

Mariana nods slowly. "I probably would have agreed with him
years ago, but not anymore. Part of my journey was realizing that
my parents are flawed, and they only forced these things on me

out of fear. Because they love me so much. And ultimately, it's not that big of a deal to me—"

"If they really loved you, they'd accept you for who you are."

Mariana blinks once. She lifts a hand and tucks a strand of hair behind her ear, and there's a sudden spark in her eyes. "Wow, you really got to the heart of it." Her voice is hushed.

Nolan narrows his eyes. "Yeah. It's fucked up."

"It is." She sighs, sounding so melancholy I want to take her into my arms.

I can't let this go on any longer. Not when it's making her sad, and I'm the one who instigated it.

"So where do you want to go from here, Nolan?" I ask to redirect the conversation. "Do you want your parents to give you answers? Do you want me to give you answers, even when you know they probably won't satisfy you?"

Nolan's expression is so thoughtful and somber, I can hardly even call to mind that cocky smirk I know was there only minutes ago.

"I guess not," he says.

"What do you want?"

He shrugs. "I want to quit going to church, and I want my mom and dad to be okay with it."

"Do you want me to have your mom come in here?"

He's quiet for a moment. "Yeah, I guess."

I shoot Mariana a look, and she smiles warmly before standing up. "I'll go get her."

Something loosens in my chest. She's so good at this. I love the way she read my intentions from the moment she walked into this office, like there's an invisible connection between us.

This is a sign.

We already have some kind of spiritual connection I can't quite articulate. Something I felt from my first real conversation with her.

This is why God called me to help her. My lust is a distraction, sure, but not one I can't overcome.

Chapter Nine

M ariana

"Would you mind talking to me about why you took an internship at a church when you don't believe?" Brandon asks in a soft, melodic voice.

I lower my eyes to my plate to hide my disappointment. I should have known the only reason he invited me to dinner after work was to minister to me. It was too much to hope that he's starting to see me as a friend.

Or a potential lover.

Fuck, I'm so dumb. Even if he weren't celibate, he'd have no interest in me. I'm a child in his eyes. This attraction is one-sided.

Besides, if he doesn't even want Sofia—the objectively better-looking daughter—there's no way in hell he's thought twice about me. I was only imagining that he wanted to kiss me yesterday.

I plant a smile on my face. "Are you trying to initiate some pastoral counseling right now?"

"No." He licks a spot of sauce at the corner of his lips, drawing my attention to his tongue. A shiver runs over my skin. "I'm asking you as a friend who's curious."

Friend. The word is so warm and comforting and dependable coming from his mouth, like the steady rhythm of a clock.

Too bad it's bullshit.

I drop my fork to knead the knots in the back of my neck. "You of all people should know that my dad is a hard ass. For as long as I have even the slightest financial dependence on him and my mom, I have to tread lightly." My smile doesn't reach my eyes. "And it'll be another two years before I finish graduate school so..."

He smiles warmly. "I know I'm biased here, but I think he'd handle the atheist news better than you think. He wouldn't cut you off financially."

I snort. "You *are* biased. In fact, I don't even really understand how you two are so close. I mean, I love him to death, but your beliefs are so different. He truly believes I'll go to hell if I don't change."

Brandon reaches out and touches my arm, and I hope he doesn't hear my sharp inhale. "He doesn't want to believe it. You know that right? He thinks it's the truth."

I groan. "Why doesn't he listen to you on this topic? You obviously know more about the Bible than he does."

He smiles. "Hector won't listen to a pastor who he's seen in his boxers."

In an instant, the tension leaves my whole body, and a giggle bubbles from my chest. "How did that happen? He won't go into detail about any of your pre-Christian days."

Brandon looks down at the table, his eyes growing unfocused. "Your dad was determined to meet me where I was, and I wasn't a Christian when I started going to First Covenant. I think he sensed that I was in need, and he took any opportunity he got to talk to me about God. He even started showing up at the bars. It annoyed the hell out of me, actually. At first." A warm smile rises to his lips. "He wouldn't drink much, so he'd usually drive me home, and that particular time..." He shakes his head. "I was plowed. He helped me into my house, and according to him—because I don't remember a damn thing—I immediately stripped down to my boxers and passed out face down on my couch. It was like I didn't even know he was there."

Warmth fills my belly at the thought of it. My dad has mentioned this story several times, never in detail. But the words "Brandon" and "boxers" was enough.

More than enough.

I'd love to have been the one taking care of him while he was drunk. I'd love to see him acting silly and vulnerable for a change. I'd love to see him in only his boxers...

"Why did you go to First Covenant if you weren't a Christian?" I ask to change the subject, hoping my cheeks don't look as flushed as they feel.

He's quiet for a moment. "I thought it would remind me of my mom. She went to a Pentecostal church, and I had just lost her."

"You were really close to her," I say, because he's mentioned his mom a few times at family gatherings. Never his dad, though.

He nods. "I had a really hard time when she died. She had an aggressive cancer, and I knew it was coming, but you're never prepared."

His dark eyes grow vacant for a moment, as if he's drifting into the past. I want to touch his arm, like he did mine a moment ago, but I'm not sure if it would give him any comfort. He seems to be avoiding any physical closeness with me since I started working at the church.

"I'd probably do the same thing," I say softly. "Church is so important to my family. If I lost any one of them, it's probably the first place I'd go to feel close to them."

His dark eyes meet mine, growing intense. "I never really felt her there, though. It wasn't the same church I went to as a kid. That's in Healdsburg, where I grew up. First Covenant just didn't give me the same feeling."

I lean forward, placing my elbows on the table. "You think she wouldn't have liked First Covenant, huh? She never would have gone there. Pastor Dave is a misogynistic prick. Your mom wouldn't have liked him."

Because she would have been like Brandon.

He smiles, his eyes crinkling at the corners. "You never hold back, Mariana. You're fearless."

A shiver skates over my skin. There's reverence in his voice. I'm not imagining it.

This might be the first time he's ever made me feel like an equal instead of a little girl. There was nothing patronizing of the way his beautiful mouth caressed the word "fearless."

"You're right, by the way," he continues. "I don't think she would have liked First Covenant, but it was meant to be. I found your dad, who became one of the most important people in my life. He's more than a friend. He's..." He lowers his gaze to his beer. "I look up to him a lot."

"He's kind of like a father figure, huh?"

Brandon smiles ruefully, and it makes my stomach flutter. I like seeing him like this. He's so sweet when he's vulnerable.

"Anyway." His smile fades, his face growing stoic. I could almost laugh. He's clearly not as comfortable showing vulnerability to me as I am receiving it. "I love him. I love all of you—"

My gut clenches at his use of the word "love."

"Which is why I want to help bridge the gap between you guys, if I can. I know it's not really my business, but I get the feeling you're comfortable opening up to me." His dark eyes probe mine, shooting straight into my gut.

"Yes." I swallow. "You're kind of like a mentor." *A mentor I'd like to fuck, that is.* "I always feel better after talking to you."

He smiles tightly. "I'm glad."

For some reason, he doesn't sound like he means that.

He sighs. "At the risk of sounding patronizing, I think it might help if you at least work toward being more open with your family. Part of becoming an adult is learning to let go of the fact that you might disappoint the people you love. It's hard, but it's worth it."

I let out an exhausted sigh. "It's easy for you to say. My whole family's in awe of you—except for my dad, of course."

"You're right. I have no idea what it's like for you. You're real family. They love you more than they love me, which means there's more fear involved. But I do know what it's like to lose my community."

I frown. "What do you mean?"

"I lived a very different life before I became a pastor."

"Oh, you mean your old gym business?" When my gaze drifts to his huge, muscular arms, he smiles mischievously. My cheeks grow warm. I lift my chin, refusing to cower. "You still look like a gym rat. I think you'd fit right in with that community, even as a pastor."

He narrows his eyes, and heat fills my stomach. I love this look he gives me from time to time.

Like he wants to spank me.

"People in health and wellness have a hard time relating to a career like mine," he says.

"So you really got dropped by everyone?"

He shrugs as he takes a sip of his beer. "Not really. They just all sort of...fell away. They have no interest in my life anymore."

I nod slowly. "I could see that happening with my family too. Not that they would actually fall away. I'd still be a part of everything, but they'd... I think they'd be more distant with me if I told them I'm an atheist."

"And that's something that you'll have to weigh out. You'll have to figure out if it's more important to you to have honesty or closeness. I'll be frank though, if you keep doing what you're doing now—going to church and keeping your mouth shut about what you really think—it'll be hard to have true closeness."

His words strike my heart, making it hard to take a breath. What he's really saying is that I'm condemned to always being an outcast, regardless of the choice I make. Always being lonely, the way I've felt since I was a teenager.

Even though I was far from the most rebellious in our family based on stories I've heard from Abuelita, everyone seemed to sense it was different with me. The questions I asked about existence and proof for God scared them.

It didn't matter that I did all the things I was supposed to do. I wore a purity ring until I was eighteen even though I had already had sex by that age. I went to church and youth group every week. Hell, I even got baptized.

None of it made me closer to them. I've been delusional, holding onto a hope that made me repress who I am deep down.

"You're right," I mutter.

Brandon sets his hand on my forearm again. The warmth of his skin radiates through my whole body. "You have every reason to grieve."

I swallow, forcing a smile. "Do I seem like I'm grieving?"

His gaze roams my face. "You seem a little...thoughtful."

I nod. "I was just remembering how I got baptized to make my parents happy, and it didn't work."

He smiles sadly.

"I didn't believe even then. It felt fake while I was doing it." I pin him with a hard stare. "What if I got baptized right now?"

He frowns. "I'm not following."

I raise both hands in the air, unable to contain the energy surging through my body at my sudden idea. "What if you baptized me not as a Christian, but as an atheist?"

He looks at me for a prolonged moment. "I don't think it's a ritual atheists usually take part in."

"It *should* be for atheists like me. We were raised with rituals and symbolism. It will be committing my life to atheism, the same way I pretended to commit it to Christ when I was a kid. I'm having a hard time accepting myself. Maybe a ritual would help."

He sighs. "Will you be disappointed if it doesn't?"

"No," I say quickly. "I promise. I just want to try it."

He sighs. "Your dad would kill me if he knew. This is not what he meant when he asked me to help you."

I roll my eyes. "It wasn't his place to ask you."

"Don't think I don't know that, but I still agreed."

"Stop being a pushover."

He narrows his eyes, his lips quirking. "Do you want me to help you or not, young lady?"

My stomach clenches. "Yes, Pastor." I'm surprised how light my voice sounds. "I just want you to stop acting on behalf of my dad."

He's quiet for a moment, but then he leans forward. The smile that overtakes his face sends arrows of heat straight to my groin. It's a wicked smile. There's no other way to describe it.

It's the smile he used to give women in his kinky past.

"I'm a man of the cloth, young lady. I don't answer to your dad. I don't answer to anyone but God."

"Does that mean you'll do it?" I nearly shout.

He leans back into his seat. "If it'll really help you."

When I squeal, his smile grows. "We usually do it in the ocean at New Morning. I could find a time on my schedule, maybe this week or—"

"Why not right now?"

His eyes widen.

I gesture at the restaurant patio deck, which has an expansive view of the ocean. "It'll probably be sunset by the time we're out in the water. What a perfect symbol. My faith in God will leave with the sun. I've never been afraid of darkness."

He looks at me for a prolonged time, and my heart thumps as I try to read his thoughts. The corner of his lips are slightly lifted, and there are creases at the corners of his eyes. Something about this look makes heat shoot into my groin.

"We won't have time to get swimsuits," he finally says, and I know I've won.

"I don't want one." My voice is shaky in my giddiness. "I wore an oversized T-shirt the first time. My mom thought a bathing suit was too immodest."

He glances out at the water. "You're going to freeze when we get out there."

I nod once. "A symbol of how uncomfortable it is to embrace who you really are. The cold will be worth it, like you said."

"You are something else, Mariana." He's almost grinning now. "Alright. You've convinced me."

I shriek as he pulls out several bills from his wallet and sets them on the table. "Let's do it."

A short while later, we're standing with bare feet at the edge of the water. As the waves lap gently at the shore, I let the melody of the ocean wash over me.

This is right.

This is what I need.

"Are you sure you want to do this just the two of us?" Brandon asks. "You don't want Livvy here?"

I shake my head. "This is something I need to do alone."

"But I'm with you."

There's something in his tone... Something warm and dark. I don't have time to interpret it, because he huffs out a laugh. "Alright, let's do it before we chicken out."

My heart races as he sets his hand on my back and leads me into the water. Coldness washes across my feet, and a shiver runs up my spine. We wade out until the water is just below our hips. The waves roll over us, occasionally throwing me off balance.

Brandon's expression grows grave. "What does this mean for you?"

I know exactly what he's asking, and a stillness descends over me. "It means that I'm accepting who I am. Even if I'm not ready to tell my family, I know what I'm about, and I'm not afraid of it."

He stares at me with an intensity I've never seen before. Those inky-dark eyes bore into mine. His lips quirk slightly, as if he's impressed with me, and my heart grows light.

I think he might be proud of me.

He sets his hands on my shoulders, and I'm suddenly engulfed with his big frame. Those huge arms of his and that muscled chest. Even with the heavy aroma of seawater, tendrils of his musky scent reach my nose.

God, he smells so fucking good.

This is so much more intimate than I thought it would be. If I weren't so overwhelmed with what I'm about to do, I'd probably be turned on.

"I'm not quite sure what to say as I baptize you." Brandon's smile grows sheepish. "Usually, I do it in the name of Jesus Christ."

I smile. "Improvise."

His eyes crinkle at the corners before he shuts them, and his expression grows somber. "As you enter the waters, Mariana, may your...self-acceptance surround you. Let this moment be a testament of your journey to becoming an atheist, and your commitment to loving yourself for who you are."

He lifts me by my shoulders as if I'm as light as a doll. The shock of cold makes me gasp when he dips me back into the water, completely submerging me. For a moment, everything is dark and quiet, and my body is weightless. When he pulls me back up, the cool air fills my lungs.

The moment is over as quickly as it began, but my heart is as light as a helium balloon.

Tears rise to my eyes even as a giggle escapes my chest. "I feel different. I really do."

His dark eyes are nearly black as he stares back at me. "I'm glad."

We fix our eyes on each other in an electric silence. It's only when his gaze drops to my mouth that I realize his big hands are still gripping my shoulders.

Holy shit, is he going to kiss me?

I swallow and lick my lips, and his gaze grows hooded. He lifts his hand to my face and grips my chin. His thumb brushes my bottom lip, and my stomach turns into molten lead.

As if recalling himself, his eyes grow wide, and he nearly shoves me away. "I have towels in my trunk," he says.

"Okay," I say.

But he's already nearly to the beach, like he can't get away from me fast enough.

* * *

His knuckles are almost white as they clench the steering wheel. He hasn't looked at me for the entire drive.

I wish I knew what he's thinking. Is he angry with me?

No. He's too reasonable a person. He knows that touch was all him.

But damn, I liked it.

And maybe he caught on to my feelings.

The silence hanging between us gnaws at the edges of my sanity. I pick at the hem of my soaked dress, my fingers trembling slightly. The memory of his touch on my lip sends a shiver down my spine.

He pulls into the parking lot of my apartment building, shutting off the car without a word. The silence in the air grows thick as I wait for him to say something.

"Can you come to my office tomorrow morning?" he finally says, his voice low. I glance at him, hoping to read his expression, but all I see is his stoic profile illuminated by the faint glow of the streetlamps.

I swallow. "What for?"

Dread washes over me when he doesn't respond.

He's going to fire me. He's decided it's not worth doing this favor for my dad if we're attracted to each other.

Holy shit. Is he really attracted to me? Even a half hour ago, I would have said it was impossible, but there was no mistaking that molten darkness in his eyes when he gripped my chin.

Slippery wetness gathers between my legs. I never thought I could be so turned on by a gesture so small.

But this is Brandon.

"I just..." He shuts his eyes. "We need to have a talk."

When I lift my hand to tuck a strand of hair behind my ear, I notice my hands are shaking. "We can't have it now?"

"No," he says immediately, reaching his hand to the door and clicking the unlock button.

I've been dismissed.

I'm going to be on pins and needles until tomorrow morning.

Brandon

"You're kind of like a mentor to me."

She said those words less than an hour before I fondled her mouth.

What has gotten into me? She trusted me to baptize her, for fuck's sake, and I touched her. I don't think I ever behaved that recklessly even before I found God. I certainly never had the urge to touch one of my employees, and this was so much worse. Even if she's an atheist, baptism is still sacred, a moment of spiritual cleansing, and I allowed carnal desire to taint it.

A small touch. A fraction of a second. Yet the softness of her lips against my thumb sent a surge of electricity through my body that was so potent, I could have fallen into the water.

My mind is still racing as I walk inside my house. I make my way to Ethan's room immediately. The door is open, and he's sitting at his desk, surrounded by books and notes. His head perks up when I walk inside, and he frowns.

"What's wrong?" he asks.

I let out a deep breath before telling him everything. How I touched Mariana after the baptism, and how my self-control seems to have been stretched into oblivion.

Ethan listens quietly, his expression thoughtful. "Maybe you should court Mari instead of Sofia."

I scowl at him. "It would be the end of my relationship with Hector. I would lose the only family I have besides you."

A notch forms between his brows. "You really think he'd be that upset about it?"

"Yes," I say immediately. "It would be a betrayal of his trust. He asked me to counsel her. He sees me as a father figure to her."

He cringes, and I want to cringe myself. A father figure to beautiful, mischievous Mariana. It's ludicrous.

"In that case..." He expels a breath through pursed lips. "You probably should avoid being alone with her."

I let out a groan that reverberates through the room. "I thought the same thing. I'll have to implement a rule that we always need someone in the room with us at the church."

Ethan smirks. "Billy Graham rules."

I narrow my eyes at him. "No. This is just for me. And only with her. Because I crossed a line. This is to show her that I know I messed up, and I want to make it right. I don't want her to be uncomfortable at work."

His lips quirk. "The lip touch sounded consensual to me."

I shut my eyes. "I'm her pastor. She trusted me to baptize her."

He gets up from his chair and pats my shoulder. "I'd pray about it before you set up any rules at the church. If I know anything about Mari, she's not going to like being told what to do."

A smile tugs at my lips against my own will. No, she'll probably tell me I'm overstepping. Her eyes will flash, and that cute little chin will lower as she leans back into her chair.

"*I don't agree, Pastor.*"

"*I don't care, young lady. You'll obey me, or else...*"

Fuck.

When my eyes shoot to Ethan, he's smirking at me, clearly sensing the direction of my thoughts. With a final glare at him, I march out of the room.

God help me tomorrow.

Chapter Ten

M ariana

"Alright, you need to get out of here," I say to my friend Zac. "You're distracting me."

Not that I really want him to leave. Sure, he's been sitting on my desk for the last half hour, and I've gotten almost nothing done. He's been talking so much, I've barely even been able to eat the lunch he brought me.

But at least I haven't thought about Brandon.

Much.

My head has been pounding today. Screaming. What is going to happen? I came to Brandon's office this morning to have our "talk." He told me we'd have it at the end of the day without even looking up from his computer. Since then, he's been as cold and remote as a marble statue.

"Alright, I'll leave you alone," Zac says. "Are you coming to happy hour tomorrow night?"

I wrinkle my nose. "Not unless Livvy's coming. I'm not a big baseball fan. It's boring."

"My little hater." Zac leans forward and touches the tip of my nose. "Don't tell Cole. He'll start crying."

I snort. "As if I care about soothing his—"

My lips close as Brandon's face appears in the doorway. His jaw is set, and his eyes are dark.

"Do you need something?" I ask.

"Nope." He quickly disappears, and my bafflement expands like a balloon.

Why did he seem angry? I didn't do anything wrong last night, damn it.

"I want to do something with you on Saturday," Zac says. "No spending the day with Livvy. It's my turn."

I giggle. "Your turn? Is this a competition now between you and Livvy? You know she'll always win."

He grins. "Hey, I'll fight. She's going to be married soon. She won't have the stamina."

"She'll still win, honey. Besties always win."

He leans forward, stopping an inch away from my face. "Yeah, but I've got something she doesn't."

I burst into laughter, and he narrows his eyes playfully. "Don't act like you don't—"

"Mariana," Brandon's voice booms from the doorway, "can you come in my office for a second?"

The sharpness in his tone startles me. "Just a second."

Brandon hesitates for a moment, glancing at Zac and then back to me before walking away.

Oh fuck.

He's going to fire me. That's what our talk is going to be about. Apparently, I've irritated him so much that he can't even wait until the end of the day.

"That didn't sound good," Zac says.

Heat washes over my skin. "No, it doesn't. You really need to get out of here."

He winces as he starts walking away. "Sorry if I got you in

trouble."

I wave a hand. "It's not you, it's...something else. But I don't want to piss him off even more. I'll text you later if I decide to come to happy hour."

As soon as Zac disappears, I head toward Brandon's office, my heart pounding louder and louder with each step, like a warrior's drum.

When I walk through the door, my attention is immediately drawn to the rigid set of his jaw and furrow in his brow, and that familiar rebellion grows like a flame within me. After the silent treatment I've been getting, I'm ready for a fight.

It's unfair that he thinks he messed up, and now I have to pay for it. I didn't ask him to touch my damn lip.

Though I did love it when he did.

"What can I do for you, Pastor?" At the word "pastor", his jaw ticks, and I could almost smile. He caught on to my intended insolence.

"Sit," he says, and I jerk back at the abruptness in the command.

Tendrils of heat fill my gut as I sit on a small couch in front of his desk. Why does it always turn me on when he scolds me?

Probably because after yesterday, I'm not so sure it comes from a fatherly place like I used to.

Brandon takes a heavy breath. "We need to have a sort of...uncomfortable conversation."

My stomach plummets. Oh, fuck. He really is going to fire me. Ice skitters through my veins at the thought.

I shouldn't care. I didn't even want this internship to begin with.

I hate myself for wanting to cry.

"I hope you understand that I appreciate how much you're helping me out right now, Mariana." He emphasizes my name. Is that a taunt because I called him "pastor"?

"Thank you," I say, my voice brittle.

"But even though this is an unpaid position, I can't have you fraternizing while you're working." His voice is stern.

His words don't compute at first. What the fuck is he talking about? He was the one who invited me out to dinner last night. He was the one who...

When his meaning finally dawns, I have to clench my jaw to keep from smiling.

He's talking about Zac.

I lean back into my chair. "Fraternizing? Did you really just use that word?"

He shuts his eyes. "You know what I mean. This may be a volunteer position, but the rules are the same."

"I wasn't *fraternizing*."

"He was sitting on your desk." Brandon's nostrils flare. "He's not an employee. He's not a member of the church. It's not appropriate. Your door was wide open. Anyone could have seen you."

My lips quirk. "Isn't that how it's supposed to be? Aren't the doors always supposed to be open when men and women are together at churches?"

He averts his gaze. "We don't have gendered rules like that here."

I scowl. "Then what is this about?"

He leans forward. "I wouldn't tolerate this among my gym employees either. This has nothing to do with working at a church."

I lift my chin. "Tolerate what exactly, Brandon?"

Those dark eyes grow wide, and his cheeks flush. His voice drops to a whisper. "I won't tolerate insubordination, Mariana."

My breath hitches, and heat rushes between my legs. Oh my God. Is it just my imagination, or does he feel this electricity between us, too?

I lick my lips and lean forward, meeting his gaze with a challenge in my eyes. "Insubordination? I'm not even a real employee." I can't help the way my voice drops to a low, sultry tone. "Are you sure this isn't about something else?"

When his eyes darken, I let my body melt back into the chair and flip a chunk of hair over my shoulder. My God, I can't believe I'm behaving this way. My taut nerves are making me reckless.

"You won't tolerate insubordination from me, but I have to let you touch me without complaint. Is that it?"

His eyes grow huge, and a wicked heat sizzles through my veins. "I never..." He grits his teeth. "I never should have done that."

An itch for rebellion quakes through my whole body. I lean forward, setting my elbows on his desk. "What if I liked it?"

His face grows flushed, and that big chest rises and falls rapidly. "I'm courting your sister."

I snort. "She and I both know you're not even into her. You only asked her out to make my dad happy."

He averts his gaze. "You don't know that."

"Yes, I do." I lift my hand and rub my index finger along my bottom lip. Brandon jerks back, looking utterly baffled by my behavior.

I'm a little baffled too. Why am I pushing him so hard when I really don't want to get fired?

I enjoy being around him every day.

Brandon stands up suddenly, his rolling chair shooting out behind him like a rocket. "I need a moment. We'll talk at the end of the day."

A split second later, the door slams, and I sit in silence for several minutes, listening to the pounding rhythm of my racing heart.

Mariana

He didn't come back.

The sun sets behind the ocean as I drive through the hills of an upscale Santa Barbara neighborhood, my eyes getting bigger with each house I pass. Damn. My dad mentioned that Brandon lives in a nice house, but I never expected this.

No wonder he didn't come back today. If I lived in this neighborhood, I would never leave.

A small smile tugs at my lips. He's going to be outraged when he sees me.

He called the office a half hour ago asking for several books from his office shelf. I overheard bits and pieces of Harper's conversation with him, and as soon as she hung up, I volunteered to drive them to his house, even though he requested her.

I won't let him avoid me.

My navigation tells me I've arrived, and I park on the sidewalk next to a house at the top of the hill. Holy shit. This house has to be worth at least a couple million. And here I thought my dad was exaggerating when he said Brandon was a multimillionaire.

As I approach the front door, a tingle runs over my skin. I'm going to see Brandon's private space. His home. Why does the thought of it give me a naughty thrill?

After I ring the bell, the door opens, and his huge form hovers over me. He smells damn good, like he just took a shower.

His eyes widen. "What are you doing here?"

I let my lids grow heavy as I smile. "Delivering your books."

"What happened to Harper?"

"She had a final to study for. I told her it was no problem for me."

He looks at me skeptically, probably because I infused such a smarmy cheerfulness into my voice. I can't help it.

I'm angry.

"You're avoiding me," I say.

His expression shutters. "I hadn't figured out what to say to you yet. I've been praying about it."

I cross my arms over my chest. "Did God tell you to fire me?"

His eyes grow huge. "Of course not. I would never fire you for something that's my fault."

"It's just a volunteer position. I don't really need it."

We stare at each other in charged silence. Then his eyes flicker to the books in my hand, as if he's ready for the conversation to be over.

"Well, I'll leave you alone to pray," I say quickly. "Here you go."

Something flashes in his eyes as I hand him the books. "You want to come in for a second so I can thank you with a cup of coffee?"

"No, I'm fine."

"Are you sure?" He smiles. "I have French vanilla creamer."

My tummy flutters. It's sweet that he thinks I like that creamer. The only reason I use so much of it at the church is because the coffee is usually sour from sitting in the carafe for so many hours. I glance through the doorway at the floor-to-ceiling windows overlooking the ocean, and curiosity gets the better of me.

"That sounds good," I say and follow him inside.

While he fetches my coffee, I try to absorb every inch of his home, wishing I could pour through his rooms and learn more about him. He has a minimalist style, with beige walls, abstract expressionist art, and scattered midcentury modern furniture. Why do the houses of rich people always look this way, as if they have to be completely scrubbed of humanity in order to look clean?

I spot a book lying on the coffee table. When I walk closer, I see that it's about hiking the highest peaks in the world. I smile to myself. I'd love to go on a hike with him. Be a quiet presence while he—

Brandon emerges from the entryway with two steaming mugs, yanking me out of my silly fantasy.

"Your house is beautiful." I hold the cup to my lips and blow on the hot liquid. "I'd never leave here if I had a view like this."

His gaze drifts to the glass wall of ocean. "It's surprising how soon you get used to it. Now it's like beautiful wallpaper. I hardly even notice it."

As I glance out at the water, I catch glimpses of sailboats bobbing in the distance. My God, how much wealth would it take to see a view like this as wallpaper? "You really are humble, Pastor. I had no idea your gym business was *this* successful."

He smiles. "We had eighteen gyms total in California and Nevada when my partner bought me out."

"Damn," I mutter. "I thought there were just gyms in Santa Barbara and Goleta. You must be loaded. Why would you give all that up to make nothing as a pastor?"

He chuckles. "I love how direct you are."

My cheeks warm at his use of the word "love." He's used it before in reference to me and my family, but never with so much warmth in his voice.

Heat is a better word.

"Quitting was the best decision I ever made," he says. "I was thoroughly burnt out when I finally sold my share of the company. I wouldn't have done anyone any good had I stayed. Damon—my partner and best friend at the time—probably would have tried to force me to sell eventually."

I wrinkle my nose. "What a dick."

He grins, his eyes crinkling at the corners. "He would've been justified. My mom had just passed away, and I was completely checked out. I had been since she got sick, really. I didn't even show up to our last few board meetings."

"That doesn't sound like you, even if you were grieving. I guess...you must have been really devastated."

"I was." His gaze grows unfocused. "She was my anchor, even as a grown man. I didn't form strong bonds with anyone else back then. I didn't... I had a hard time being vulnerable before I came to God."

I lift my chin. "Like most men I know."

"Yes." His smile fades. "My dad is the same way. He deals with his emotions by finding new, younger woman."

A chill skates over my skin at the bitterness in his voice. I've never heard him talk this way before. In his sermons, he always sounds so quietly accepting of life's trials, probably partially by design. He wants his congregation to look to him for guidance.

No wonder he never talks about his dad. He wouldn't want people to see this side of him.

I soften my voice. "That must have been hard for your mom."

"It was." His jaw clenches. "He left her for one of his younger women. I'm not sure if she ever really recovered from it. Cancer's a complicated disease, and I sometimes wonder if..." He shakes his head. "There's no point dwelling on things that can't be changed."

He stares down at his coffee mug for a moment. Then, as if a thought occurs to him, a cynical smile tugs at his lips. "He left *that* woman too, for an even younger woman."

I frown. "Which one was Ethan's mom?"

"Wife number two." That cynical smile grows. "He's now on wife number three. She's probably only a little older than Sofia."

A wave of melancholy washes over me. Everything is starting to click into place. No wonder he's agonizing over touching my lip yesterday. Any attraction to a woman as young as me probably reminds him of his dad.

"Don't feel sorry for me," he says abruptly. "I'd probably still be a selfish prick if things hadn't happened the way they did. I used to be the type of person who saw people only for what they could do for me, and it was a shitty way to go through life. For me and for the people I treated like garbage. I had so many shallow friendships and..." His jaw tightens. "Relationships with women that were only about...one thing. Now I know that all people have value. All people are worthy. I believe this from the bottom of my soul, and it didn't come from within. It came from God."

I smile faintly. "I guess I'm fucked then."

He shakes his head sharply. "You don't need God. You're that way all on your own."

The atmosphere between us changes, like smoke drifting through the air, I can almost see it. No one has ever told me anything like that before, not even the people who accept me just as I am—like Livvy and Vanessa.

What would it be like to be in this house all the time? What would it be like to become part of the beautiful wallpaper—sitting out there on the patio with him looking at me like he is right now, telling me I'm perfect as I am?

Oh fuck, I hope this doesn't mean the lip touch got to my head. Wanting him physically is one thing, but I can't develop deeper feelings for him. What would he do if he caught on?

He'd probably pity me. Think I'm a silly girl, like the young women in his church who have stars in their eyes when they approach him after his sermons.

"Well, I should head out," I say quickly.

He jerks back a little, as if surprised by my change in mood. "I'll see you tomorrow, I guess."

I smile. "Tomorrow's Saturday, Pastor."

"I'll be at dinner."

My stomach drops. Oh, that's right. The dinner with my family. "Damn, I forgot. Everyone's going to be there. They're all going to be asking me how this whole...internship with you is going."

He smiles faintly. "You'll tell them it's going great, that you're doing an excellent job."

I let out a groan. "They're going to ask me what I've learned about the Bible."

He reaches out and sets his hand on my shoulder, sending tingles up my neck. "You don't need to say anything to appease them. Wasn't that what yesterday was about? You accept yourself as you are, even if they don't."

Warmth spreads slowly from my chest out to my limbs, making my whole body lighter. How does he do it? How does he provide comfort while also pushing me to be braver? With anyone else, I'd probably get defensive. Or consider his gentle encouragement condescending.

Brandon seems to see right through me, straight into my heart.

I'm not sure if I like it.

"I'm going to try to get to know Sofia better," he says.

His words hit me like a shockwave. How could I forget about Sofia? I can't start catching feelings for him when he's technically dating my sister.

I force what I hope looks like a light smile. "You weren't doing that already—you know—by courting her?"

His expression grows grave. "I've been thinking about what you said this morning. About not being into her... It isn't right that she thinks that. She's a wonderful woman. She deserves someone who'll give it his all. Give things a real chance."

My throat grows tight. "So you're going to actually talk to someone besides my dad at this family dinner?"

His lips quirk. "Watch it, young lady. I'm still your boss. I won't give your family a good report tomorrow if you keep sassing me."

I snort. Thankfully, my thoughts are too twisted for me to be turned on by his playful sternness. "Maybe you should tell them you baptized me as an atheist. That way I won't be the only outcast."

His smile vanishes. "Oh, Mariana." His voice grows hushed. "You'll never be an outcast. Even if you disappoint your family, you'll always have people who love you." He clears his throat. "Including me."

Mist rises to my eyes as a lulling warmth fills my body. I know what he means by "love." It's a Godly love. Maybe even a fatherly love. But it doesn't make it any less devastating as he stares at me with eyes as deep and dark as a cavern.

I can't let it get to my head when the best pastors are good at this. Good at providing quiet comfort that makes you feel like you've been roaming the earth alone until you found them. It's where the belief in deities comes from. It's why cult leaders can charm people to their death.

It won't happen to me.

I won't fall for him.

Chapter Eleven

M ariana

Three hours. I just have to get through the next three hours.

I adjust the tablecloth, trying to ignore the weight in my chest as Brandon settles into his seat beside Sofia. He leans in to say something to her, their heads close together, and my throat squeezes.

What the fuck is wrong with me? It's good that he's actually trying to pursue her now. He might be able to help her heart finally heal. No one on earth would choose Finn over Brandon.

His eyes meet mine for a moment, and his gaze is so dark and intense that I have to look away, my heart pounding in my ears.

Make it two hours. I'll leave right after dessert. I'll say I have a headache and ask my brother and Nora to take Sofia home later.

"Mari, can you come in here?" my mom calls from the kitchen.

Just as I start to turn around, Brandon's eyes flash, and I quicken my step. I can't keep looking at him all night long.

Oh God, what if this really becomes something with Sofia, and they get married someday? At all these family dinners, Brandon will be sitting right next to her like he is right now. I'll catch him brushing his hand along her thigh and stealing kisses in the hallway when he thinks no one is watching.

As I walk into the kitchen, the smell of Mom's garlic shrimp fills my nose. At least I'll have good food to get me through the evening.

My mom points to the kitchen island. "Can you finish up the salad?"

I walk to the counter. "Sure."

As I turn to the sink and start washing my hands, my mom shoots me a mischievous grin. "They look like they're getting cozy in there."

I smile tightly. "Hopefully not too cozy. They'd better keep the holy spirit between them. We don't want Sofi to get pregnant."

My mom wrinkles her nose as she fluffs the rice. "Don't be gross. As if Brandon would ever do that."

I smile. "I don't know, Mom. Sounds like he was pretty wild before he became a pastor."

She chuckles as she turns off the heat under the pot. "Stop it, Mari, before I come over there and spank you. I don't want Brandon hearing you talk like this."

"I'm his intern now." I shoot her a smile. "We're practically besties."

Her delighted smile makes my stomach drop. She loves that I'm working for him now.

It gives her hope for me.

"He told your dad you're the fastest learner he's ever met, even compared to the people he knew in the business world."

I snort. "That has the hand of Dad all over it. Brandon probably said, 'She's doing fine,' and Dad was like, 'My daughter is a genius.'"

"No." Her voice is hushed. "We don't need our kids to be geniuses. It doesn't take a genius to be a strong woman of God."

Her words hit me like a punch in the gut, making me momentarily senseless to the world around me.

Why does it hurt so much to hear her say something like that? I know that's my parents' biggest priority, and it doesn't come purely from judgment. They're genuinely fearful that I'll go to hell if I don't change my ways.

But fuck. She knows what *my* priorities are. She knows I want to travel the world and learn about every scrap of human history. She knows I want to be a professor someday.

She doesn't care. The parts of myself that are so meaningful to me are nothing to her.

I'm still in a fog by the time dinner starts. It isn't difficult to tune everyone out. As usual, they're all vying for Brandon's attention. Mom has a million questions for him. Even Abuelita is making occasional comments when she's usually shy around him. They're all making an extra effort, because they must sense that he's being more attentive to Sofia, and they're encouraging him. They want him to officially become part of the family.

They want him to be Sofi's husband.

Dad turns to Brandon with a smile. "How's Mari doing in her new position? She hasn't caused a church schism yet, has she?"

My dad shoots me a teasing glance, and I give him the same long stare I've been giving him since I was twelve years old.

"I don't know how to respond to Dad jokes, Hector," Brandon says. "Am I supposed to make one back?"

Chuckles break out around the table, and Sofi smiles up at him. "He's had over thirty years of practice. They just roll off the tongue for him."

Dad takes a sip of his wine. "Brandon will understand soon. He won't be a single man forever."

Dad's pointed glance at Sofia makes my skin crawl. Why can't he be more subtle than this? Why isn't he even slightly self-conscious about his overt intervention in all his kids' lives?

Brandon smiles. "I'm not going to respond to that, so I'll answer your question as if you asked it in good faith. No, Mariana has not caused a schism. She's an excellent volunteer. I've barely had to explain anything to her, and just last week she organized my entire office library. We're lucky to have her."

Warmth fills my chest at his words, though I try not to let it show. Our gazes meet for a brief moment. There's that familiar softness in those inky-dark eyes. I hate that it makes my stomach flutter.

Sofia leans in to whisper something to him, and he turns away. The warmth inside me abruptly fades, replaced by a cold emptiness.

I push my salad around my plate, my throat so tight I couldn't take a bite if I wanted to.

Dad chuckles. "Well, hopefully by the end of this, it will be good for her too. Maybe you can bring her back to the Lord."

I grow still, and my cheeks burn. There was no mistaking the passive aggression in that statement, as much as he was trying to sound playful.

How can he talk about things like this in front of our whole family? How does he think he has the right?

Brandon's expression grows stern. "It's important to have people like Mariana in the church. Sometimes congregations can be echo chambers. For my part, having someone challenge my faith always strengthens it."

A lightness blooms in my chest. Brandon is usually honest with my dad, but I don't think he's ever stood up for me before.

I don't think anyone has.

I smile faintly at him, and his eyes soften in response.

"I agree that we need people like that," my dad says, "but I'd rather it not be my daughter."

I twist around to scowl at him. "Can we not talk about this at the dinner table?"

My dad's expression softens. He reaches out to pat my shoulder. "My little firecracker. You're going to do amazing things someday."

For God, he means.

Fuck, I have to get out of here. I'm going to make a scene if I don't.

I stand up from the table and grab my plate. "I have a bad headache," I say, inwardly cringing at the triteness of the excuse.

"Where do you think you're going?" my dad calls out.

"Your grandma has extra strength Ibuprofen," my mom says. Her voice grows hushed as she asks Abuelita in Spanish if she minds that I use the medication leftover from her surgery.

"Ibuprofen makes me nauseous," I shout over the rushing sink water.

As I walk into the living room to grab my purse, I catch sight of my mom's stern gaze. I'll no doubt be getting some scathing texts after I leave, but it will be worth not lashing out at my dad. Not in front of Brandon.

I can't reinforce his belief that I'm just an unruly child.

As I turn the corner of the dining room into the hallway, I catch sight of Brandon's intense expression.

He knows.

He knows my feelings as if they were his own.

Am I crazy, or is this invisible connection between us something real?

Brandon

I inhale deeply, attempting to calm the tornado of feelings that have been swirling since Mariana left. "I need to be upfront with you," I say to Hector. "You hurt Mariana tonight. Everyone saw it."

His face falls as he stares into the glass of amber liquid. He doesn't drink whiskey very often—or any form of alcohol for that matter—so he's probably already feeling regret. "I shouldn't have talked about it in front of everyone." His voice is hushed.

"I don't think you should have talked about it at all."

His brow furrows, his dark eyes meeting mine. "I can't be dishonest. That's not how I raised my kids. I have to be real with her, and we both know she's drifting. If we can't get through to her soon..." He shakes his head.

"We?" I pin him with a hard stare. "I told you I'd talk to her. You know it's not in my power to bring her back to God."

Especially since I don't think she was ever with God to begin with.

He leans forward, his eyes alighting. "Here's the thing, though, I'm finally starting to see a change in her. Every night, I pray. I tell God the deepest desire of my heart. 'Protect my children,' I say. 'Keep them with you, God.'" When he pauses, I inhale a breath to prepare myself for what I know he's about to say.

"Ever since she started working with you, I've had this feeling." He places his palm against his chest. "I think it's a message from the Holy Spirit, Brandon, I really do. You're the one who's going to finally get through to her. I really believe it. She admires you. You're a cool, liberal pastor, you know?"

I grunt. "It sounds like a pretty shallow reason to come back to Christianity."

"It's not though. You can speak her language. She looks up to you."

And I want to fuck her.

The words echo in my head, as clear as the word of God.

It's a warning.

Self-recrimination squeezes my chest like a fist. I don't believe that God is telling Hector that I'll be the one to bring Mariana to Christ, but I do believe God is sending me a message through him.

Crossing this line will be an abuse of power.

83

I can't ever touch her again. Not when she looks up to me as a mentor. It's reprehensible.

"I'll keep talking to her." My voice is barely above a whisper. "But that's all I can promise."

"That's all I'd ever expect of you." His smile grows so affectionate, my chest squeezes with guilt.

Mariana

My head pounds. It turns out I have a real headache. A punishment for faking one, I guess.

The front door bursts open, and Sofia's beaming face comes into view. "Guess what?" she squeals as she sets her purse on the couch.

I clench my facial muscles to keep from grimacing. "What?"

"Brandon asked me to be his date for Livvy's wedding!"

Her words are like ice through my veins, and it's so silly. Here I am suddenly wanting Brandon to stay away from her—my beloved sister—when their relationship couldn't be anything but good for her. It might even mend *my* relationship with her, since it would help her forget about Finn.

What is wrong with me?

I force a smile. "That's awesome."

"I'll be sitting at his table," she continues, bouncing on her toes. "Can you imagine what Finn will think?"

My stomach plummets to the floor. "So you're using Brandon? That's fucked up."

She halts, turning to me with wrath in her eyes. "How dare you say something like that."

Heat creeps into my cheeks. She doesn't realize what she's doing. I know this. Finn's betrayal has pulled her into a deep, dark hole. She can't see anything but her own pain.

I sigh. "Why do you still care what Finn thinks?"

She crosses her arms over her chest. "I'm not letting Brandon court me just to make Finn jealous. I know that's what you think."

It is what I think, but I can't tell her that.

"I know you aren't, but why are you... Why make Livvy's wedding all about Finn?"

She flutters her eyelids dramatically. "How would you feel if you were forced to spend hours at a wedding of all places with your ex-fiancé who dumped you for the woman he got pregnant?"

I let out a long sigh. "Livvy said she would have her dad ask him not to come. She never would have even invited him if you hadn't given her the okay."

Sofia grimaces. "I'm not going to be the reason Livvy excludes her *cousin* and his wife from her wedding. It's embarrassing. I don't want him thinking he still gets to me."

I raise both hands in the air. "But he *does* still get to you!"

Her jaw tightens as she walks into the kitchen. Oh fuck, no. I won't let her dismiss me.

"I don't want you to fuck over your relationship with Brandon," I lie, "because you're still hung up on Finn."

She rolls her eyes as she gulps down a bottle of water. "I would never do that," she says breathlessly as she lowers the bottle. "But I can't help that my heart is still in pain."

I grit my teeth. I know I should feel compassion. I did, for so long. It was a disgusting thing that Finn did.

But it's been three years.

And why doesn't she have any pain in her heart for what she and I lost? Finn left her, but I'm right here, damn it. And I was right about him. How does she not see it?

She blames me for everything that went wrong between them, just like Brandon said. I saw it coming, and she superstitiously considers me the cause.

I thought our bond was stronger than this. Finding out that it wasn't is a physical pain in my chest. I miss my big sister.

Maybe the person I thought she was never existed.

Chapter Twelve

Brandon

Mariana drops to her knees and reaches for my hips. I glance down and see my own bare thighs. Why am I naked?

There's no resisting her now. I'd have to be a saint. I'll just give in. God will forgive me.

She smiles cheekily before leaning forward and slipping that beautiful mouth around my cock.

"Naughty girl," I whisper.

Unbearable pleasure rushes through my gut with the force of a deluge, my heart pounding like a hammer. My office blurs, morphing into a dark room. The feel of Mari's hot mouth becomes my hard, dry fist.

Fuck.

I shouldn't be this disappointed. I always wake up when it gets to be too much. When her sweetness makes me so wild, I can no longer hold on to the ghostly hand of sleep.

I grit my teeth. I won't jack off. I won't do it.

Dreams are involuntary, but masturbating isn't. Sure, God would forgive me. I'm already halfway to ecstasy. But I couldn't forgive myself. Indulging lust only makes it more potent, and I have to stop fantasizing about the young woman who sees me as a mentor.

After a deep, steadying breath, I step out of bed. I'll just have to start my day early. Staying in bed will only be a temptation.

Hours later, I'm in the church auditorium. The real-life Mariana stretches one long arm up to the top of the corkboard, and a swath of brown skin on her lower back is exposed.

She has beautiful skin that looks so, so soft.

"What do you think?" Gurshan asks.

When my head jerks up, he's smirking at me. His gaze shoots to Mariana, then back to me.

Fuck. It's all over his expression that he knows exactly what I was looking at.

I haven't been able to stop. After that dream, I've been sensitive to her every movement.

It doesn't make any sense. It wasn't my first dream about her. I've been having them for weeks now.

Naughty girl. I desperately want to say those words to her. I want her to behave like such a bad girl that I lose my power to resist her. Then I want to bend her over my lap and spank her for it.

Fuck. Gurshan just said something.

"I'm sorry," I say. "Can you repeat that?"

"I was thinking of swapping 'In Christ Alone' with 'Oh Come Thou Fount of Every Blessing.'" He sets his guitar on a stand at the edge of the stage. "It's a banger of a hymn."

I nod, trying to maintain a placid expression. "Sure, that sounds good. We'll try it at rehearsal."

Gurshan looks at me for a moment longer before heading out of the church sanctuary. I take a deep breath and close my eyes, trying to shake fantasies of Mariana from my senses.

I haven't jacked off thinking about her. Not once since this strange lust for her began to stir within me.

That's the one thing I have.

I make my way to the back of the church. "Hey, do you have a minute?"

She turns around, her dark hair swinging over her shoulder. Her brown eyes meet mine, and my stomach does a little turn.

"Sure, what's up?"

I clear my throat, trying to ignore the wash of her sweet floral scent over me. "I just wanted to check in and make sure everything's okay. You seemed upset last night."

She waves a hand. "I was more irritated than anything. I didn't want to snap at my dad."

I lower my chin. "I had a talk with him after you left. I didn't like the way he treated you."

Her eyes grow wide at first—as if she's surprised—but then that mischievous smile tugs at her lips. "My big strong protector. I should start calling *you* Daddy."

My whole body ignites into flames. *Yes, you should, naughty girl. Get on your knees and thank me.*

Oh fuck.

Fucking fuck. This isn't good.

I glance at the corkboard, searching for a change of subject. "What are you doing?"

Her smile fades. "I'm rearranging the prayer requests. I hope you don't mind."

I take a breath to calm my racing pulse. "Why would you do that?"

Her eyes spark. "I decided to categorize them by topic. Loss of a loved one is this big section right here." She points to the middle of the board. "I subdivided it by pets and people. These right here are family struggles, but I put breakups and divorce in their own category up there. And these are miscellaneous."

The warmth blooming in my chest is calming my raging lust. I'm thankful for it. Mariana's excitement fizzes out of her like champagne bubbles. I always found it adorable and infectious, long before I started seeing her differently.

I smile. "What was your rationale for rearranging them?"

She licks the corner of her mouth, drawing my attention to that full bottom lip. "I figured people who are going through some kind of trial probably want to pray for people going through a similar thing. This way, they can easily find it."

I tilt my head. "Is this for the benefit of the one praying or the prayee, so to speak?"

She shrugs. "Both, probably. It'll help the person praying sort through their own troubles, for one thing, and don't pastors usually encourage people to pray with specificity?"

I smile. "We do, but why would an atheist care about this?"

A notch pulls between her dark brows. "I respect all the rituals, even if I don't believe in them."

"I never doubted it." I take a step forward, as if pulled by a force from outside of me. "You're very kind and thoughtful."

She tilts her head up to look at me, and a molten liquid heat floods my gut. Those lips are full and slightly pouted. The temptation to lean in and kiss her is overwhelming.

Fuck.

"Well, I'll leave you to your project," I clip out.

The last image I see before turning away is a flash of surprise in her dark eyes. I don't care if I was abrupt. She's too fucking tempting.

Mariana

"I'm going to head out," I say.

Brandon's head snaps up, his expression grim. "Alright." His voice is hoarse. "I'll see you tomorrow."

I pause, trying to read the strange energy that lingers in the air between us. He averts his gaze and stays silent.

He was about to kiss me today. I wasn't imagining it. That's why he's been cold ever since.

Goddamn it, why can't he just give in? If he's willing to stand up to my dad when he oversteps, why not in this area, too? It was stupid of my dad to push Brandon and Sofia to get together. She's still obsessed with Finn, and Brandon is trying to force a connection with her that he doesn't feel.

I wait a moment longer before turning around and walking down the hall. A door is shut behind his eyes, and I refuse to force my way through it.

When I make it to my car, I rummage through my purse to find my phone. I can't drive without music. After digging through pockets and pushing around receipts and lip glosses, I still can't find it.

"Damn it," I mutter before turning around and marching back inside the church. When I get back to my desk, my phone is sitting face up on my desk. I roll my eyes at myself, grab it and set it in my purse. I walk back into the hallway, and an odd sound halts me in my tracks.

Was that a groan?

Curiosity prickles over my skin like the adrenaline rush from a rollercoaster. That was Brandon's voice, and it was the sound of...

Pleasure.

I tiptoe closer until I reach the door and open it as quietly as I can. The sight in front of me sends an otherworldly chill down my spine.

It can't be.

I'm not really seeing this.

Brandon is standing with one hand braced on the corner of his desk while the other moves rapidly up and down as he strokes his...

Holy shit, that's his penis.

It's big and thick and veiny, just like I imagined. How is this happening? Am I dreaming?

His breathing quickens, and heat pools between my legs as I

stand and watch, unable to move. I need to walk away. I don't want him to see me, but my body is frozen.

"Mari," he whispers my name like a prayer, using that Saturday-night service voice.

He never calls me Mari. It's always Mariana.

His groaning gets louder, his face grimaced as if in pain, but it's those eyes. Those inky-dark eyes are heavy lidded and dreamy.

He's thinking about me right now. An almost unbearable tingle runs into my groin.

"My naughty girl," he whispers, and my head jerks back. Oh my God. I'm witnessing his private fantasy.

About me.

Clenching his jaw and gritting his teeth, he pumps and strokes, faster and harder until sparkling droplets of sweat bead up on his forehead. His breathing quickens as ropes of come flood over his fist, intensifying until a gushing stream splashes on the wood floor beneath him. He lets out an animalistic roar before finally releasing the last drop.

I snap into action and start running down the hallway. I need to get out of here before he catches me. When I make it to the door, I slow my pace, lifting the metal knob as lightly as if it were the page of an antique book.

Before I know it, I'm sitting in my car, breathing heavily.

I just witnessed possibly the hottest thing I've ever seen in my life. So hot and so, so forbidden.

Brandon.

Masturbating and thinking about me.

Calling me his naughty girl.

He must have liked it when I called him Daddy earlier today.

My belly is on fire. Without a moment's reflection, I slip my hand under my skirt until I find the seam of my underwear. The moment my finger reaches my clit, I release a moan.

When I close my eyes, I'm back in Brandon's office, bent over his wooden desk with my ass in the air. "Naughty," he says, but that's as far as I get. The next moment, I'm panting as waves of heat shoot like arrows through my veins.

"Yes, Brandon," I moan. "I'm your naughty girl."

And I mean it.

I can't be good after this. Not after what he revealed.

I'm going to tempt him, and I don't even feel guilty about it.

Chapter Thirteen

M ariana

"You're shitting me," Livvy says, her eyes huge.

We came to this cafe to talk about wedding details, but I doubt we'll get much done now that I've told her the whole story.

I huff out an almost hysterical laugh. "I honestly still feel like I dreamed it, but it was real."

She shakes her head slowly, her eyes wide and dazed. "I can't believe it." Her eyes narrow. "Do you think he's going to break up with Sofi after this?"

I snort. "No. As a matter of fact, he's arranged a coffee date with her and his little brother tomorrow because he wants her to get to know him better."

She frowns. "It's so strange. Does he really feel that much pressure from your dad?"

I roll my eyes. "At this point, I'm wondering if he's in denial."

A childlike grin spreads over Livvy's face. "About wanting you, huh?"

I nod, taking a sip of my chai latte. "He's very weird about age. He thought Sofia was too young for him at first."

Livvy's nose wrinkles. "It's silly, though. You're both grown ass women."

"I know." I expel a breath through my closed lips. "It's my damn dad who fucked this up. Brandon looks up to him."

"Yeah, but... Do you think your dad would be mad if he got with you instead?"

"Yes," I say immediately. "He's so different with me than he is with the rest of the family. Being the baby sucks. They all treat me like a little kid."

Livvy's warm hand settles on mine. "I think you need to have a talk with Brandon. You're not a little kid, and after what you saw last night... You know he doesn't see you that way. I know you wouldn't actually mention it outright—"

"Oh, but I'm not going to just pretend it didn't happen either." A thrill runs up my spine. "I'm going to drop hints that I know and make him sweat over it."

Livvy's face lights up. "What are you going to say?"

I grin as I tell her my plan for tomorrow.

Brandon

As I roll down the window, the misty ocean air cools my face, but it does nothing to calm me. I can't reason away the grip of guilt squeezing my heart.

What would the Hernandez family think if they knew what I did last night? I'm on my way to meet Sofia for coffee, and less than twenty-four hours ago, I jacked off thinking about the baby of the family. In my damn church office.

In the house of the Lord.

I know a church building is no more significant than anywhere else. God is everywhere. The thought isn't comforting, though. Not when I felt more alive last night than I ever have in that office.

I glance over at Ethan. He has Sofia's Instagram page pulled up on his phone. "She still has pictures up of her ex," he says.

I flip on the turn signal. "Not recent pictures, I hope."

He snorts. "You don't sound hopeful at all. You don't sound like you even care."

Guilt sinks my gut. How could I care when I'm consumed with lust for her younger sister?

"Don't say anything like that around her. I've made up my mind to give her my all. She has a lot of good qualities. She's a smart woman and very sweet."

Smart. Sweet. The words feel dull on my lips, like I've rehearsed them. Like they rise to my tongue because I can't think of anything else to say. Why can't I think of better words to describe her?

Bright. Intense. Eyes that cut into you and clench your stomach muscles.

But those aren't words to describe Sofia.

"Mariana, though..." Ethan mutters, startling me. When I look in his direction, a mosaic wall of pictures of Mariana are pulled up on his phone. "If you don't go for her, I might. Those eyes of hers."

My jaw clenches, but I try to keep my expression placid. He's only trying to goad me. He'd never actually pursue someone who doesn't share his faith.

But fuck if I don't hate hearing anyone else talk about her eyes.

Those incredible eyes. Inky dark and dusted with gold, but that's not what makes them sparkle. It's her expressions. She's so full of emotion, that woman.

I'd love to see what ecstasy looks like on her face.

Ethan chuckles, and heat washes over my face. I know what he's about to say. It's as if we can read each other's minds.

"You so want Mari. It's obvious."

I grit my teeth. "It's not something to joke about. I'm old enough to be her dad."

Ethan scoffs. "Yeah, if you had her at fourteen. I think you've let Hector get in your head."

I run a hand through my hair. "Please let's not talk about this now. Not when we're about to hang out with Sofia. I feel guilty enough that I'm attracted to Mariana."

"The solution is to stop letting Hector pressure you into dating someone when you don't really want to. I'm seriously worried you might end up marrying Sofia just because you're lonely."

A chuckle rumbles from my chest, easing my frayed nerves. "You have a really high opinion of my character."

Ethan smiles. "It's so clear you're dying to find a wife. You're more of a stereotypical evangelical than I am."

I punch his shoulder before stepping out of the car. "I'm not a virgin."

Ethan chuckles. "You're a born-again virgin."

I'm relieved by the lightness between us as we walk to the cafe, yet I can't fully stifle the stirring of guilt inside me. Maybe he's right that I should stop pursuing Sofia. If I haven't felt a spark with her yet, maybe it's never going to happen.

No. I have to give her a chance. I owe Hector at least that after everything he's done for me, even if I don't agree with his attempt to manage his grown daughters' lives.

My stomach plummets to the floor when we walk into the coffee shop, and I see Mariana sitting right next to her sister.

Sofia waves, and Mariana shoots me a cheeky, heavy-lidded smile.

Naughty girl.

Oh fuck, not these fantasies again. Not here of all places. Goddamn it, what is she even doing here?

I force myself to focus on Sofia and greet her with a warm hug. As we sit, Mariana's eyes bore into me, and tingles run down the length of my spine.

Why do I get the feeling she can read my thoughts? That she knows I beat my cock last night with thoughts of her pretty tongue lapping up my come?

I force a smile. "You don't trust me and Ethan alone with your big sister?"

That mischievous smile returns to Mari's face, and my stomach ties into knots. Just as she opens her mouth, Sofia speaks over her. "I hope you don't mind. I figured since Ethan was coming..."

When Sofia swallows, my gut sinks. It must have been obvious that I'm disconcerted by Mariana's presence.

I can't have that.

"I don't mind at all," I say, "and I can tell you right away that you've made my brother's day."

"You sure did." Ethan grins, his gaze shifting to Mariana. "Good thing we have two chaperones, or else you'd be in trouble."

My teeth clench. Why did I have to encourage him? Now he's going to flirt with her all morning.

And I'm going to want to punch him.

Mariana shoots Ethan that cheeky smile I've come to adore. "Oh, Ethan, honey, you're the one who needs a chaperone with me around."

Ethan's jaw drops into an open-mouthed smile. "You're a wild one, Mari. That's what I love about you."

Sofia shoots Ethan a playful frown. "You're not sounding like the good Christian boy I know, Ethan Harrington."

He frowns at her. "Boy? I can legally drink now."

I pat Ethan's back, but the gesture is much harder than I intended. Shit. I don't want him to know that his attempt to annoy me—as I'm now almost certain this is—is a raving success. "But you don't drink. Because you're a good Christian boy. So maybe you should stop sexually harassing our coffee date."

"Hey," Ethan says. "I didn't say anything sexual. You all read into it."

I cock a brow. "I'm surprised you would say you like wild

women when you tell me over and over again you don't have a thing for Lily."

Ethan's smile fades, and a pang of guilt tugs at my chest. Why the fuck did I do that? He's obviously infatuated with the troubled girl, and it's a betrayal of his confidence to bring it up with strangers.

What is going on with me? My lust for Mariana is loosening my grip on my integrity.

But I suppose that's what I've learned about my own integrity. I'm not built like people who have an inward compass. I inherited my dad's morality. I have to keep my eyes on the stars. Even a momentary lapse could find me lost beneath an unexpected veil of clouds.

"Who's Lily?"

"She not— She's..." Ethan shuts his eyes, smiling. "He's just saying that to get back at me for flirting with you two. She's a girl I've been ministering to."

"Ministering." Mariana hums the word. "I'll bet you are."

Ethan chuckles, and it's a relief after his earlier discomfort. How does she always do this? She always knows exactly what to say to break the tension.

She's so adorably playful all the time.

"It really is about ministry," Ethan says. "Believe me, she's not my type. She's beyond wild. She's kind of a...disaster. And I know that sounds really judgmental, and I kind of hate saying it, but..." He shrugs.

Mariana leans forward and places her elbows on her thighs. "How is she a disaster?"

He rolls his eyes. "She's the biggest partier I've ever met. She's notorious in my frat, and they all party."

Mariana makes a little O with those pretty lips. "Imagine that. She's a college student who parties."

Ethan narrows his eyes as he smiles at her. "I promise you I'm not being judgmental. She's not a normal partier. She's...crazy. We have beer pong at my frat on Thursday nights—not a party or anything, just a low-key hangout. Anyway, last week, she left to go to the bathroom, and when she came back, she was fully naked. She said she fell in the toilet because the lid was up." His frown turns incredulous. "She took off every lick of clothing because she got her pants a little wet and then just walked out in the open like it was nothing."

Mariana cocks a brow. "Sounds like she made quite an impression on you."

Ethan grunts. "How could she not when she was butt naked?"

Mariana giggles as she leans back into the couch. "If that's appalling to you, I probably shouldn't tell you any stories about my freshman year of college. I was a very naughty girl."

I jerk back in my seat. Is it just my imagination, or is there a challenge in those dark eyes?

Holy fuck. Does she know? Does she know what I did last night?

No.

It's just a coincidence. How could she know?

Fuck, why did I have to be so reckless? Pulling my cock out the second she left my office like a kid sneaking sweets. If I had had a little more self-control, I wouldn't be going out of my mind right now.

I shift in my seat, trying to maintain my cool, but my face is as hot as a broiling oven.

"So Ethan likes wild ones as long as they aren't too wild," Mariana says, that intensity still in those dark eyes. "What's your type, Brandon?"

She caresses my name with her lips. Oh fuck. She knows.

She fucking knows.

Or am I going crazy?

I lick my lips. "Um..." I glance at Sofia. "Gentle. Kind. With a sweet disposit—"

"So the typical Christian wifey," Mariana says, and anger begins to flame in my chest.

She's taunting me.

She's taunting me at her sister's expense.

I sit up straight and lower my chin. "Those are qualities I value in any human being. Man or woman. But in this case, I was describing your sister. I'm sure you wouldn't dismiss her as just a... What do you say? Typical Christian wifey."

Mariana's eyes widen slightly before falling on her coffee, and a pang shoots into my chest. I didn't mean to sound so scolding, but she should think more before she opens that bold mouth of hers.

"She's not gentle." Mariana's voice is small. "You don't know her very well."

Sofia's brow knits. "What do you mean I'm not gentle?"

Mariana smiles sheepishly at her. "You know you're not."

Sofia laughs, but it sounds forced. "Don't listen to her, Brandon. It's that historian memory of hers. She remembers every single fight we've ever gotten into, and she loves to tell the stories."

I make an effort to smile warmly, though my muscles are as tight as guitar strings. "I'll have to ask her for stories at work tomorrow."

Sofia laughs genuinely this time, and the tension is diffused, but for the rest of our visit, my shoulders are tense and my reflexes alert.

Mariana knows.

I'm almost sure of it.

Mariana

As we drive home, Sofia turns to me. "Why did you say that to Brandon?"

I let out a sigh. She doesn't have to tell me what she means. I knew this question would come, and there's no use trying to placate her. "Because you aren't gentle."

I feel her scowl even though I can't see it.

"I wouldn't say I'm pointedly not gentle. Like, I'm as gentle as most people." When I don't say anything, she grunts. "It's almost like you don't want him to court me anymore."

The word "court" makes irritation sizzle under my skin. It's an antiquated practice that the evangelical church coopted as just one more way to control the sexuality of its youth.

Sofia is almost thirty years old, and she's still being oppressed by it.

"Don't you hate the fact that Dad orchestrated this whole thing?" I ask. "Brandon hardly knows you."

"Yeah, because he wasn't going to hit on his friend's daughter. He kept his distance from both of us out of respect for Dad. I love that about him." Her voice has a dreamy quality. "He has such strong principles."

I snort. "Well, he is a pastor."

"You of all people should know that doesn't equate to high character."

Her words settle over me slowly. I'm so used to coldness from her, it takes me a moment to realize there was no sarcasm or bitterness in the statement.

She's trying to connect with me. She's admitting that my frustration with the hypocrisy in the church has some truth to it.

She's never done that before.

I smile. "He's definitely not power hungry like a lot of pastors."

"Not at all," Sofia says, and for a moment, I'm not even jealous that she's the sister Dad pushed on Brandon. This understanding between us is so heady, I almost tell her right now that I'm an atheist.

Of course I won't. I'm not there yet.

But I feel like I could be soon.

Thanks to Brandon.

Throughout the day, I keep expecting the connection between Sofi and I to fade, for her to slip back into cool indifference. But something seems to have changed in her. She's noticeably warmer and kinder, and she even offers to drive to the In-N-Out in Goleta to get us dinner.

"Guess who texted me last night?" she says after popping a fry into her mouth.

I've been so lulled into complacency that I didn't see that coming. Something ominous vibrates over my skin.

"Who?" I ask, but I already know.

"Finn," she answers with the faintest quirk of her lips, and coldness descends over my whole body.

Of course. This explains her cheerful mood. This explains her kindness toward me.

It had nothing to do with mutual understanding. It had nothing to do with Brandon, even.

It's always about Finn.

I frown. "Why is a married man texting his ex-fiancée?"

That faint quirk of her lips morphs into what could almost be described as a sneer. "That's exactly what I asked him."

I groan. "Why did you even respond at all?"

She keeps her gaze fixed on her fry as she swirls it around a puddle of ketchup. "I probably shouldn't have, but I wanted to give him the benefit of the doubt."

"What did he say?"

She's silent for a while. "He told me he heard that I'm dating Brandon," she says, "and that he's happy for me."

I snort. "We know that's bullshit."

"Yes," she says softly.

"Be careful, Sofi. Texting your ex can be...dangerous."

She scowls, tossing the ketchup-soaked fry onto her plate. "How dare you even insinuate something like that? I'd never do to Finn's wife what he did to me."

I let out a groan. "I didn't mean it like that. I'm just saying be careful."

She raises her chin. "Even if I was that kind of woman, he has nothing to offer me. I'm dating Pastor Brandon. There's not a single Christian woman in Santa Barbara who would take Finn over Pastor Brandon."

I clench my teeth, using all my willpower to keep ugly words from spilling off my tongue.

Brandon is just a prize to you. You don't actually care about him.

Not the way I'm starting to...

Or already do.

Fuck. I think I've fallen for him.

Chapter Fourteen

M ariana

I halt my typing to reach out and grab my bagel from the Styrofoam plate, placing my fingers carefully to avoid getting cream cheese on them. I can't stand it when my keyboard gets greasy spots on it. Just as I take a big bite, Brandon appears in my doorway.

Perfect. Now I have an excuse to be short with him since my mouth is full.

I've been giving him one-word answers all day, and he's noticed. I'm annoyed with myself for being passive aggressive, but I can't help it.

I hate that he's courting Sofia—a woman who doesn't really interest him—when he won't even consider me. Is it really because I'm fourteen years younger or is it something else?

Maybe it's because I'm an atheist.

Maybe he doesn't really think I'm worthy "all on my own" or whatever lip service he gave me that day at his house.

"What are you working on?" he asks.

I lift a finger in the air and purposely chew my food slowly. God, why am I so childish? When I finally swallow, I take a big sip of my coffee. "I'm writing the CEO of Beach Burger to see if we can hold the baptism on their private beach."

He seems to perk up at that. "What a great idea."

"I know his grandson. He'll definitely say yes."

I turn back to my computer, but he lingers in the doorway.

I wish I didn't enjoy it. I wish I weren't so petty that I made my silent treatment even worse when I saw how much it affected him.

"When you're done with that..." In my periphery, I see him scratch the back of his head. "Do you think— Can you come to my office and help me with something?"

I keep my face carefully blank. "Sure. I'll be there in a sec."

I take my sweet time finishing my bagel before making my way to Brandon's office. As soon as I step inside, I can tell something is off. I feel it in the air.

"What's going on with you?" His voice is abrupt.

I avert my gaze. "What do you mean?"

"You've been short with me today."

I shrug. "I didn't sleep well last night."

"Is that it, or is it..." His swallow is audible. "Is it something else?"

Is he trying to get me to admit what I know? He definitely seemed flustered yesterday after I called myself a naughty girl.

I probe him with a hard stare, and his eyes widen minutely. Is it just my imagination, or is a bit of his tan color leeching from his face? "What else could it be?" I ask with a faint tilt of my head.

His gaze falls to his lap. "I thought maybe you have a problem with what I said about your sister yesterday."

Oh, right. The "gentle" comment.

"Yeah, I am a little annoyed with what you said about her." I set my hands on my hips. "It shows how little you know her."

His jaw clenches. "I'm trying to get to know her."

"It also annoys me that you want a meek, submissive woman. I thought you were a different kind of pastor."

His eyes flash. "What does it matter to you what kind of woman I want?"

His words hit me in the chest. I take a deep breath, trying to ease the stab of pain that he still doesn't even consider me as a possible partner, even when he wants me physically.

"Are we back to where we were before?" My voice is quiet. "I thought we were starting to become friends."

He blinks once. "We've always been friends."

I shake my head sharply. "No, we haven't. Until recently, you treated me like a little kid."

He stands up and crosses those big arms over his chest. "I'm your pastor. There has to be some form of a boundary between us."

"You're like family," I say, my voice rising.

"Exactly. I'm a father figure to you."

When I snort out a laugh, his eyes grow wide. He's so close now that his breath is hot on my face, and the tension between us is as tangible as a live wire. I lift my chin, smiling slowly. "Daddy."

His jaw clenches so tightly it looks like it might snap in half, which sends a malicious thrill up my spine.

"I'll be a good girl for you... Oh, wait. You prefer me naughty, right?"

His eyes grow huge, but I don't wait for him to respond. I turn around and rush from the room, barely able to comprehend my own audacity.

* * *

Regret squeezes my chest when I glance at my computer clock. 5:03. I haven't even seen Brandon since our conversation six hours ago. He's been hiding out all day, even during lunchtime.

After I grab my purse, I head to his office. That shut wooden door looms in front of me, but I don't let it deter me. After knocking once, I open the door without waiting for him to answer. His head jerks up. I'm just about to rush through an apology when my tongue freezes. He's standing at his desk with a wad of toilet paper wrapped around his hand. A massive red spot sits at the center of the makeshift bandage.

"What happened?" I nearly shout.

He smiles sheepishly. "It's almost too embarrassing to tell you."

I place my hand on my hips. "Is that why you didn't get the first aid kit? You didn't want anyone to see."

"We're the only people here," he says, and a chill skitters over my skin.

We're all alone.

I swallow. "I'll go get the first aid kit. Meet me in the nursery bathroom."

A while later, we're standing over the sink. Brandon's hand is warm inside of mine. I try to ignore the fluttering in my stomach.

The dim lighting of the bathroom casts shadows over his face, hiding his expression, but the air is thick with unspoken words.

I turn on the faucet and run cold water over the wound. God, his hands are so big. What would they feel like roaming over my body?

I clear my throat. "How did you get this?"

"I was cutting an avocado."

I frown. "An avocado? In your office?"

That sheepish smile returns, easing the tautness vibrating in the air between us. "Yes."

"Why didn't you go to the kitchen?"

His expression shutters. "I wasn't making a whole meal. I was just going to eat the avocado as a snack."

I snort. "A plain avocado as a snack. What a gym rat thing to eat."

"Old habits. I'm not much of a cook, unfortunately."

"Well, I'm an excellent cook." As I dab the moisture with a

paper towel, every brush of his skin sends tingles up my arm. "I can always throw something together for you if you're hungry."

He doesn't say anything. He doesn't even smile.

"It's time for the peroxide." I use the same cheerful voice I use with my littlest nephew, Mateo. "It's going to sting, but it's necessary."

He smiles. "I've used peroxide before, Mariana."

Mariana. I guess I'm only "Mari" in the heat of the moment. I smile. "I was hoping you wouldn't try to be tough."

He winces as I pour the peroxide over the gash on his palm. It bubbles and hisses, and once it's clear, I run the faucet again. After drying his wound, I place a big circular Band-Aid on his palm. As soon as I have it smoothed down, I lean down and press a kiss against his palm.

Holy fuck. What did I just do?

My pulse starts to pound. Heat washes over my cheeks and chest. "I'm so sorry. I was on autopilot. That's what I do with Mateo."

When I'm finally able to lift my face, Brandon's eyes are almost black. He's closer than he was just a split second ago. His swallow is audible. "Mari," he croaks out.

Mari. It's a whisper. A prayer.

"What?" My voice is breathless.

His mouth moves closer. Those full lips hover, and my head grows heavy. A moment later, his soft lips are on my neck. I gasp at the sensation of his hot mouth against my skin.

My hands instinctively go to his shoulders as I tilt my head, giving him better access to my neck. His hands are on my waist, holding me tightly as he kisses a trail up to my earlobe. His tongue must be peeking out of his mouth, because a warm wetness on my skin sends jolts of heat into my belly. I moan softly, my mind spinning with the realization of what's happening.

He's kissing me.

Holy shit. He's kissing me.

He pulls back slightly, his breath hot against my ear. Those strong hands cut into my waist. His breathing grows ragged. He stays silent for what feels like an eternity.

"I knew it was a mistake," he eventually says, his voice thick and husky. "I knew it was a mistake to let you touch me."

"Please don't stop," I rasp.

His head jerks up, those dark eyes almost wild as they roam my face. "I want to stop. I want to stop so badly, but I can't. I fucking can't." His big fingers thread into my hair before tightening into a fist, yanking my head back. The tingles of pain make me cry out as pleasure rushes into my belly.

"God, forgive me," he whispers.

His lips crash against mine, and he devours my mouth. He kisses me like I've never been kissed before. Like I'm sustenance.

Like he'll die if he doesn't have me now.

His mouth roams everywhere—my cheeks, my neck, even my eyelids. He grips my waist, and a moment later, my body grows weightless. He sets me on the cold bathroom sink and lifts the skirt of my dress. He stares between my legs with wild eyes.

"Oh, fuck." He winces as if in pain. "You're so fucking beautiful."

I let out a whimper.

"I'm going to worship you." He gets down on his knees. His large hands settle on my legs, and he presses a kiss against my inner thigh. The warmth of his lips sends a tingle straight to the spot between my legs that aches to be filled. I moan and move restlessly against him.

His warm breath tickles my pussy as he pulls my panties to the side. And then he's there, his warm tongue rubbing up and down my clit. My hips flail from side to side, and he grips my hips to still me.

"Be my good girl," he whispers against my clit. "Let me love you."

Love. The word curls through my body like a vine seeking the light.

He slips a finger inside of me, and I clench around him. The groan that emanates from his chest sounds almost like a roar.

"So tight. My sweet girl." His lips brush against my aching clit as he thrusts a second finger inside of me. I clench around him, arching my back. He adds a third finger, and my hips curl upward helplessly. I whimper, and he presses his mouth to my clit, sucking. My body begins to shudder, and I let out a low, mewling cry.

"That's it, my girl." He flicks his tongue against my clit. "You're mine."

Mine. A magical word coming from his lips.

"Yes!" I moan.

He pulls away, and I whimper at the loss of his hot mouth. His big palm pats my thigh. "Look at me. Now."

My eyes fly open to meet his predatory gaze. "You're going to come for me, and you'll keep your eyes on me while you do it."

"Yes."

He squeezes my thigh. "Yes, what?"

"Yes, sir."

He groans. "That's my girl."

Those big fingers are inside me again, and I arch up off the floor. His thumb flicks against my clit. It's a soft motion at first, but then he begins to move as rhythmically and rapidly as a hummingbird's wings. "Come for me, Mari."

I let out a cry, and the world around me falls away. All that exists is heat and skin and his heavenly voice.

"Good girl." His voice comes from far away.

Brandon

My chest is so heavy, it's hard to take a breath. The realization that hit me a few minutes ago is now threatening to strangle my throat.

It can't be true. I wish it weren't true.

But I can't deny it.

The euphoria of tasting her was more heady than the moment I gave my life to Christ.

She's dangerous, by no fault of her own. I never covet in moderation. If I give her even a little of myself, she might take my soul with her when it's over.

It must stop now.

"Mari," I croak out.

She looks at me dreamily. The image of her languid eyes and tussled hair is so sweet it will probably be burned into my memory forever.

"What?" she whispers.

"I'm so sorry."

She lets out a sweet sigh. "I'm not sorry at all."

I wince, brushing her hair from her face so I can get a better look at those clear, dark eyes. "You have nothing to be sorry for. That wasn't your fault, Mari. I took advantage of you."

Her adorable little brow furrows. "That's the dumbest thing I've ever heard."

"I'm your boss." I swallow. "I'm your pastor."

That cheeky smile I love tugs at her lips, though her eyes are still sleepy. "My father figure." A soft laugh emanates from her chest. "Brandon, you're not really my boss. Or my pastor. What you are is codependent."

I frown. "What are you talking about?"

She stares at me for a beat. "You know you never should have indulged my dad."

I grit my teeth. "What you call codependent, I call basic human decency. He's my best friend, and he asked me to talk to you."

"Yeah, but you're also letting him get into your head. Who cares if I'm younger than you? We're both—"

"I care."

When she flinches, I realize I raised my voice louder than I intended.

"My integrity is important to me. As a pastor, a Christian... As a human being."

Her nostrils flair. "And how has your integrity been compromised?"

"I'm courting your sister, Mariana. Has that not even occurred to you?"

Hesitation creeps into her eyes, but it fades almost as quickly as it came. "She's not invested in you. Gorgeous women like Sofia don't waste their energy on men who clearly aren't into them."

"And how would she feel if she saw us right now?"

The vulnerability that flashes on her face makes me want to reach out and stroke her cheek, but I can't. I can never touch her again.

What a miserable thought.

"She'd be upset," Mari eventually says. "But mostly because..."

I lean forward, my hands straining at my sides as I fight to keep them off her. "Because she'd feel betrayed. By *me*. A man she trusts, one who's supposed to be courting her. A pastor and friend of her dad's. Who just mauled her sister in the bathroom of his own church."

A languid little smile tugs at her lips. God, she's so adorable after an orgasm, like a sleepy kitten. God must be testing me to give me just a taste of this and expect me to never slip up again.

"Is this a kink of yours?" she asks.

My head jerks back. "What?"

"Making me out to be some innocent young woman who doesn't know how to stop a big strong man like you when he wants her."

My lips twitch, but I try to keep my expression stern. "Watch it, young lady."

Her smile grows. "So it is a kink?"

I avert my gaze to the tiled wall. I can't indulge in a conversation like this with her, no matter how much I want to. "I'm going to have to end things with your sister. Tomorrow, if I can arrange a time to see her."

Out of the corner of my eye, I see her move her skirt down her hips. I'm dying to get one last look at that pretty pink pussy, but I keep my gaze fixed on the wall.

"That's for the best," she says as she steps down onto the floor. "For her too. I get the feeling she wants to show you off to Finn at Livvy's wedding. She needs to get over him."

"Maybe you need to get over him too."

Her head whips in my direction. "What do you mean?"

"Why is it your place to decide when she gets over a man she loved deeply? Maybe you should let her heal on her own time."

Her nostrils flare as she pulls down her skirt. "It's been three years."

"Yeah, you've mentioned that. Many times."

"Okay, well—" She crosses her arms over her chest and glances at the door "That was lovely, Brandon. We should make it a regular thing after you break up with Sofia."

I reach out and grab her chin, forcing her to look at me. "I know you're joking, but I want to be clear that this can never happen again."

Her expression shutters. "Yeah, you've made it clear, Daddy."

"None of that, either. You seem to have an understanding of... what it does to me."

She snorts. "Yeah, I understand kink. I have sex like a normal person. Just like you used to before your whole celibacy thing. I'm not a baby like you seem to think I am."

I lift my head heavenward. God, help me with this bold woman. "I'll stop calling you 'young lady.' I don't want us to even tease when it comes to this. Our relationship has to be different from now on."

"Right. We'll go back to you treating me like a child."

"My volunteer PA." I correct, squeezing her chin. "That's what you are, Mariana. Do you have any idea what kind of scandal would erupt if people found out about what just happened in here?"

Those dark, gold-tinted eyes grow bewildered. "Could you get fired?"

I sigh. "I'm not sure. But what I just did is not okay."

She scoffs. "Those rules are arbitrary. You didn't coerce me."

"It doesn't matter. Men of God aren't supposed to eat out their interns in the house of God."

"Fuck," she says, and the word on her lips sends a lick of heat over my cock like a slippery tongue. "It's so hot when you say it like that."

I let out a low groan. "Please. Don't talk that way. Never again."

She's quiet for a while. Am I imagining that those lips are quivering? She's not the only one who wants to cry that the magic between us is over forever.

"I can do that for you," she eventually says. "We could have had a lot of fun. It's a bummer you had to take me on as your intern."

With that, she walks out of the bathroom and quietly shuts the metal door behind her, and I want to weep.

Chapter Fifteen

Brandon

Sofia smiles sweetly at me from across the table and my chest constricts like a vise. I texted her as soon as I left the church last night, asking her to meet up for coffee. Her enthusiastic response made me feel like an asshole.

I devoured her sister in the bathroom of the church, and she doesn't have the slightest clue.

Fuck, what if Hector found out? He'd never speak to me again. I'd never be included as an honorary family member again. No more Sunday barbeques or praying at the Thanksgiving meal or being called "Uncle Brandon" by his grandchildren. I'd be cut out from the haven I found after all the warmth seemed to leave the world with my mother.

I'd lose everything.

I clear my throat. "I have something to tell you."

Her eyes widen before lowering to her lap. "This doesn't sound good."

The dejection in her voice makes me want to reach out and grab her hand. "Sofia, I'm so sorry. I never should have started something with you when I've been struggling with... Having my own struggles. It isn't the right time."

She licks her lips. "What do you mean?"

I let out a long sigh. "I've been having some internal struggles. Struggles with sin if I'm being completely honest. It wouldn't be fair to you to start something now."

"We all struggle with sin. Anyone who says they don't is a liar."

"I agree with that, but this particular sin..." I shake my head. "If you knew what it was, I'm not sure if you would be so forgiving."

Those clear brown eyes meet mine. "Try me."

There's a challenge in those eyes, and it's as clear and sparkling as the water glass in my hand.

If you're going to dump me, at least have the decency to tell me the truth.

I ought to be as honest with her as I can, leaving Mariana out of it, of course. It's a pastor's duty to show his humanity when appropriate. The fact that I'm terrified of Hector finding out only reinforces that it's the right thing to do. It's time to stop being selfish.

This is about Sofia, not Hector.

I shut my eyes and let out a heavy breath. "I've been struggling with lust lately..."

"Oh." Her eyes grow wide before lowering to her lap. "Do you mean..." She licks her lips. "Did you maybe watch something..."

Her cheeks darken, and my chest sinks. She thinks I watched porn. She thinks I would break up with her over something so trifling, because the people who raised her wouldn't find it trifling at all. Hector and Ana are staunchly anti-porn and believe that even one viewing is the equivalent of infidelity.

Fuck. They would loathe me if they knew what I really did.

"No," I say. "It's worse than that. I... I messed around with a woman."

Her head jerks up, those big eyes of hers widening. It would be so much worse if she knew it was Mariana. That the woman who consumes my thoughts at all hours of the day is her sister.

"Is she someone you have feelings for?" she asks.

"No." The word comes out too quickly to sound sincere even to my own ears. "It's only lust. She's not someone I'd ever want to be in a relationship with."

Sofia lets out a breath, her features softening. "I see. So she's kind of...easy."

The word steals the breath from my lungs. *Easy.* It's such an ugly word to describe a woman like Mariana. Such an ugly word in general, as if a woman's worth is determined by how difficult she is for a man to acquire.

Sofia doesn't know what she's saying. She doesn't know who she's talking about, first of all, and she can't help that she was raised to think this way. First Covenant taught her these ideas. She's a victim of a misogynistic self-serving view of the Bible.

Still, a deep part of me can't help but hate her a little bit for saying something so ugly about Mariana.

I shake my head. The weight of my sins bears down on my body, making my movements sluggish. "No, I wouldn't say that about her. But my feelings for her are only physical."

Liar.

The word is as clear and resonant as if God spoke it from heaven. How could my feelings for her be only physical when I came into this already loving her like my own flesh and blood?

Fuck. What if that familial love becomes something more? What if I fall in love with her for real?

God help me if that ever happens.

"I forgive you."

The words jerk me out of my head. "What?" I nearly shout at her.

She licks her lips. "I do. I know it must be so hard for a man to stay celibate until marriage. You're so physically driven. I sin every day. My sins are different, granted, but I'd be a hypocrite to judge you for your struggles. Look what you did." She smiles faintly. "You came to me right after it happened. That shows that you're aware of your sin and trying to make it right."

"Sofia, I don't want you to give me credit for—"

"No, let me finish." Her voice grows louder. "I don't expect my boyfriend to be perfect. He can't expect perfection from me either. I believe we'll have to work together every day to make our relationship work. And that means frequently having to say the words 'I'm sorry' and 'I forgive you.' I know we're not fully dating but..." She lowers her eyes to the table.

My throat squeezes so tight I have to cough to clear it. God, she's so sweet. Never in the months that I've been courting her have my feelings for her ever been so clear to me. What was I thinking starting this? Unlike what I feel for her sister, my love for Sofia is truly familial.

She's like a little sister to me.

"Sofia..." I groan as I run a hand through my hair. "I can't keep courting you. It was never right to begin with. I'm starting to realize that my feelings for you are more—"

"You're not into me."

I jerk back. When my gaze roams her face, a small smile tugs at her lips.

"I know," she says. "And I won't lie and say it doesn't hurt my feelings a little bit, but I can understand, in a way. Hearing my dad talk about me like I'm a pathetic loser who will never get married probably didn't help."

"Sofi," I say, softening my voice. "He never said anything like—"

"I know he didn't say it outright, but don't lie to me and say that he doesn't constantly talk about the fact that I'm almost thirty and still single."

Heat washes over my skin, and I lower my eyes to the wooden table. I can't deny it. He talks about it constantly.

"I won't ask you to betray his trust. You're his friend, and he needs to be able to vent to you, but just think of what it's like for me. I lost everything three years ago..."

When she takes a deep breath and lifts her coffee to her mouth, I reach out and set my hand on hers. "I know, honey."

Honey. It's the word I used to call Ethan when he was a baby, and here it just rolled off the tongue. How could I have ever thought I could have a physical relationship with this woman?

"Can we at least wait until Livvy's wedding to stop officially courting?" she asks, her voice firm and clear. "You know being there is going to be really hard for me. It would be even worse if I didn't have a date."

Mariana's words from yesterday echo in my head. *She needs to get over him.* Though it's not my place to decide when Sofia's heart heals, I don't love the idea of indulging her pride this far.

"Finn is Livvy's cousin," Sofia says. "There's no way I can escape him. He'll be there with his wife and baby. The baby he conceived while I was making wedding favors—" Her voice chokes, and she shuts her eyes.

I wrap my hand around her tiny one. "We can wait. It's not like I'm going to pursue this other woman. We can wait to call things off officially until after the wedding."

Her eyes pop open, and a joyous smile overtakes her face. "And we won't tell my family?"

My chest squeezes. I hate the idea of lying to Hector, but I'm already lying by omission on another count.

I usually tell him my struggles. If I had violated my celibacy vow with any other woman, I would have unburdened myself to him immediately.

That sin will be taken to my grave. He'll never know what I did to his daughter.

I smile faintly, though my lips quiver. "We won't tell your family."

· · ·

119

Mariana

A tingle of discomfort skitters over my skin. Sofia got home hours ago, and she didn't say a word. She went straight to her room.

Is she sad that Brandon broke up with her? I wouldn't have expected it. Irritated maybe, but not sad.

Guilt claws my insides.

Even if she isn't invested in Brandon, it still must have hurt to be rejected by him. Finn's defection left her heart in a fragile state. If she's grieving behind that shut door, it's from the resurrected pain of her broken engagement.

Years ago, I would have gone into her bedroom on the second story of our old house. I would have plopped down on her bed with the white comforter and bright-blue sheets. She would have been sitting at her desk, pretending to work on college homework. She'd roll her eyes at me and tell me she needed privacy, but then I'd ask her what's wrong in a voice just for her. She'd break down crying—like she did with her first boyfriend—and I'd rush over to her and wrap my arms around her shoulders. She'd say she was fine in a voice mixed with tearfulness and exasperation, but she wouldn't push me away.

What would she do if I went in there now?

She'd be as silent as death, and it would feel like it too. Like how I knew Abuelo was gone as soon as we walked into his hospital room a decade ago. The silence of death is so thick you can almost touch it. I feel the death of my relationship with Sofia every moment I'm around her.

The door opens, and Sofia walks to the kitchen. She doesn't acknowledge my presence, but there's nothing unusual about that.

"How was your coffee date?" I ask, unable to help myself.

As she opens the fridge, she lets out a soft little laugh, which eases the tension in my shoulders.

She's not sad that he broke up with her.

"He wanted to end our...whatever you call it. Relationship, I guess." Her smile grows. "Because he messed around with someone."

My stomach does a little turn. She wouldn't be smiling right now if she knew who it was. In fact, she'd probably be at our parents' house telling on both me and Brandon.

I clear my throat. "He told you that?"

A little giggle escapes her mouth as her eyes grow unfocused, as if she's reflecting. "You know how honest he is about sin. I've always admired that about him. I know pastors are human, but..." Her dark eyes probe into my face. "Who do you think it was?"

I can't help but smile. She rarely ever initiates gossip with me like she used to when we were younger. This is the kind of conversation she would now have with Dani.

"I don't know," I say, unable to stop from indulging her even in my deceit. "It wouldn't be someone in his congregation."

She frowns. "Well, of course not."

My throat grows tight. I cough to clear it. "Maybe someone he met at the gym."

Her eyes grow wide as she smiles. "I think he still has a contact list full of women. You know he was a big man-whore before he was saved. I bet he called up an old hookup buddy."

Her childish grin makes mist rise to my eyes. Oh God, I miss this so much. This is how she and I used to talk to each other. This was part of my everyday life.

I smile. "Maybe two. He seems like a threesome guy."

"Mariana Isabel!" she scolds, though her chest shakes with laughter. "Don't you dare give me that mental image. I have to listen to this man preach the word of God."

I wave a hand. "No one will expect you to help out on Saturdays if you guys aren't dating anymore."

Her smile fades. "No, that's just between us. We're not going to tell the rest of the family until after Livvy's wedding."

My skin heats. "Why?"

But I already know the answer.

"I don't want to go alone." Her eyes narrow. "You already know why."

"Sofi..."

She lifts a hand. "I don't want to hear whatever it is you have to say. You can't relate to what I'm going through. Even if it happened to you, you'd never understand."

"And why is that?"

She shrugs, her expression growing prim. It's the snotty look she used to give me as a child when she was disappointed in me. "Because you're not following God."

Ice fills my veins, and the world around me grows a shade darker. Was there really warmth between us a moment ago? I hardly even remember.

I refuse to accept crumbs from her as if that's all I deserve. If she wants to ostracize me from her life because of my lack of faith, it's her loss.

That she doesn't feel the loss as acutely as I do is painful, but that pain will fade.

I'm resilient.

I'm resilient because I choose to be.

Chapter Sixteen

M ariana

I've hardly seen Brandon at all this week. At the very least, I can call him a man of his word. He said our relationship would be different from now on.

We're as good as strangers now.

Today, I'll have to change that, however little he might like it. I had a conversation with Harper this morning about a retreat he's planning to go on next week. He's leading most of the conference sessions and will hardly have a single moment of free time. He needs his PA with him.

But he told Harper he's planning to go alone.

I can't have it. If he really wants us to be strangers, he should have fired me.

He'd never do that, though. It would require too many lies. He certainly won't tell my dad what happened between us, but he has too much integrity to invent a lie that would save my ass from looking like a fallen woman.

We're stuck together for the next two weeks and for this retreat.

My heart pounds as I knock on his office door. When I walk inside, he's sitting at his desk looking grim-faced,

"Can I talk to you about something?" I ask.

His posture grows rigid, like he's bracing himself. I force a smile as I sit on the chair in front of his desk. I'll do anything to lighten the tension between us, so I adopt a cheerful voice. "Harper told me you're planning on going to the retreat alone."

His eyes widen minutely. He takes a moment to answer. "I can handle everything on my own."

I sigh. "I don't think you can. I think you need your PA with you."

"Mariana, you know it's not right for us—"

"Not right for us to what?" His head jerks back at my raised voice. "Be alone together? What's going to happen after Daisy's maternity leave is over? Will we always have to avoid each other? People in my family will pick up on it." I huff, shaking my head. "They'll assume it's my fault."

His eyes flash. "I'd never let them think that. I won't avoid you forever. I just... I need time."

"You'll have until next week." I stand up from my chair, hoping I look like a boss babe who won't take no for an answer. "You need me at that retreat."

He frowns. "I'll be fine on my own."

I flip my hair as I turn toward the door. "Well, I want to go on that retreat. I love Big Sur. Would you really make me miss out on that because you want to bend me over your desk?"

His body grows utterly still, and I want to kick myself. I've ruined my chances of ever changing his mind with one little slip of the tongue.

"Mari," he whispers, and my legs turn to jelly.

My nickname. It's so rare that he says it that, when he does, I wish I could absorb his voice into my skin.

There's so much heat between us. It's not fair that it can never be realized. It's not fair that my dad had to intervene and make him feel like the desire he feels for me is a betrayal. It's not fair that there's now a church congregation between me and Brandon because of my dad's intervention.

I swallow. "I was just teasing. I promise I won't talk that way ever again. It only slipped out because I was frustrated."

An emotion flashes in his eyes... Something that looks like disappointment. He lowers his gaze to his desk. "You can go on the trip. I don't want to deprive you of a nice little getaway if you were looking forward to it, especially after all you've done for me. But please..." He shuts his eyes.

"I know."

"We have to be mindful."

"I understand that. I'll keep my distance. It'll be like I'm not even there."

His expression grows somehow grimmer.

Brandon

I promise I won't talk that way ever again.

Why do those words make me feel like I've been sent to the guillotine?

She's handling this with much more maturity than I expected, and I'm a bastard for being disappointed. Was I really hoping that she'd throw herself at me, making me feel less responsible for my betrayal to the Hernandez family?

Thank God, I've learned that it's my actions that determine my integrity, or else I'd probably hate myself.

My phone chimes and I see I have a text from Sofia.

Sofia: Do you want to be my date to mini golf tonight?

. . .

I let out a low groan. Mariana said something about mini golf to Harper the other day, and it sounded like a big group activity. I only overheard because I was straining my ears to listen like a lovesick teenage boy.

Sofia probably wants me to go so she can mention something to Hector. She wants to keep up appearances until the wedding, and I can't blame her. Her dad is observant. If Sofi and I aren't careful, he'll pick up on our deception. Depending on the mood he's in, he might even call us out in front of the rest of the family, which would be embarrassing for her.

I have to be careful.

But damn. I really don't want to have to spend an evening with Mariana and all her twenty-something friends. I'd feel even more like an old lecher who couldn't keep his hands off her.

I'll ask if Sofia wants to go on a coffee date on another day instead. That will serve the same purpose. Just as I place my thumbs on the keyboard, another text appears.

Sofia: I don't want to be the third wheel haha.

I frown. Third wheel? I guess she's not asking me to attend a group activity but a double date, which means...

Oh fuck.

Mariana has a date.

Something dark and primitive clenches my gut and makes heat prickle all over my skin. It's completely irrational to be possessive. I know this. But somehow, I can't stop my thumbs from typing out a response.

Me: That sounds great.

I won't do anything stupid. It might even be good for me to watch Mariana out with a young guy. I'll see in action how she's living a different life, one I left behind many years ago.

But even if I want to kill the little prick—whoever he is—it won't matter, because I'll behave myself.

Please God, help me behave myself.

Chapter Seventeen

B randon

The modern chandelier is relentlessly bright, and all the servers seem especially cheerful and talkative. I'm not in the mood for a place like this. I want to stay quietly in my head while I prepare myself for how I'll react when Mariana finally shows up for her date.

Thankfully, Sofia has been quieter than usual as well. One hand is set primly in her lap while she uses the other to scroll on her phone.

"Where is she?" I ask, hating how impatient I sound.

I inhale deeply and slowly. This is so stupid. Here I am itching with anxiety when I could have avoided this all together by just saying I couldn't make it.

But would my anxiety be worse if I were waiting alone at home, thinking about her out with another man?

No matter how bad my anxiety is, I'll have to get over it eventually. Mariana will be in my life forever. I might even officiate her wedding someday.

The thought is like a blow to the chest.

Why didn't I consider what all of this would mean before now? I knew I'd never be able to touch her again, and yet it didn't occur to me that I'd have to watch someone else do it.

"There she is," Sofia says, and when my head jerks up, heat engulfs my whole body like a flame.

She's wearing a tight black dress that reveals every inch of her beautiful skin. I would give anything to be able to touch her again.

And the motherfucker behind her is staring at her ass.

Zac.

Of course it's him. Zac who brought her lunch. Zac who touched the tip of her nose.

He might even fuck her tonight.

My chest seizes with an unbearable tightness. I set my water glass down, and a bit of it splashes onto the table.

I need to calm the fuck down. I never should have touched her to begin with. Zac is much better for her, if only because he's her age. He understands her in a way that I never could.

The thought isn't comforting.

Sofia follows my gaze to Mariana's tall escort. Her eyes widen. "Do you know Zac?"

I shake my head. "He stopped by once to bring her lunch, but we weren't introduced."

"Of course he brought her lunch." Sofia lowers her voice as Mariana and Zac approach our table. "He's always had a crush on her."

Heat washes over my skin.

"Look at you two all dressed up." Sofia smiles. "Mari, I don't know how you're going to play mini golf in that."

Mariana grins as she sits down, and now that she's in full view, I see that her cleavage is out of control, and Zac's gaze once again falls to her beautiful skin.

Little prick.

"Hey, Pastor," Mariana says, her voice sultry and low. "Now that I'm here, I can say that you're both sitting way too close. You got to leave room for the Holy Spirit."

I can't even bring myself to respond to her little tease. I'm consumed by every inch of her bare flesh in that skimpy dress, every movement of her lips. Just a week ago, I had that woman with her legs open for me as I brought her to ecstasy.

Now I'm forced to watch her from afar.

"I thought I might try a cocktail, Mariana." Sofia lifts the menu. "Looks like they have a bunch of different daiquiris. Do you want to split one with me?"

Mariana pouts. "My lightweight sister. No, I shouldn't even split one. We just came from happy hour with the whole crew." Mariana shoots Zac an intimate smile that makes my skin crawl. "I already had a few too many."

Zac reaches his hand around her shoulder and gives it a squeeze, and my jaw clenches of its own will. "You didn't introduce us," I mutter.

Mariana frowns at me, and I wonder if the words came out more biting than I'd intended.

"You met Zac." She smiles slowly. "He was the guy I was...fraternizing with."

I shoot her a warning look, and those beautiful dark eyes of hers grow hooded. Oh God, it's that sultry look of hers.

She's being defiant tonight.

Because she's tipsy.

Naughty girl. I wish I could drag her into that bathroom and turn her over my lap.

With effort, I smile at Zac. "I don't think we officially met. I'm Brandon."

"Pastor Brandon, right?" Zac asks. "Mari has great things to say about you. And you know she's a heathen, so—"

Mariana punches Zac in the shoulder, and they both start laughing.

I shut my eyes for a moment, letting self-recrimination wash over me in a flood. They're both so young, flirting the way they are. I'm an old man over here wishing I could be in the place of a twenty-something kid.

It has to stop.

Thankfully, our food comes, and I'm able to pull my attention away from Mariana and Zac. It isn't difficult since they spend the next half hour talking mostly to themselves about people and circumstances unfamiliar to me. I use the opportunity to converse with Sofia, and it's a balm to my shitty mood. She truly feels like family—the little sister I never had.

Somehow, Mariana escaped those brotherly feelings.

By the time we leave the restaurant, the late afternoon sun is reflecting off the downtown buildings. The air smells like a combination of hot asphalt and ocean.

"Ugh," Mariana says. "It's too hot for mini golf."

Zac lowers his sunglasses as he looks at her. "It's my turn to pick. We did your little boat thing last week, and I was ready to puke the whole time."

She giggles. "Your sea legs are pretty weak."

Since Sofia and I are walking behind them, I take the opportunity to ask the question that's been burning in my gut since the moment I got the text from her yesterday. "Are Zac and Mariana dating?"

Sofia smiles. "No. Technically they're just good friends. But Zac has been trying for years."

I look ahead, and Zac sets his hand on Mari's lower back.

Oh fuck. The clawing jealousy in my gut is a physical pain.

Jesus, please help me to be civil.

After we make it to the course and start playing mini golf, Zac starts getting more touchy than he was in the restaurant. His hands are everywhere. On her arm, her back, her shoulder. The touches are gentle, not overtly intimate, but they're enough. Enough to make me want to grind my teeth into chalk dust.

"Actually, why don't we make this a bit more interesting?" I say after sinking a hole in one, feeling like a child for what I'm about to propose, but unable to help myself.

"What do you have in mind?" Zac's tone is playful, but I can sense a hint of competitiveness in his eyes.

"Sofia never got her daiquiri. How about losers pay for a round afterward." I keep my eyes locked with Zac's.

He smiles, the corners of his mouth curling into a cocky grin. "You're on."

"Uh-oh." Sofia winces. "I hope it's only one round. Mari's right about me being kind of a lightweight when it comes to alcohol."

I smile at her and set my hand on her shoulder. "You can have as much or as little as you want. I'm driving you."

"Wow, Pastor." Mariana tosses her hair as she bends forward to putt. "Getting the young people drunk. Don't worry—" she smiles slowly "—we won't tell Dad." Her tone has that usual playfulness, but I sense an underlying edge to her words.

If you're going to act like a father figure, I'm going to treat you like one.

I swallow and lower my head to Sofia's ear. "You know I would never try to get you or Mariana drunk, right? You can tell your dad whatever you want."

"Of course. You don't even have to say it." Sofia frowns at Mariana as she lowers her voice. "She's already drunk. Or buzzed, I guess. Dad would be happy you're here to watch out for her."

The thought isn't the slightest bit comforting. Fuck me, I don't want to act as Mariana's elderly chaperone. Not after having my mouth all over her body just a week ago.

She's *mine.*

But she's not. She never will be, and I must come to terms with it, however much my body is battling my head.

These troubling thoughts drift away like smoke as the game continues. Zac seems to love the competition. And it's cathartic for me to be able to score on him when he has his hands all over Mariana's bare skin.

The holes become a battlefield. Every successful shot from one of us is met with a smirk, a raised eyebrow, a snarky comment. The girls look on, a mix of amusement and bafflement on their faces.

We're both acting like children, and I started it—the pastor who's over a decade older than him.

I promised myself I wouldn't do anything stupid tonight. Yet here I am, acting like a fool and unable to stop myself.

"Damn, Pastor!" Zac shouts when I manage to score another hole in one. He wrinkles his nose. "Is it alright if I swear in front of you?"

I roll my eyes. "I'm not your mom."

Zac smirks as he putts his ball. It ends up in a tricky position just at the edge of a small hill on the course. I watch as he aligns his shot, his brow furrowed in concentration. With a quick, fluid motion, he strikes the ball, and it rolls up the hill...only to roll right back down again. I look away to hide my smile.

"Maybe the Holy Spirit isn't with you today, Zac." I pat his shoulder.

Mariana's eyes grow huge. She grabs my arm and pulls me in the direction of the next hole. "I need to talk to my boss for a minute."

I ought to be dreading whatever she has to say. I've been acting like an ass for the last half hour. She's probably going to give me a scolding, but holy fuck, she smells so good. It's wonderful to have her to myself after what I've had to witness all evening.

"What is going on with you?" she asks as soon as we're out of earshot.

I can't tell her I'm raging with jealousy.

Even though she must know.

"Just trying to make the most out of the evening. It's awkward being as old as I am and—"

"Oh no." Mariana raises one finger in the air. "You don't get to use the old man excuse. Not when I feel like I stepped into a time machine and have just met high school Brandon. The star point guard with the prom queen girlfriend. The guy who flushed nerds' heads in the toilet for fun."

I laugh, and the tension leaves my shoulders in an instant. "Do you think I went to high school in an eighties movie?"

She widens her eyes innocently. "That was when you went to high school, wasn't it?"

I step forward. "Watch it, young lady."

Her smile fades, and heat tingles over my skin.

Fuck.

"Sorry." I step back, scratching the back of my head. "I really need to get out of the habit of saying that. Especially with our trip two days away."

She places her hands on her hips. "I'm a grown woman, Brandon. I'm not offended by a little dirty talk."

I frown at her and open my mouth to speak, but she raises her hand to halt me. That adorably playful smile tugs at her lips. "We don't need to go over it again, though you do look like you're about to scold me like the stern boss daddy you are."

My gut clenches, and I let out a groan. "Mari, please. Don't call me Daddy."

She sighs. "I won't. We need to get back to the game before Sofia starts getting suspicious. You don't have anything to fear from me. I'll be a saint at the pastor conference."

As she walks slowly back to Sofia and Zac, the fight seems to have left her body, which leaves me dejected.

I'm two people at once. One who wants this pastor retreat to come and go without ever coming close to touching Mariana again.

The other is a devil.

He wants to fuck her raw all weekend long.

Chapter Eighteen

M ariana

The morning sun casts long shadows across the empty church parking lot. When I step out of my car, the cool morning air makes me shiver. My gaze falls on Brandon. He's waiting for me by his Audi, and my heart flutters at the sight.

Such a daddy.

He stands tall and imposing, his deep-brown eyes narrowing as he takes in my appearance. His jaw is tight, and his gaze lingers on the contours of my body revealed by the form-fitting tank top. A wave of delightful defiance washes over me.

I didn't dress sexy on purpose. I can't help it if he likes what he sees.

"Well, you're dressed comfortably," he says, his voice low and tight.

A teasing smirk tugs at my lips. He's not even trying to hide the fact that his eyes are on my tits right now. His stern gaze makes my heart race, but I refuse to let him see how much it turns me on.

If he wants polite distance, I'll give it to him.

"It's a four-hour drive," I say. "Would you prefer I dress uncomfortably?"

His expression shutters. "No...but I'm going to be introducing you to a group of pastors. I'd prefer you be dressed professionally so they don't think—" His lips close.

My smile grows. "Don't think what?"

He lets out a long sigh. "Nothing. I'm sorry. I shouldn't be commenting on the way you're dressed." He flinches. "It's sexist."

"It's okay. I should have worn a bra."

His teeth clench, and I have to fight the smile rising to my lips as I hand him a stainless-steel mug filled with hot coffee. "Black and strong as gasoline. Just the way you like it. I've also loaded up some history podcasts for the drive."

His brows lift at that. "What kind of history?"

Lightness fills my chest. My friends and family groan whenever I suggest listening to history podcasts on a road trip, but Brandon loves history as much as I do.

Ugh. I'm actually excited to spend the next four hours alone in a car with him, and it fucking sucks.

I'll never have him all to myself again after this trip.

"You're going to lose your mind over one of the podcasts I found," I say. "It's all about the badass women in the Bible. We've got Esther, Mary Magdalene, Bathsheba... My role models growing up. Bunch of strong-willed hoes, just like me."

He chuckles. "The strong-willed hoes of the Bible," he says under his breath. "You're so cute, Mariana."

I inhale a sharp breath, and he winces. "I'm sorry.

"It's okay," I say, my heart pounding.

"I'm still on edge about this weekend."

"Me too," I say, but it's a lie. I've been looking forward to it ever since he agreed to let me come.

Maybe we'll finally have a breakthrough. Maybe he'll finally let go of his obsession with my age and what my dad thinks of him.

A fool's hope, most likely.

The thought is confirmed a while later when we're driving to Big Sur. The tension in the car is thick. Brandon's hardly said a word, and he's shot down any conversation I've tried to initiate. His walls are up.

Fuck this.

I reach for my phone and plug it into the aux cord. "Do you mind if I play that podcast?"

"That sounds great." It's the most enthusiastic he's sounded since we started driving.

The spirit of rebellion—as my mom always calls it—rises within me. Without giving myself a chance to reflect, I press the podcast episode about David and Bathsheba.

A kinky Bible story.

My cheeks warm as the melodious voice of the podcast host fills the car. I shouldn't be so immature, but damn him. Why does he have to be so rigid in his thinking?

I smile at him from under my lashes, even though I know he can't see me. "This story made me...feel things. Growing up, I mean."

The atmosphere in the car grows suddenly stifling. I chance a glance at Brandon, my breath hitching as I take in his stiff posture, his knuckles white on the steering wheel. His face is flushed.

"Oh yeah?" Brandon finally asks, his voice tight. His gaze remains glued to the road ahead. He knows exactly where I'm going with this, but he's giving me the benefit of the doubt.

"I mean..." I pick at the loose thread on my yoga pants. "It's one of the sexier Bible stories, and my parents sheltered me so much, it was my only opportunity to hear something like that."

His jaw clenches, a muscle ticking in his cheek. "I think it's pretty sad. David essentially raped her. And then he had her husband killed."

I bite my bottom lip and scrape it with my teeth. "Well, of

course. If I think of the fact that they were real people—I mean, historians are pretty sure they were real but probably not the details. To me, it was just a story. And it was a hot story. David was the king, and he saw her naked once and had to have her. He wanted her so badly, he eliminated all barriers between them."

My skin grows hot and tingly. I shouldn't be talking this way with him, but it's so hard to resist.

It's fun to be able to have a conversation like this with him, given how reasonable he is about his faith and his deep knowledge of the Bible. I could never say something like this to any of my family members.

"I used to think about this story when I took baths," I say. "I'd imagine a man watching me and wanting me."

"Mari," he says, his voice full of warning.

"I'm sorry."

Frantically, I fumble with my phone, hitting the pause button. The car plunges into silence.

"I wasn't trying to turn you on. I really mean it."

He's quiet for a while, and my guilt makes my skin tingly and itchy.

"I honestly just..." I shut my eyes. "I want to be able to talk to you about this stuff. I feel like we could have before..."

His hand leaves the wheel for a moment, hovering over mine before returning to its place. "It's okay," he murmurs. "I want to be able to talk to you about the Bible. Answer all your questions. But this topic in particular..."

"I know."

"We can talk plenty this weekend, but let's keep the topic off sex." He smiles faintly. "Even if it's sex in the Bible."

I grin. "Such a kinky book."

"Watch it, young—" His lips close.

Goddamn it, Brandon. Just say it. Call me young lady. Call me your naughty girl.

The rest of the drive is rife with tension, and all I can think is what a long weekend it's going to be if he stays this bottled up.

Chapter Nineteen

B randon

I'm about to check into a hotel with the woman I'm dying to get my hands on but can never touch again.

Fuck this.

Fuck everything.

I can't even enjoy the gorgeous resort, which would normally make me feel as close to God as ever. Redwood trees surround us, and the ocean crashes against the cliffs in the distance.

I'm in a romantic setting with the object of my desires. For two whole days. And nights.

Please God. Help me get through the weekend without sinning again.

Not a kiss.

Not even a light brush of the hand against her beautiful skin.

The receptionist hands over our keys. "Pastor, Ms. Hernandez, you're in bungalows five and six. They're side by side for your convenience." She smiles warmly.

"No," I say too sharply. I swallow, attempting a casual tone. "Ms. Hernandez should be closer to the conference hall. For logistical reasons."

Mari turns to me—probably frowning in question—but I can't look at her. Not when I'm telling a bald-faced lie.

The receptionist blinks at me. "We're all booked. I thought you..." She looks at Mariana. "Your PA arranged it all."

"Yes, I did." Mariana's tone is sharp. "You never told me you wanted me next to the conference hall for...*logistical* reasons."

I inhale a deep breath, trying to calm my nerves.

I can't have her right next to me.

I'll go utterly insane.

I shoot Mariana a hard look, and she raises her chin. Fuck, I love how she does that. I love how she never lets me steamroll her.

Just as I'm about to tell her she's right, the receptionist speaks. "Bungalow twenty-seven is available. We don't usually book it, but we could...make an exception."

Twenty-seven. That sounds far away. My breath stutters out of me in a rush of relief. "That's fine. Thank you."

Mariana

The key turns in the lock with a rusty squeak, and the door swings open, revealing my accommodations for the night.

Oh my God.

No wonder the hotel clerk seemed so horrified when Brandon insisted I stay in this room.

I cringe as I step inside, the door creaking shut behind me. There's an earthy, damp smell to the place, like old wood and mildew. I make my way to the tiny bathroom.

Pink.

A pink sink, and a pink toilet.

A wave of irritation crashes over me. It's not just the fact that this damn bungalow clearly hasn't been renovated since the nineteen eighties. It's the reason I'm here in the first place. Brandon's damn piousness.

What is so wrong with messing around with a woman fourteen years younger than him who happens to be his best friend's daughter? I've wanted him since the moment I first saw him leading worship at First Covenant four years ago. I was a goddamn adult back then.

There's something more to it. I can feel it. He's afraid to get close to me.

It's probably because I'm an atheist. He doesn't want to fall for someone like me.

I take a deep breath to ease the tightness in my chest. After turning from the bathroom, my gaze falls on my suitcase. An idea sprouts.

I pull out my black dress. It's long with heavy material that hugs the contours of my body, but it's casual enough that no one will question why I'd wear it at a pastor's conference. Brandon will notice though.

He always notices.

A pang of guilt shoots into my chest, but I try to ignore it. It's not like I'm crossing any of the lines he established for us. Wearing a flattering dress isn't the same thing as calling him Daddy.

Still, I wish I had more mature ways of dealing with rejection.

I dress quickly, applying a touch more makeup than usual, giving my lips an extra gloss. God, I'm childish. I shouldn't be trying to taunt him when he's so troubled by his attraction to me.

But if he "slips up" again on this trip and touches me, I certainly won't cry about it.

Brandon

Fuck, I need to get out of here.

The restaurant is brimming with conversation. Our group maxed out the entire resort, which means everyone here is either a pastor or someone who works for one.

My guilt has grown as heavy as a mountain. These people came to this conference to hear my wisdom.

And all I want to do is fuck my PA intern, who's the youngest daughter of the man who brought me to Christ.

As I scan the room, my gaze lands on the subject of my thoughts. Even in the crowded hall, Mariana stands out like a flame in the darkness. The long black dress she's wearing clings to her curves, accentuating her body. A body I know she'd let me touch if I only asked.

She's like the fruit of the tree in the middle of the garden, and in moments like these, letting my whole fucking life implode almost feels worth the fleeting heaven of tasting her.

Beside me, Jeremy, a young pastor from Santa Monica follows my gaze. "Who is that?" His voice is full of appreciation.

"Mariana," I say a touch too sharply. "She's my temporary PA."

He turns back to me, a teasing glint in his eye. "How are you still single with women like that around you?"

I force a tight smile.

Don't lose your temper. Lots of married men comment on the appearance of other women.

"I'd never date my PA."

But I would go down on her in my own church.

As Mariana approaches, Pastor Jeremy flashes her a big smile. "The PA joins us. He hasn't scared you away yet with those tattoo sleeves?"

Mariana returns his smile and takes a seat. "All of New Morning loves his tattoos. They make him seem more human."

Jeremy smirks as he turns to me. "I'll bet that's why they love your tattoos. Especially the ladies."

I roll my eyes. "It's not like I wear sleeveless shirts at Sunday service."

"No." Mari shoots me a saucy little smirk that hits me right in the groin. "But one time he wore this short-sleeved shirt that was a little too small...for his arms, at least. My sister and I talk about it to this day. We call that service 'the gun show.'"

Heat fills my gut at the thought of Mariana talking about my body. Has she always been attracted to me? It never even crossed my mind before my lust for her first sprouted. I thought she saw me as an old man.

A bitter taste fills my mouth. How am I going to live as a stranger to her from now on, knowing that she wants me? How will I even stand it? I made a colossal miscalculation allowing us to get close these last few weeks, and now it's become a runaway train.

I force myself to focus on my plate, and eventually, the murmur of conversation lulls me into my head. There's nothing I can do right now. I just have to focus on getting through the weekend without sinning again.

"Pliny the Elder is hands down the best," Jeremy says to Mariana, pulling me out of my head. "It's a double IPA."

I grit my teeth. His voice is a little too enthusiastic.

"Santa Barbara bars only have it in bottles," Mariana says. "I'll bet it's much better on tap."

Jeremy grins at her. "They actually have it at a bar not far from here. Maybe we could sneak out after our meeting tonight."

I nearly choke on my steak. Sneak out? I clear my throat, shooting Jeremy a stern look. "I don't think so."

Understanding seems to dawn in his eyes. "I meant all three of us, of course."

Mariana meets my gaze steadily, a mischievous spark in her eyes. "Everyone needs a day off now and then, Pastor. Even you."

Pastor. She's back to her usual cheekiness.

Defiance.

My naughty girl, I'd pull you over my lap and spank you right now if I could.

Jeremy seems oblivious to the tension, his attention fully on

Mariana. "Why don't we sneak out right now?" He lifts his wrist and glances at his iWatch. "We have an hour and a half before the meeting starts."

"No." I stand up from my seat. "Mariana, are you done? I need to talk to you."

She glances down at her half-full plate, and my stomach sinks. I'm making her abandon her food.

"Sure," she says in a small voice.

Mariana

I clench my teeth to fight my smile.

He's jealous of that annoying pastor. So jealous that we're now about to spend the evening together. Alone. Just what he's been trying to avoid.

The air is cool and crisp, and my heels crunch over the gravel as we walk toward the bar. The tension between us is thick.

"I'm sorry about dinner." His voice is strained as he opens the screeching wooden door. "I wanted you to get a meal since you didn't get to finish yours."

"Why didn't we bring Jeremy?" I ask, feigning innocence.

Brandon sighs. "He's married."

Embarrassment heats my skin. My God, I didn't realize I was flirting with a married man to get a rise out of Brandon. Though I suppose I should have guessed it. Most pastors are married. But Jeremy seemed like just another young single bro I might meet at a bar.

Images of his eager expression flash in my mind. "He was definitely flirting with me."

"Yes." The word is clipped.

"And he wanted to hang out. It was me he was really inviting out. You were an afterthought."

Brandon grunts. "I don't think he would have given me any thought at all if I hadn't called him out."

I frown. "He's a pastor?"

He's quiet for a long moment. "Pastors are human, Mariana. We have frailties just like anyone else."

A laugh escapes me, bitter and humorless. "Seems like an odd place to let out your frailties. At a pastor's conference. Right in front of the pastor who's leading it."

His gaze is intent on the host's stand while we wait to get a table, but there's something in those dark eyes that makes the hairs on my arms stand up.

"What about in the bathroom of your own church?" he eventually asks. "With your temporary PA?"

His questions hit me in the chest. He's ridden with guilt. It's so palpable, I could almost reach out and touch it.

It was selfish of me to toy with him. Just because I think his reasons for resisting me are silly doesn't mean they aren't deeply meaningful to him. If I keep doing this, I could hurt him.

I don't want to hurt him.

I think I might be falling in love with him.

Chapter Twenty

M ariana

The dim light from the single lamp casts shadows that dance and flicker against the sun-bleached wallpaper. In the quiet, my guilt expands within me like a balloon, robbing me of breath at times.

Dinner was tense and short, and not because of Brandon. I was too in my head to enjoy my alone time with him.

He thinks I'm a child, and here I am, acting like one almost on purpose. Is this what I do when I feel rejected?

My whole life, I've felt out of place because of my beliefs. Brandon is one of the first few Christians who have accepted me, and his acceptance means something. He's a pastor, a man of authority in a community I'll probably always be a part of. At least, if I want to be close to my family.

He makes me feel like I belong. Just as I am.

It hurts to think that he might be hiding the truth from me— that maybe he thinks an atheist is fine for a family friend but not for a lover. I don't want him to only accept me partially.

I want him to want me as intensely as I want him.

A soft hissing sound pulls me into the present. I sit up and listen. It's coming from the bathroom. Spraying water.

I get up and pad barefoot across the coarse old carpet. I flick the light switch, illuminating the grimy bathroom in harsh white light. The sink is spraying an arc of water.

I rush forward, my heart pounding like a drum in my chest. My fingers slip on the cold metal of the faucet as I turn it, trying to stop the relentless assault of water. But instead of stopping, the spray intensifies. A monstrous jet of icy water drenches me in seconds.

Water seeps into my clothes, and I stumble backward, shielding my face with my hands. I gasp, my breath catching in my throat as the cold water saturates my skin, matting my hair to my face.

I'm soaked through as the water starts to creep out of the bathroom, drenching the carpet. I jump over the growing puddle and snatch up my suitcase. Water sloshes under my feet as I make my way toward the door.

In the quiet darkness of the forest, I use the moonlight as my guide. I run in the direction of Brandon's bungalow, my soaked clothes clinging to me like a second skin. Goddamn him for making me stay in that shack. Since this is all his fault, he can deal with the aftermath.

I knock frantically on his door, my teeth chattering from the cold. When Brandon opens it and appears in front of me, his eyes grow huge. "Oh my God," he nearly shouts. "Are you okay? What happened?"

I wave a hand. "I'm fine. I'm just wet, as you can see."

His dark gaze slowly drifts from my soaked hair down my neck, lingering on my chest.

"My room is flooding."

He doesn't say anything, just continues to stare at my soaked body as if in a trance. A breeze drifts over me, sending a shiver down my spine. "Brandon," I clip out. "My room is flooding."

"Sorry." He blinks once before moving aside quickly, ushering me into his room. Even in my frantic state, I'm immediately hit by the stark contrast between his bungalow and mine. This one is big and luxurious with a fully equipped kitchenette and stainless-steel appliances. I let out an almost hysterical laugh. "Well, I see why they don't rent out bungalow twenty-seven."

He frowns. "What do you mean?"

"It's a shack. Hence this." I gesture at my clothes. "We need to hurry. The room is flooding as we speak. Can you call the front desk?"

He nods before walking to the bedside table, that troubled expression never leaving his face. He feels guilty, I know, and even ten minutes ago, I would probably want to soothe him for it.

Maybe I will later, but not now. Not while I'm soaking wet and cold because of him.

A smile rises to my lips as I roll my suitcase into his bathroom. I was too frantic to appreciate that look on his face when he first opened the door, but when I'm dry, I'll be able to drink in the memory.

Hypnotized. That's how I would have described it.

Brandon

My pulse quickens as the phone rings. I can still see the way her clothes clung to her, outlining her every curve. The image burns in my mind.

It's all my fault. I deserve this punishment.

I acted selfishly, putting her in that clearly unlivable room. What if it was worse than a busted pipe? What if the whole damn thing had caved in on her?

Icy-cold recrimination washes over me. It's all my fault, and this is what I get. I glance over at the bathroom where shadows play at the bottom of the door. She's undressing in there, shedding the clothes that were practically painted on her body.

She might be naked at this very moment.

Don't think about all that pretty skin. Don't think about the water dripping down it.

The front desk finally picks up after probably the fifteenth ring. I explain the situation briefly, my words stumbling over one another. I can't keep my gaze from sliding back to the bathroom door. An odd sense of anticipation tingles over my skin.

"I'm sorry," the office staff says after a pause. "But we're fully booked. We don't have any other rooms available."

"What about the room next to mine? It was vacant just this afternoon."

"I'm so sorry, but it's no longer available."

Dizziness descends over me, making me sway forward.

God, no.

Deliver me from this. Keep me from sinning.

I beg you.

Mariana will have to stay here. In my room. My blood runs hot and cold at the same time, my heart pounding against my chest.

As I slam down the phone, Mariana walks out of the bathroom. She's wearing a large, baggy T-shirt, and a fist clenches around my gut. This is what she looks like in her bed at night. If I were sleeping with her, I could slip my hands under that big shirt and kiss her from her naval to that beautiful pink...

No.

This isn't even a fantasy anymore. She's here. She's real. My beautiful Mariana. Sinning now feels as inevitable as the moment David ordered Bathsheba be brought into his chamber.

God, please help me.

Of all the women in the world, why does it have to be her I crave so intensely? I don't want calamity in my life if I sin with her again. I don't want to lose the family I've come to need as if it were my own.

"You'll have to stay here." My voice is hushed and husky, and Mariana's eyes widen. Fuck, I didn't mean to use that bedroom voice.

"What about the bungalow next door?"

"No." My voice feels disembodied, as if in a dream. "It's booked. There's nowhere else for you to go."

The words seem to settle over her slowly. Those big brown eyes drift around the room before settling on my bed, and a darkness rises within me. I want to grab her by the throat, punish her for making me think these wicked thoughts.

"Would you mind—" Her lips close.

"What?" My tone is sharp and commanding, and those brown eyes grow wide and vulnerable.

I need to calm the fuck down. She can't know what I'm thinking.

Then it will be over.

She licks that full bottom lip. "Would it be too much trouble if I took a bath? I'm still shivering from all that cold water."

I fight the groan about to leave my lips.

Mariana bathing. While I sit here. Left to imagine what's on the other side of that door.

"Of course," I answer. "Get to it."

Based on the slight widening of her eyes, it must have sounded like a command again, when I meant for it to be a suggestion. Why does the dominant side of me always come out with her? I thought I left these proclivities behind me with the meaningless one-night stands. With effort, I turn away from her and sit on the bed, pretending to look at my phone.

The faucet turns on, muffled through the closed door. Heat engulfs my whole body, and my skin vibrates with electricity. I try to steady myself. To focus on anything that isn't Mariana's bare, beautiful skin.

I turn on the TV, hoping the noise will drown out my thoughts. I scroll aimlessly through the hotel's limited selection of shows and movies, but my mind keeps drifting back to that bathroom.

The sound of water splashing calls to my senses. What is she doing? Scrubbing herself? No. She's bathing just to get warm.

But maybe her thoughts are going in the same direction as mine, and she's using this strange set of circumstances to touch herself. Warmth radiates from my thighs to my gut as my thumb brushes over my cock.

Oh, fuck.

This has to stop.

I clench my fist and set it firmly at my side before standing up and walking to the fridge. I pull out the bottle of beer I picked up from the market earlier. I pop the cap and take a swig.

No. This is a bad idea. Lowered inhibitions are the last thing I need when Mariana's going to sleep in my room tonight.

I frantically reach for my phone and check the time. I haven't heard a peep from her in ten minutes. What if she fell asleep? What if she's hurt?

I find myself standing in front of the bathroom door, my heart pounding in my chest. I knock lightly, my voice barely a whisper. "Mariana?"

No answer.

"Mariana," I say louder. I'm about to knock again when something wicked within me halts my fist. I've already called for her twice. I'd be entirely justified to peek inside to make sure she's okay...

I *am* justified. I *am* worried she's hurt.

I push the door open, my pulse drumming loud in my ears. The soft glow from the vanity lights spills out, casting long shadows over the room. When my gaze drifts to the tub, I nearly fall over at the sight in front of me. She rests against the back of the tub with her mouth open, but she's not asleep.

Her hand is moving rapidly under the water.

"Shit," she squeaks before lifting her hands and covering her breasts with her palms.

It only makes my cock even harder.

"Mari," I croak out. The heat that surges through me is as relentless as a desert sun.

There's no going back now.

I'm lost.

Chapter Twenty-One

Mariana

He marches toward me, his gaze boring into mine. He kneels in front of the tub. "Tell me to leave. Tell me to leave now."

I swallow. "No."

His eyes flash. He threads his fingers into my hair and yanks my head back. His face hovers over mine, his lips an inch away. "God help me," he says before standing up and walking toward the door.

No, I want to shout, but he turns around before I get the chance, crossing his arms over his chest. His expression is oddly blank, and those dark eyes have a dreamy quality. "Keep going." His voice is as soft and hushed as it is at Saturday service.

I inhale a sharp breath. "You want me to..."

"Yes," he whispers.

I've never seen him like this before. He's at the edge of his control. That's why his voice is so soft. That's why his eyes are vacant. He's in a trance.

"What are you waiting for?" Again, that hushed voice.

I return my two fingers to my clit and start rubbing. Delightful pressure builds in my tummy, and a breathy moan escapes my lips.

Brandon's eyelids grow hooded. He walks around the tub, disappearing behind me. "What are you thinking about, Mariana?"

"You," I whisper.

"No." The word sounds like it slipped through clenched teeth. "If we're going to be sinners, you'd better make it worth it. I need you to tell me much more than that."

A jolt of electricity shoots into my stomach. "I was thinking about...the night I saw you...do this."

"Do what?"

"Stroke your big cock."

He hums. "And what would you do if I had my cock out right now?"

"I'd get down on my knees and put my mouth on you. Worship you."

"No," he says softly. "I wouldn't let you worship me. I'd make you gag on my cock. Punish you for being so tempting."

I rub faster, and a whimper escapes my lips. He's so good at this. I always suspected he was kinky before he came to God, but now I'm certain of it.

"Such sweet sounds." His shadow hovers over the bathtub, and I drop my head back to stare up at him. His arms are still crossed over his chest. "Such a sweet face—" he narrows his eyes "—for such a harlot."

The sound that is pulled from me is something between a gasp and a whimper, and I start frantically rubbing my clit.

Holy shit, he's degrading me.

I never imagined he'd be like this.

"You like that, don't you?"

"Yes!" As the pressure builds and expands in my tummy, I

slow my pace into a circular rub, drawing my pleasure into an agonizing upward climb.

"You'll say my name when you come, Mariana. Do you hear me?"

"Yes," I sob.

"You won't call me Pastor, or you'll regret it."

I scream as pleasure crashes over me, and Brandon lunges for the tub, his big hands gripping the copper edges. "Say my name now," he growls. "You filthy sinner."

"Brandon," I whimper.

"Yes." Through my haze, I see his expression soften. "That's it, sweet girl. Say it again."

"Brandon," I whisper as the last wave of pleasure runs through my limbs. My body grows languid, and I exhale heavily.

I'm startled by the sound of water splashing and the next thing I know, I'm being lifted out of the tub. He cradles me against his chest before setting my feet on the damp tile floor. When I stumble a little, he holds me steady. He grabs a towel from behind him and runs it over my body almost reverently.

"Such beautiful skin. My gorgeous Mariana."

I smile dreamily up at him. "Please say that wasn't it. Please say we can do more."

He stares at me for a long moment before lifting his hand high in the air. It comes down in a flash, cracking on the skin of my pussy. I let out a gasp as a sharp sting radiates from my groin to my thighs. He sticks two big fingers inside me and grabs me by the hair, yanking my head back.

"I'm a sinner because of you," he grits out. "You can take a little pain."

"Yes, Brandon."

Oh God, I never thought he'd be like this. Dominating, yes, but this...

How will I ever be able to walk away from him after tonight?

"We can do more." His voice is softer. He lifts a hand and

strokes my wet hair from my cheeks. "Much more. I'm going to fuck you until you can't breathe."

My gut clenches, and I let out a gasp.

"Now go," he commands. "Go to my bed and get on your hands and knees. I'll be out in a moment, so don't keep me waiting."

I nod frantically, and he smiles. "My eager little whore."

My belly is on fire as I rush out of the bathroom and hop onto the bed.

Brandon

"Jesus, help me," I whisper as I run my fingers through my hair.

I shouldn't go out there. The fact that I've already sinned doesn't justify sinning more, and fuck me, I'm acting like a mad man. I never should have degraded or hit her without her permission.

I'm going mad. My skin is almost vibrating with lust.

This is not the right state of mind to do things like this, especially when we haven't talked about it first.

How can I stop myself now? She's on my bed right now on her hands and knees.

I think I'd rather die than stop.

After taking a deep breath, I turn around and walk out the bathroom. When I open the door, the sight awaiting me nearly brings me to my knees.

Her heart-shaped ass is offered like an altar while her head rests on the bed.

I make my way quietly over to her and stick two fingers inside that pretty, glistening pussy. My cock throbs at the slippery wetness, but I don't let it pull me from my purpose. I walk around the bed and kneel down, offering my fingers to her mouth. "Taste yourself."

Her eyes widen minutely, but she obeys my command. When her tongue darts out and licks at my finger, I shove it inside her mouth.

"You're tasting something sweet but very, very wicked."

She moans. "Yes, Brandon. I'm your—"

"No." I yank my hand away and lift it to silence her. "You've been a bad girl, Mari. You'll listen to me now."

"Yes, Sir."

I smile as I stroke her cheek. Such a beautiful woman with those sparkling eyes and plump lips. How is it possible that just a few weeks ago, I tried to be a father figure to her?

But I didn't really, did I? Not with Mariana. Maybe Sofia. But something about Mariana called to me like a siren's melody. I fought it. Refused to acknowledge it, but it was always just beneath the surface.

"Lay on your back, my sweet, wicked girl. I'm going to make you come."

My skin is vibrating with electricity as her beautiful body turns over on the bed, exposing those round tits and pretty brown nipples.

My cock throbs painfully as I scoot onto the bed. "I'm going to use my fingers this time." I lean forward. "You'll have your eyes on me the whole time."

She nods frantically, and I smile as I set two fingers on her clit and start rubbing in a circular pattern. "You want to be good. Don't you, baby?"

"I do, Brandon." She whimpers. "I want to be so good for you."

"Ah." I increase the speed of my fingers. "You already are. So sweet. So well-behaved, but only for me. Isn't that right?

Her eyes grow huge. "Yes! Only you."

I lean forward, gritting my teeth. "And why is that?"

She lets out a little mewling sound but doesn't answer, so I pull my fingers away until my touch is featherlight. She thrusts her hips upward. "No, I want it harder!"

157

"You'll answer me, Mari, or you'll get nothing."

"What..." She pants. "What was the question?"

"Why do you behave only for me?"

She hums. "Because you're my daddy."

Hot exhilaration rushes through my veins, and my cock strains against the elastic of my boxers. "Yes, pretty girl. I'm your daddy."

I press a little harder as I flick her clit, and I see the effect of it immediately. She shuts her eyes and grimaces, as if in pleasurable pain. I use my other hand to grab her chin. "Eyes on me, Mari."

Her eyes shoot open, and those hips flail every which way. "Brandon!"

"Yes, my sweet girl. Let it all out."

She screams as she comes, and an angelic light spreads over her face. She smiles sweetly as the pleasure crashes over her.

Jesus Christ, I've never seen anything so beautiful in my life. Not even when I reached the top of the Inca Trail. As the sunrise broke through the mist—revealing endless emerald mountains—I thought I would never again in my lifetime be so close to God.

I was wrong.

And the need for her now is as potent as my need for God.

I crawl onto the bed until her little form is beneath me. It takes all of my willpower to move gently. No matter how much I want to claim her, I can't plunder her when she's so peaceful from her orgasm.

It would be blasphemy.

"Mari," I whisper. "Open your eyes for me, baby."

Her eyes flutter open and meet mine. There's such tenderness inside them that I could get drunk on it. I swipe my thumb over her swollen lower lip. "I'm going to use my cock now. Can you take it?

Her eyes flutter closed again, but her entire body shudders. A wicked little smile plays on her lips. "I can take it, Daddy."

Electricity jolts through my veins. I reach over to the bedside table and grab my wallet, pulling out the condom I've kept in here since a few days after this obsession with her started. I'd told myself it was for another woman. A woman to help me get over what I feel for her.

What a lie.

I've been deluding myself from the beginning.

After slipping on the condom, I crawl on top of her sweet little body. I push my hips down between her thighs. My cock is so hard it's painful. I need to be inside her.

I need to claim her now.

I run my palms up her thighs to the soft skin of her ass. She whimpers as she spreads her legs wider for me. "Please, Daddy."

I growl, nudging my cock against her slick pussy. I push in just a little, and she cries out. I still my hips. "Does it hurt, my sweet Mariana?"

"No." She shakes her head frantically. "It's perfect."

I press my lips to her ear, clenching my teeth. "Maybe it doesn't hurt yet, but it will. I can't be gentle, Mari. I've waited too long."

Her low mewling sound is like raindrops over my skin. Fuck, this woman was made for me. I never thought I'd be able to play sex games like this when I came to God. I figured any woman of faith would be insulted.

I needed my bold little atheist.

"You're too tempting" I kiss the spot where her shoulder meets her neck. "There was no way I could resist."

"Please. Now."

The word "please" lights a fire in my gut. I drive my cock deep inside her, my hips rocking against hers.

Holy fucking Jesus Christ.

She's so silky and tight I could come right now. I clench all of my core muscles to keep the pleasure from taking over. I lean down and lick a nipple, sucking it into my mouth as I rock in a slow, grinding motion. "You're so perfect. I could live inside you."

"Oh God, I love the way you talk."

I kiss her hard, capturing her tongue with my own. She

clutches my shoulders as she moans, the sound vibrating through my whole body. I growl into her mouth as I thrust into her.

"You're mine, Mari," I whisper against her mouth. "Only mine."

"Yes." Her eyes widen as she writhes beneath me, her pussy clamps around my cock, and the wave starts to build in my gut. I'm close. So close.

There's no point in holding back any longer when I know this won't be the last time with her.

God help me, I'm going to fuck her until the dawn breaks. I'd fuck her for the rest of eternity if I could.

As I thrust harder, the slickness between us makes a smacking sound. I lean down and bite her shoulder. Her cries get louder, and just as she's about to come apart, I push her legs back, bending her knees up.

"Oh God!"

"Yes. Take my cock, sweet girl."

"Brandon," she whimpers, and as her pussy clenches around me in waves, I lose myself. Unbearable pleasure floods my insides, and I let out a roar.

Chapter Twenty-Two

M ariana

I can't believe I'm here.

The warmth of his breath tickles the back of my neck. His big arms are wrapped snuggly around me like he's afraid if he lets go, I'll sneak away into the darkness.

He'd never let me, and the thought is like champagne fizzing through my veins. I smile to myself as I wiggle my butt against his hips.

"You need to get some sleep." His voice is just a little scolding, which makes my tummy flutter. I used to imagine him like this every Saturday night service when I heard that delicious voice of his.

It turns out his voice is different. It's stern, yes, but it's also sweet. Affectionate.

Maybe this voice is just for me.

"How can I sleep when you're so good at making me come?"

He lets out a low growl. "Maybe I won't let you come again if you don't sleep. Did you consider that, young lady?"

I sigh as I let my cheek press against his biceps and stroke his forearm with my fingers.

This is heaven.

But how long will it last?

Not long, probably. When morning comes, he'll tell me that it was a huge mistake. That he never should have crossed this line. He might even tell me that he took advantage of me again, and I'll have to force myself not to roll my eyes.

Oh well. For now, I'll enjoy it.

I smile. "Holy shit, you're good with your fingers. I don't think a guy has ever gotten me off with just his hands before you. Men are usually so bad at it."

He squeezes me tightly. "I don't want to hear about other men, young lady."

My laughter is raspy from lack of sleep. "Even when I tell you they were bad at making me come?"

His warm mouth brushes against my cheek. "I don't want to hear about the *boys* who touched you before me."

I giggle. "My big strong boss daddy."

His palm slides over my bare ass before giving it a firm little pat. "Somehow I feel like you're making fun of me."

"Never. All I could think about when you were fucking me was how many times I imagined it while I was sitting in church watching you preach."

He's quiet for a moment, his chest rising and falling rhythmically against my back. "And I was thinking about Machu Picchu."

I gasp out a laugh. "What?"

"I hiked it just a bit after I became a Christian." The warm, rough pads of his fingers brush from my forehead over my scalp.

I flip around so that I can look at him. The room is dark, but a lamplight from outside casts shadows over the angles of his face. "I've always wanted to hike the Inca Trail. My dad did it after law school, and he said it was incredible."

Even in the darkness I can make out his smile. "He's the reason I did it. He told me about it when he was trying to bring me to Christ. Said he couldn't imagine that all that beauty could be random. It has to be the hand of God."

I snort. "I see he likes to play the old hits. He said that exact same thing to me when I was a kid asking him to prove the existence of God."

"My little skeptic." He brushes my cheek with his fingers. "I don't need proof of God, but I can see what he meant. It's a long hike. Several days. You're surrounded by green and mist for a lot of it. You start to feel like you're in another world after a while. At times, I felt like God was walking beside me. My mom, too. It was the most divine experience of my life." He brushes his lips against my cheek. "Until tonight."

Warm rushes through me, making my head fuzzy. He must be teasing me. There's no way he can really mean that.

"What..." My pulse pounds like a hammer against my throat. "What's going to happen, Brandon? Between us, I mean."

His smile fades into the shadows. "Mari."

A weight engulfs my body, and I feel like I'm sinking into the bed. The pity in his voice is unmistakable.

I'm so stupid.

Of course he wasn't serious.

"I never should have done this," he says.

My throat is choked, but I manage to huff. "You. Always you. I have no agency in this."

"Of course you have agency, but you haven't done anything wrong. I'm the one who sinned here."

"Because I'm your *intern*." I spit out the word.

"It might not mean anything to you, but it does to me. You're part of my flock."

I hum. "It sounds kinky."

"Mariana Hernandez."

My tummy does a little flip at his stern tone. Before I get the chance to say something cheeky, he leans forward and kisses my mouth. "Let's not talk about it anymore. For right now, I'm happy."

"Even though you're sinning?"

He lets out a long breath. "Yes, though I hate to say it."

"Are you implying that you want to go a few more rounds since you've already sinned?"

He smiles, stroking the hair around my face. "Cheeky girl. I don't *want* to be a sinner, but..." He swallows. "I don't know how I could possibly get through the weekend without doing this again. Telling myself I could would be setting us both up for failure."

I lean forward and kiss his cheek. "I agree."

He lets out a long sigh. "Let's just have this weekend."

"I like that." I trail my mouth from his cheek to his jaw. "Let's live like there's no tomorrow, Pastor."

* * *

Brandon sets the phone on the receiver. "I just spoke to the staff, and they'll have a room for you by three p.m."

I step out of the bathroom, running a hand through my freshly curled hair. "And what... What should we say? If the other pastors find out my room flooded?"

"We're not going to lie to anyone." His voice is stern. "We'll tell them you had to sleep in here because your room flooded, but we also don't need to tell them any more than they need to know. It's none of their business."

I smile. What a contrast he is right now to moments ago when we lay in his bed and he stroked my hair and kissed me softly. At one point, I woke up to the deep rumble of his laughter, and when I asked him what he was laughing about, he said I was talking in my sleep. There was so much affection in his voice.

Now, he's all business. My boss. My stern daddy.

It makes me want to be naughty.

He walks toward me and pins me with a glare. "I don't like that look you're giving me, Ms. Hernandez."

I cock a brow. "What look?"

"Like you want to be spanked."

Electricity shoots into my groin. "Maybe I do."

His playful expression vanishes. "I was too rough with you last night."

I scowl. "Absolutely not. I loved it. I want more."

He crosses his arms over his chest. "We'll save it for tonight. I can't have anyone finding out there's something going on between us. I'll deal with my sins when we get home. For now, we're going to be living a double life. You can be my naughty girl at night, but during the conferences today, you need to be my professional PA. I can't have any distractions while I'm teaching."

I nod. "Yes, Boss."

He smiles. "Maybe I'll even reward you for it later."

Chapter Twenty-Three

M ariana

"I can't believe you know Vanessa Gallo," Jake says.

This outside time is a welcome distraction from the stuffy auditorium at this never-ending conference. Brandon has been speaking all day, and we've barely exchanged two words.

My alone time gave me the opportunity to get to know Jake, another pastor's PA. He's charismatic, easygoing, and a fantastic distraction from thoughts of the coming night.

Which has my stomach fluttering uncontrollably.

"Not just know her," I say. "She's my best friend's baby sister. I literally grew up with her."

He shakes his head slowly, his eyes wide. "I can't believe that. I'm seriously in love with her."

I snort out a laugh. "Of course you are. Every deconstructing Christian who's ever opened TikTok is in love with her. But she's more than taken. Her boyfriend would fight you."

He narrows his eyes, still smiling. "I've seen her boyfriend in her videos, and he seems like such a tool. He doesn't deserve her. I could make her so much happier."

I burst into laughter. "Oh, is that right? Please tell me how you could make this complete stranger happier than she is right now."

He grins, but just as he opens his mouth to speak, a shadow appears behind me.

Brandon.

When I turn around, his face is like thunder, brows furrowed and lips set in a firm line. He's staring at Jake and me. "Did you take notes?" His voice is curt.

I blink at him. "Yeah, why?"

"May I see them?"

His tone is brusque, lacking any warmth. Why the hell are these notes so important? He should know I'm a good notetaker. I have a history degree, damn it.

Oh no. Is he regretting our agreement to live like there's no tomorrow?

"Sure," I mumble, pulling out my laptop and flipping it open. It takes me a moment to find the document with the notes. When I hand it to him, he doesn't look at me, his focus solely on the laptop.

"Excuse us," Brandon says without looking Jake's way. "I need to speak to Mariana privately."

Jake raises his eyebrows but shrugs. As he walks away, I turn my attention back to Brandon. His posture is stiff.

"What's wrong?" I finally ask, my voice barely above a whisper.

"Meet me in my cabin. Two minutes."

With that he turns around and walks away, and my stomach muscles tie into knots. There's no mistaking what he wants.

Sex in the middle of the day. With Brandon. At a pastor conference.

I want to squeal in delight, but instead, I take a deep breath and start counting. After what feels like an eternity, I start walking in the direction of his bungalow. When I finally reach the front door, I pause, a smile tugging at my lips. I grip the bodice of my dress and pull it down, revealing more of my cleavage.

I push open the door, and there he stands with his back to me. He looks so big and intimidating.

I love it.

"Well." My voice is breathy. "What did you need to...*talk* to me about?"

He turns around, and his dark gaze is so intense my legs turn into jelly. "We're not going to do much talking."

I smile. "We're not?"

"I wouldn't be smiling, Mariana. You've been a bad, bad girl."

Heat shoots into my groin. "Have I?"

"Yes."

After shutting the door, I step toward him, and his tall form looms over me, and that fire in his eyes sends shivers through my body. "What are you going to do to me?"

He takes my hand and leads me to the bed. "Punish you, of course."

My heart pounds. "Really?"

"Yes. You've been begging me to spank you."

"What did I do?"

After sitting on the bed, he lifts me up and places me on his lap. His big fingers brush over my cleavage. "You've been distracting me all day. With this dress." His eyes narrow on my chest. "Your bra is showing. You pulled it down."

I nuzzle my head against his shoulder. "Maybe."

"No." He grips my waist and pushes me back. "No cuddling. Not yet. Not until you've had your punishment."

"Is it a sin to wear a formfitting dress?"

"Not a sin." His voice is hushed. "But you disobeyed me."

"How?"

"I told you I needed to focus on being a pastor today. You've been distracting me on purpose."

I grin. "Have I?"

He hums in agreement. "And not just with this dress. You were shamelessly flirting, too."

I gasp out a laugh. "Flirting? With Jake, you mean?"

He grabs me by the chin, narrowing his eyes on my face, and heat shoots into my gut. "You know you were."

Oh my God, is he really jealous? How absurd.

How delightful.

"So that's why you interrupted us and all but ordered him to leave?"

"He needs to know that he's not allowed to touch what's mine." He lifts me in the air and sets my belly on his thighs. As he presses his hand on my lower back, the ache between my legs intensifies, and I groan.

"Don't move," he growls.

"Oh God."

His hand roams over my back, slipping under my dress and cupping my butt. "You're not going to be able to sit comfortably after this."

Liquid heat pools into my belly. "I'm sorry for flirting."

"It's too late for sorry."

He pushes my panties down to my ankles, and cool air hits my pussy. I shiver. A moment later, a loud crack resounds in the room, and numbness spreads over my ass. I suck in a breath as tingling heat spreads over my skin.

"Count," he orders.

An almost hysterical giggle bursts from my chest. "This is a really intense spanking, Boss."

"An intense spanking for an intense woman."

I hear the smile in my voice, and warmth fills my chest. I breathe deeply. "One."

Crack.

"Two."

Crack.

"Three."

"Good girl." He rubs his hand gently over my burning cheeks.

"You're doing such a good job, Mariana. But are you going to obey me?"

"Yes, Sir."

Crack. "That was four."

He rubs his palm over my burning skin. "You're getting one more, but it's going to be really hard. I'm going to give you a chance to take some deep breaths. I'll pet you while you do it."

His fingers stroke into my hair, and I take the deep breaths, though I don't really need them. A warm smile tugs at my lips. God, I love him like this. What would it be like if we had this relationship all the time?

A loud smack echoes through the bathroom, distracting me from a fantasy that probably wouldn't do me any good anyway.

"You did so well," he says softly, "taking your punishment."

I smile. "Thank you, Sir."

He groans as he slides two fingers into my soaking wet pussy. "My good girl wants to be taken right here, doesn't she?"

"Yes." I moan as he works his fingers in and out of my pussy. "Yes."

He removes his fingers suddenly. "Not now. We need to head back."

My eyes grow wide as he lifts me up and sets me between his legs. "We have at least another five minutes. Let's just have a quickie."

He grins. "Oh, no. When I finally get my cock in you again, I'm going to enjoy it. You'll have to wait."

I glare at him. "You're trying to torture me."

He shrugs one shoulder. "Like you've been torturing me since the moment you started working for me."

Brandon

. . .

Warm contentment seeps through my veins as I gaze out over the assembly of pastors. Laughter and chatter fills the room. They're just as glad as I am that the last conference of the day is now over, and that it's time for relaxation.

I won't be relaxing a bit. Not when I have the whole night with her.

The whole fucking night.

How is it possible that my body is so light and unburdened? I'm technically deceiving all the people in the room. They'd never think that the pastor who just spoke about Paul's sexual ethic would turn around and fuck his young PA in his cabin afterward.

It's like I've been living in a dreamworld these past twelve hours.

I don't want to leave it.

As I descend the steps of the stage, my gaze immediately finds Mariana. She's sitting in the front row, tapping away on her laptop, taking the last notes for the day. The soft glow from the screen illuminates her face. Her dress has slipped off one shoulder and one thought comes to mind.

Mine.

This perfect woman is all mine.

As I approach her, she looks up from her laptop. "Hey, Pastor." There's that saucy lilt to her voice that used to drive me insane.

Before she was mine.

"You've been sitting for a long time." A deep, satisfied possessiveness wraps around me like a blanket. I lean forward and whisper in her ear. "Are you sore?"

"I am, actually." Her eyes narrow. "My butt's sore from all the...sitting."

A deep laughter is pulled out of my chest.

She narrows her eyes, mouthing, "Kinky bastard."

I'm not even worried that someone around us might be watching closely enough to pick up what's going on.

I care for nothing but her.

* * *

How will I ever give this up?

She swivels her hips, grinding into my cock as she rides me. I grip her hips tightly, thrusting upward to get more of her.

Fuck, I need more.

I could have her for eternity and never be satisfied.

"Kiss me," I command, and she smiles dreamily before leaning forward.

As our lips touch, her body melts into mine. She runs her hands along my back, exploring my skin. When I pull her closer, her chest moves rapidly against mine. "Are you tired, love?" I ask.

"No," she pants.

I smile. "Liar."

She laughs breathily. "I'm tired, but I don't want to stop."

That frantic, fevered tone... I recognize it immediately, because it's how I feel, too. We only have a few hours before the sun comes up.

It will all be over soon, and I want to weep at the unfairness of it. Why God? Why did you allow this to happen? It's misery to experience bliss like this, only to be forced to give it all up.

I need to extend it as long as I can.

I move my hands down to her hips, and in one swift motion, I flip her beneath me. I reach for her wrists and pin them above her head. "I'll do all the work from now on."

She smiles sweetly, and my heart swells. Oh fuck, this feels like love.

It can't be love. Not *that* kind of love, at least. Sin and true love can't coexist, and everything about this situation is all wrong. She's my best friend's daughter. She's my intern. Having her long term would mean losing everything I hold dear.

But in this moment, it feels worth it.

"You don't have to." She reaches between our bodies to cup my balls. "I want to make you happy."

I hiss at the exquisite pleasure. "I could already die of happiness." Her lips open, and I thrust my tongue deep into her mouth.

More.

I need so much more.

My fingers dig into the flesh of her ass as I roll my hips against hers. She groans and I feel the vibration deep inside of her. I lick my tongue along her neck, nibbling as I move toward her collarbone. I move my mouth to the spot between her throat and her shoulder, sucking hard. Her pulse flickers against my tongue, and it feels like my own. Like her body is mine.

Mine.

Oh fuck, she feels like she belongs to me and only me. How will I ever be able to stand by while another man touches her?

I see myself sitting impotently across the table from her at a family dinner. Another man is beside her, his arm draped over her shoulder. His fingers idly stroke this very spot of skin that is in this moment so dear to me.

This is heavenly hell.

I thread my fingers through her hair before gripping hard. I pound my hips into hers, my balls slapping against her skin.

"Oh God," she moans, her body trembling.

"You'll take all of me, Mariana. This pussy is mine."

"Yes," she pants. She lowers her chin as those wicked dark eyes stare up at me. "And your cock is *mine.*"

Pleasure shoots through my veins. Oh fuck, she's so perfect.

"Yes, sweet girl. I'm entirely yours."

And I mean it.

I really mean it.

"Then come for me," she whispers.

The words hit me like a meteor. I pump into her one final time before I explode. As wave after wave of ecstasy ripples through my body, the warmth of my come shoots out of me, but not far enough.

I wish I weren't wearing a condom.

I want to fill her with my come. I want to put a baby in her, watch her belly grow with a part of me.

Holy fucking shit, this is madness.

Exquisite madness.

Mariana

The soft purple morning light peeks through the slits in the blinds, illuminating the room. I'm sitting at the small vanity, running a brush through my long, tangled hair.

Tangled because he had those big hands all over it.

Brandon stirs behind me, his sleepy groan resonating in the quiet room. He rises from the bed, the sheet slipping off his muscled chest. After walking over to me, he leans against the wall, watching me with curious eyes. "What are you doing?" His voice raspy from sleep.

"Just taking care of this now." I divide my hair into sections. "I know I'll be too tired to get ready in the morning." A naughty smile tugs at my lips. "It's morning now, actually."

He walks behind me, and those pensive dark eyes study my hands. "Can I do it?"

My reflection shows huge eyes. "You want to French braid my hair?"

He nods. "You have such beautiful hair." He brushes a loose strand off my shoulder and then leans down and kisses my neck. "And neck. I love your neck. I couldn't stop staring at it when you organized my bookshelf."

Warmth fills me everywhere. "Alright." My voice is strangely hoarse. "I'll tell you how to do it."

He nods sharply and steps directly behind my back. "Command me, my queen."

"Okay, it's not easy on your first try. Your fingers have to do multiple things at once."

He grins. "I'm good with my fingers."

I cock a brow. "Let's see how good you are, Pastor."

I show him how to divide the hair into sections and then intertwine them. He's quiet, focused on the movements of my hands with a furrowed brow, looking thoroughly absorbed, and something about it is achingly sweet, making my chest tight.

"That seems pretty straightforward," he says.

I smile. "Let's see what you've got."

He doesn't waste a moment before reaching out for my head. His fingers are surprisingly agile for his first time braiding, and the rhythmic pull on my hair is soothing.

"You have so much hair," he says.

I snort. "It's my one beauty."

His hands grow still. "What the fuck are you talking about?"

He sounds so sweetly indignant that the ache in my chest grows sharper. "I'm not trying to fish for compliments, but it was hard growing up with someone who looks like Sofia. Every guy I knew had a crush on her."

He frowns as he continues his task. "You're every bit as beautiful as her, if not more so."

When I snort, he tugs at my hair. "I mean it, young lady."

"And yet you started courting her. Not me."

His eyes soften as he stares down at my hair. "I didn't start courting her because I thought she was more beautiful than you. You weren't even an option."

"Why not?" I ask a touch too sharply.

For a moment, he quietly works on my hair, but I know he's thinking of the right response.

The right response to placate me.

"Don't say I'm too young," I add. "That's bullshit. I'm only six years younger than Sofia."

He chuckles humorlessly. "*Only* six years."

"I'm not some naïve Christian girl who thinks getting married will solve all her problems. I'm probably more mature than Sofia in that respect. The church tried to groom me to become a man's possession, and they failed. I know my own mind, and I know what I want. I want *you*."

What am I asking? Am I asking for more than this weekend? He can't give me that. Won't.

His hands grow still, and his eyes meet mine in the mirror. "I'm supposed to be mentoring you. I don't know if you realize this, but it's wrong to fuck someone you mentor."

I scoff. "I never asked you to mentor me."

"No." His gaze returns to his hands as they work through my hair. "But someone did."

Tightness grips my chest. When will he ever get over this thing with my dad? It's not fair that my dad's unwanted intervention in my life has to drive away the man I love.

Oh fuck.

I love him.

"I can't lose him, Mari." Brandon's voice is so sweet and vulnerable, that a coil wraps around my heart. "He's like family."

I nod, even as that coil grows tighter, making it hard to breathe. I'd be selfish to try to convince him otherwise. Even if I'm pretty sure my dad would forgive Brandon eventually, it doesn't matter if he's not willing to take the risk. He loves my dad.

I want him to love me more.

We sit quietly while he braids my hair. It's so hauntingly domestic that I can't help but imagine we're in our own room, sometime years down the road when all this turmoil is behind us.

It's a heartbreaking fantasy.

"Okay, what do I do when I reach the bottom?" he asks with an adorable little wrinkle in his brow, and something about that earnest, concentrated frown squeezes around my heart so tight I can hardly breathe.

I love him.

I love him, and this will be over soon.

Chapter Twenty-Four

B randon

She snores softly, her face pressed against the passenger window, and I can't help but smile. I tired her out. That's what happens when a woman comes along who's too tempting to make a celibacy vow worth keeping.

A part of me knows this is so much more than lust. Mariana feels like she was made for me.

I want to uncover her endlessly, learn her every secret. I want to simply exist with her. Have her become a staple in my home. Someone whose presence I get used to seeing. I want to become so intimate with her that her mere existence will no longer make my heart pound in my chest. Instead, there will be a warm stillness, my restlessness will be gone, because she'll be a permanent fixture in my life.

Fuck.

I'm in love.

She stirs slightly in her sleep, her lips parting to let out a tiny sigh, and my heart clenches.

Oh God, this pain is a tight fist around my heart that will never let go. I never thought love could feel this way, and I knew it could be painful. I watched my mom slowly fade away. But I've never had to let someone go who's still a part of my life. Years stretch ahead of me. Years of being around this precious woman, but not nearly close enough.

Not close enough to touch.

I reach out and stroke a soft strand of hair that's escaped the orderly braid. How like Mariana. Sweet and soft and unable to be like everyone else.

I take a deep breath, my grip tightening on the steering wheel. I need more time with her.

Just a little more time.

I know it's wrong. That shadow in the distance is God's voice in my heart, telling me I'm being selfish, that I should end it all now. I'm risking more than just my friendship with Hector. I'm risking Mariana's heart as well.

But I need more time. I think I might die if I don't have it.

I squeeze Mariana's thigh, and she jerks up, making a sweet little breathy sound I wish I could record in my mind and store with me forever.

"Darling," I say. "Sorry to wake you up, but I have to talk to you about something."

"What?" she asks in a raspy voice.

My fingers clench on the steering wheel. "I want to extend our time together a bit. Let's have lunch tomorrow. Maybe I could..." I flinch, hating myself for my deliberate sin, but unable to stop myself. "Take you to my house. Make something for you."

And fuck you raw afterward.

"That sounds great," she says, and the delight in her voice brings a smile to my face that quickly fades.

It will be over after tomorrow.

It has to be. I already hate myself. In my next conversation with Hector, I'll update him on my "progress" with Mariana's faith while blithely ignoring the fact that I just spent the weekend fucking her brains out at a pastor's conference. It will feel that much worse if I keep doing it behind his back.

I've never lied to him before. After all the lies my dad told my mom growing up, I vowed to tell the truth like a witness on the stand after I became a Christian. Turns out my integrity is even more fragile than I thought it was.

Which is even more reason to end things permanently after tomorrow. How could I continue to lead my congregation as a willful sinner?

Fuck, this is misery. Misery and bliss at the same time. I'm itching for tomorrow to begin, and yet dark dread swarms within me like a plague of locusts.

Chapter Twenty-Five

M ariana

The bright lilt of my sister's voice pulls me from the deep darkness of sleep.

I jerk up to an unfamiliar room that gradually morphs into my own. Oh, that's right. Brandon and I came home, and based on that orange glow of sunlight on the floor, I must have slept until the afternoon.

Shaking off the remnants of sleep, I pad out of my room, the murmur of voices growing louder as I near the living room.

"Do you think heels would be too much?" Sofia asks, excitement bubbling in her voice.

I pause in the hallway, leaning against the wall and trying to stay out of sight. Sofia stands in a tight emerald dress that clings to her every curve. Danielle sits on the couch, her eyes narrowed in assessment. "I would do strappy sandals. Let's make him think this meetup is an afterthought."

Sofia laughs again, and a chill runs down my spine. What the fuck is going on? Please say "him" doesn't refer to who I think it does.

"Oh man, that dress, Sofi." Danielle shakes her head slowly. "You have no idea."

Sofia grins. "Really?"

"Yes!"

"You don't think it's too sexy?"

"No, I mean, it's definitely modest. No cleavage is showing. But with the curves you've got, girl, you can't help but look kind of sexy."

They both break out into giggles, and I want to roll my eyes. *Modest.* One of the dumbest words in the evangelical vernacular, as if revealing certain body parts is inherently sinful.

"I shouldn't be saying this, but..." Danielle giggles. "No, I'm not going to say it."

"What?" Sofia's grin grows.

"Okay, so I'm not saying you should lie, but I think you should make it sound like you just came from a date. With Pastor Brandon. You know it would drive him crazy."

Sofi nods. "Maybe I'll stop by New Morning before we hang out so it won't be a lie. I've been meaning to..."

Sofi's voice fades into the raging buzz in my ears. Holy fuck. This really is what I feared.

She's meeting up with Finn.

I march forward, and both of their heads turn to me. "What's going on?" I ask firmly.

Sofi's smile fades. "Nothing that concerns you."

"Are you meeting up with Finn?"

"I told you it's none of your business."

"Well, if you're not going to tell me, maybe I should call up Mom. You usually tell her everything, so I assume—"

"Don't you dare," she says through clenched teeth.

When I continue to stare steadily at her, that outraged expression of hers falters. "Okay, yes. I'm meeting with Finn, but it's not what it sounds like. Apparently, he's had a big breakthrough recently in his counseling with his pastor, and he wants to apologize. He never really—"

"So he's meeting you somewhere? Why can't he just do it over the phone?"

She averts her gaze. "It's a big apology. He thinks it needs to be in person."

"I'm assuming his wife is coming since married Christian men don't believe in meeting other women alone."

Indignation flashes in Sofia's eyes. "We're meeting in public. His wife isn't walking with the Lord right now, so it wouldn't—"

When I burst into incredulous laughter, Sofia's indignant expression shifts into what looks like rage, but I don't care.

I've reached my limit with her obsession with Finn.

"You of all people should know that I believe in marriage above all," she says, her voice quivering with anger. "I would never do anything to jeopardize what he has with his wife. No matter what he did to me."

Even in my rage, my chest aches. She really believes from the bottom of her heart she would never do what he did to her.

"You're making a mistake doing this," I say softly.

Her nostrils flare. "We'll have to agree to disagree."

I grunt. "I guess we will."

Dread clamps my chest. I never really thought my sister would have an affair with Finn, though everything seems to be pointing in that direction.

* * *

"You're stressed," Livvy says, her fingers momentarily freezing around the delicate dried flower she's about to place into a small glass bottle.

A sigh escapes me as I halt my fingers, holding another wedding favor we're crafting for her wedding, which is now less than two weeks away. I'm not as groggy as I was earlier, but I can't keep my mind from wandering during the rote task.

Livvy can always sense my inner turmoil.

"I can't help it. What do you think of this?" I ask as I lift a nearly finished favor, trying to redirect our attention back to the task.

She squints at it, her mind seeming elsewhere. "Pretty. But... what is it exactly? Are you worried Brandon's going to be stubborn forever?"

I press another petite blossom into the glass enclosure. "He's not going to change his mind, Livvy. He's set on ending things between us."

"Maybe for now." Her gaze is fixed on the dried flower between her fingers. "But I don't see how he could stay that way. Every time he's around your dad, he'll be reminded of you."

I seal the bottle and set it next to the row of others we've completed. "I think it's more than just my dad, to be honest. I don't think he wants a partner who's an atheist."

Livvy sighs. "It doesn't make sense, though. He's so level-headed. If I was able to accept Cole as an atheist, how can Brandon not accept you? You're so wonderful."

A smile rises to my lips even as coldness settles in my gut. "Thank you."

A momentary silence fills the room, and a sluggish melancholy drifts over me, making my body heavy. I love him, but I'll get over him. Daisy's maternity leave will be over soon, and then I won't have to be in his warm presence all the time.

Plus, I'll start avoiding family gatherings.

The thought of that leaves a heavy loneliness in my gut.

"Mari..." Livvy's voice cuts through my inner turmoil. "What if you told your dad about everything? Maybe... What if you got him on your side? You're so logical and convincing when you're sure of something, and your dad's a lawyer. He's more reasonable than most fundy Christians. Way more reasonable than my dad, for example. I think you could make him understand."

"No," I say immediately.

Her eyes widen. "Why not?"

I fix my eyes on my fingers as I put a tiny flower in a bottle, willing away the small flutter in my heart at the thought of being with Brandon long-term. "I don't want to get Brandon that way. I want him to be willing to take a risk for me."

Her eyes grow so sad that I have to look away. As much as I adore her quiet empathy, I can't bear seeing my own heartbreak reflected in her.

I don't want to taint tomorrow. If it's the last few hours we'll have together, I want to enjoy them.

I'll deal with the heartache when it's well and truly over.

Chapter Twenty-Six

B randon

"How did the weekend go?" Ethan asks.

I take a sip of my beer, guilt gripping my chest like a vise. I'll tell him eventually. Tell him everything, but not now, damn it.

Not when I have one more blissful day with Mariana.

Tomorrow.

"Fine," I say, the word surprisingly smooth on my lips. Deception has gotten much easier these past few weeks.

Ethan's quiet for a long moment. Maybe my lie wasn't as convincing as I thought. "Even though you were with Mariana for forty-eight hours?"

I take a sip of my beer and glance at the basketball game on the screen high above us. "It was a busy trip. I was speaking most of the time."

"You weren't speaking at night."

I set down my beer and pin him with a stare. "What's that supposed to mean?"

His wide eyes tell me I overreacted. Fuck.

"Nothing." He scratches the back of his head. "I just mean you had time to hang out with her. At dinner and... I don't know. I really wasn't implying anything. I know you'd never do that."

My jaw clenches, and I look back at the screen, pretending to watch the game. Fuck, what will he think when I tell him?

Maybe I don't have to. When I became a Christian, I opened up to him about the careless way I used to treat my sexual partners. I wanted him to see how Christ changed me.

What would he think, especially given what our worthless father has done?

A loud giggle resounds behind us, drawing Ethan's attention. His confused expression fades. His posture stiffens, and his eyes grow alert. I'm thankful for the distraction.

I don't want to have to answer the question I know he's going to ask.

Not when I still have tomorrow. Eight precious hours of work.

"That's Lily," Ethan says, his voice hard. His gaze is still fixed on wherever the laughter is coming from.

"Oh." A smile quirks at my lips. At least I'm not the only one pining over a woman I can't have.

"Yes," he grits out, those watchdog eyes darting over the scene. "She's wasted and surrounded by men. And I do mean men. They don't look like college students."

I follow Ethan's line of sight to a group at the bar. Three guys stand around a woman with bright-red hair. She releases another high-pitched giggle.

"She's pretty," I say.

"Yes," he answers absently, his eyes fixed on Lily. "I need a favor."

I frown. "What kind of favor?"

"I need you to walk over there and pretend to be her boyfriend."

"What? Why can't you do it?"

His nostrils flare. "She'll throw a fit if I do it, but with you, she'll probably just be...confused."

Ah. My sweet little brother, protecting the woman he wishes he didn't want. What would I do if Mariana were wasted and surrounded by a bunch of creepy men?

Probably something stupid. Something that would wind me up in jail.

"So what do you want me to do?"

"Make it seem like she's your girlfriend and lead her outside. Use your pastor coaxing to get her to go home with you. I'll order an Uber for her."

I drain the last of my beer and set it back down on the counter. I turn to Ethan, holding his gaze. "Okay, I'll do it."

Ethan's shoulders visibly relax. "Thank you."

After pushing off my chair, I make my way through the crowded bar. As I get closer, Lily's giggles grow louder, and the three men surrounding her are closer than before. One of them has his hand on her lap, making my skin crawl. What if that were Mariana's delicate thigh?

No wonder Ethan wants me to do this. I'd be far less calm right now if one of these men tried to touch my Mari.

I square my shoulders and take a deep breath, fixing a smile on my face as I approach. "Hey, love."

Lily turns to look at me, her bright-red hair tumbling over her shoulders. Her eyes are wide and glazed. "Who are you?" The lilt of her voice tells me she likes what she sees.

Good. That'll make it easier.

I shoot her a teasing smile. "We can play that game when we get home. You've had a few too many."

She laughs again, this time into my chest, and it's a relief to see the men backing off, each one looking down at their drink or phone, likely to avoid a confrontation. I don't wait around to explain, leading Lily away from them and toward the exit.

With Lily leaning heavily against me, I walk her outside into the cool night air.

"So you're my knight in shining armor?" she asks, the words thick with drink, "or were you just trying to get rid of the competition?"

"You're going home," Ethan says. "I've already called your roommate."

Lily's wide eyes dart to Ethan. "I should have known."

"The Uber's around the corner," Ethan says, not meeting her gaze.

A saucy smile spreads over Lily's face. "My lord and master, Ethan Harrington."

Ethan only rolls his eyes, and I fight the urge to laugh. My poor brother. This one is even more trouble than Mariana.

He's in for it.

The Uber comes shortly after, and I lead Lily to the car. She doesn't put up any resistance, which is a relief. After the car drives off, I turn to Ethan. "You've done this before."

His jaw is set. "She needs a lot of hand-holding. She's a fucking mess."

I pat his back. "You can't take care of her forever. If you don't want her for yourself, eventually you're going to have to let someone else do this."

He doesn't seem to like that. His expression clouds over, and that same darkness fills me from the inside, threatening to burst its way out.

Let someone else take care of Mariana? Watch while he touches and kisses and protects her while I sit on the sidelines with her damn father?

The thought is agony.

Chapter Twenty-Seven

M ariana

The murmur of the ocean fades as we make our way from the beach, and I feel like I could die of contentment. Brandon and I just spent the morning walking along the water with our coffee.

Like we're a couple.

It's heavenly anguish, but I'm surviving. I'm trying to live in the moment and enjoy our last day.

Or maybe I'm hoping he'll change his mind...

"I need you to behave yourself at work today," Brandon suddenly says, breaking the silence. His voice is firm, authoritative. A spark of something wicked flickers in his eyes, and it's all I can do not to melt into the sand.

I turn to him, smiling innocently. "Behave myself? And how have I been misbehaving, Pastor?"

A ghost of a smile flits across his lips. "You know exactly what I'm talking about. I can't be seen groping my PA—

"Volunteer PA."

He snorts. "As if that would make it any less of a scandal. No, we both need to behave today, but especially you, young lady."

My tummy flips at the pet name. I never thought Brandon would use kink to cope with his biggest insecurity about our relationship.

I love that he's this way. There's so much we could explore if we had the time to do it. Maybe I could even work out some of my insecurities over living as an atheist in a church community. Maybe we could play out some priest fantasies...

God, I need to stop thinking this way.

Live in the moment, Mari.

"No bending over and showing me those beautiful tits," he says. "No talking back to me."

"Talking back?" I giggle. "There isn't a more daddy phrase than that."

He grabs me by the chin, those dark eyes narrowed but with a spark of amusement. "I am your daddy, for the next eight hours."

Coldness washes over me, and I look down at my bare feet in the sand. Eight hours. How final.

How sad.

"I'll behave," I say, forcing a smile.

He must sense the change in my mood, because his grip on my chin softens. His hand slowly trails up my cheek. He leans forward and presses a featherlight kiss on my forehead. "Even though I've sinned," he whispers. "I have no regrets. I wish I did. God knows I wish I did."

I swallow. "Then why end this?"

He sighs. "I know it's hard for you to understand, but relationships that begin in sin—"

"That's bullshit, Brandon." He jerks back at the sharpness in my tone. "It's black and white thinking."

He laughs humorlessly. "I'm a man of God. Part of the bargain is black and white thinking. I know the world is full of nuance, but some of us just aren't cut out to navigate it without strict principles. Mariana, think of all the people we would hurt if we continued this. My congregation would probably never trust me again if they knew that I slept with my intern. Your family..."

When his voice quivers, I have to look away. Tears hover behind my eyes, and I don't want them to fall.

"I'm already deceiving them." His voice has regained some of its firmness. "I don't want to compound my sin."

I nod rapidly as I pull away from him. "Let's get to the office. I want to enjoy our last day together."

And I mean it. Even though there's a physical ache in my chest that feels like it might never leave, I don't want to spend our final moments wishing for something that can never be. If he's set on living in black and white, at the very least, I can give him a few hours of vibrant color.

Brandon

"Mariana," I say, my voice husky. "I have a job for you in my office. Come now."

A smile tugs at her lips as she stands up from her computer, but I turn away before I'm tempted to return it. I don't want to be soft with her right now. Not yet. Not until after she's behaved herself.

This is so wrong, and somehow, I don't even care. Sin has made me reckless. I sent Harper home early today, and it's now just another dead Monday evening. No worship practice or Bible studies. My associate pastor and worship leader are already home with their families.

It's just me and Mari.

After she follows me into my office, I gesture at my bookshelf. "The top shelves are a mess. I need you to organize them for me."

She follows my hand with her gaze. "Why does it look like they were messed up on purpose?"

I take a step in her direction, gripping her chin. "What did I say about talking back to me?"

She smiles. "It won't happen again, Sir."

I stroke her cheek with my thumb. "Good girl. Now get to work."

Just as she walks toward the bookshelf, I grab the stepladder I fished through the storage closet to find. Just for this.

"You'll be using a ladder this time," I say through clenched teeth. "And you'll be taking off those shoes. If you do try anything like you did on your first day, I'll bend you over that desk."

Mariana's beautiful dark eyes grow huge, but then she slowly bends and starts removing her shoes. "Maybe I want you to." Her words are faint, whispered.

"What was that?"

She purses her lips, as if to fight a smile. "Nothing, Sir."

I narrow my eyes. "Good. Get to work. I'm going to be reading my Bible, so you'd better not distract me."

She grins like a naughty little kid. God forgive me, if anyone walked in on us right now, they'd think I was committing blasphemy.

Mariana climbs up the stepladder, giving me a view of her toned calves. She has such a lithe, athletic body with delicate curves. I love having the pleasure of gawking at it as much as I want. After sitting in my desk chair and setting my Bible in my lap, I turn to the side to get the best view of her.

For the next few minutes, she slowly arranges books on the shelf. Occasionally, she glances over her shoulder and smiles mischievously at me.

"Mariana." I say sternly.

Her eyes grow hooded. "Yes, Pastor?"

"What did I tell you about distracting me?"

She widens her eyes in mock innocence. "How am I distracting you?"

I lean back into my chair and set a hand behind my head. "I've told you how much I like your neck. You're drawing attention to it."

Her smile grows. "Am I? By turning it toward you?"

I frown, though I can't stop my lips from twitching. "Watch it."

"I'm sorry, Sir."

"Get back to work now, young lady. I promise you the next time you distract me, there will be consequences."

I return to my task of pretending to read my Bible, never keeping my eyes very far from her. After a few minutes, a loud thud makes me look up. Mariana is making her way down the ladder to retrieve a fallen book. She smiles at me before bending down, arching her back and sticking her ass out much farther than necessary.

"Stop right there." I keep my voice low and dark.

She looks up at me innocently. "Sorry, Sir. I accidentally dropped a book.

I slam my Bible shut. "I don't think it was an accident."

She bites that delectable bottom lip. "It was. I promise."

I cross my arms over my chest. "First you drop a book on purpose. Then you lie to me. Get over here. Now."

Her excited little grin makes heat flood my gut.

"What do you need me to do?"

I stand up and gesture at the desk. "Bend over, and don't make me wait."

She glances at the desk and back at me, those beautiful dark eyes growing hooded.

I narrow my eyes on her sweet little face. "Don't test me, little girl."

"What are you going to do?"

"I'm going to punish you with my cock."

She squeals as she makes her way over to my desk. When she bends over the front of it and extends her hands forward, I could come at the sight of her. Here she is, offered to me as if on an altar to atone for her sins. I rub my palm along the silky material of her skirt. She has such a pretty ass, plump and shaped like an upside-down heart. I want to memorize every inch of it before the day is over.

I lift my hand in the air and bring it down hard on her skin. The cracking sound resonates through the room.

She inhales sharply. "You didn't say I was getting a spanking."

"That was for making me wait. Now lift your skirt for me. Slowly."

She reaches her hands back and finds the hem of her dress. As she gradually pulls it up her thighs, a groan is pulled from my chest. "That's a good girl. Keep going. Take those panties off."

She follows my command. By the time her ass is bare, the tingling ache in my cock is almost unbearable. I'm going to come quickly from this. I grip her underwear and yank it down her thighs. When I set my fingers between her thighs, I'm greeted with a slippery wetness. "Oh, Mari. You're soaking for me."

She lets out a low moan as I unzip my pants and yank out my aching cock. "I'm already as hard as a rock. This is your fault."

"I'm sorry, Sir."

"You'll really be sorry in a minute." I rub the tip of my cock against the soft skin of her ass. "I'm only doing this for your own good. You know that right?"

"Yes, Sir."

"What a good girl you are," I croon, "taking your punishment."

"What is going on?" a voice that sounds like Sofia asks.

The shaking words are so faint, I could almost believe that I dreamed them.

Chapter Twenty-Eight

M ariana

"Sofia..." Brandon's voice is strangled as he frantically zips up his pants.

Sofia stands frozen in the doorway, her eyes darting up and down. And her face... Oh God, her face. I don't think I'll ever forget it—those wide eyes, that quivering mouth.

She's terrified.

The room spins around me, and my heart pounds violently in my chest. My hand instinctively moves to smooth down my skirt over my bare skin.

"What..." Brandon blinks. "What are you doing here?"

Sofia's quiet for a long moment. "I texted you." Her voice is small. Faint. "I wanted to see your office."

It's only now that I'm able to take in her appearance—her emerald dress and perfectly curled hair. Of course. She's going to see Finn. She mentioned something yesterday about wanting to see Brandon first so that she could rub it in Finn's face.

Maybe she won't go see Finn now. Maybe she'll go straight to my parents' house to let them know what she walked in on.

The thought isn't the least bit comforting.

"Oh, I..." Brandon swallows. "I didn't see your text."

Sofia's jaw ticks. "No, you were busy."

Brandon flinches as if physically struck. "Yes." His voice is just above a whisper.

For a moment, there's silence. Then Sofia laughs, a brittle, haunting sound that drifts through the room like smoke. "I can't believe this, Brandon. I can't believe this is who you are. You're a fucking liar. A charlatan pastor like the..." She shakes her head. "You're like the pastors who have affairs and order call girls and then have the audacity to preach on Sunday as if nothing happened. Except it's my baby sister you took advantage of."

"Sofi, I'm a grown woman." The words are out before I can think, and I want to bite them back into my mouth. Now is not the time to try reasoning with her.

She pins me with a hard stare. "How long has this been going on?"

"Since two weeks ago," Brandon says, his voice unsteady.

Sofia huffs. "So Mariana is the woman you sinned with. Your PA."

Brandon shuts his eyes. "Yes."

"And you kept sinning." She gestures at the desk.

"Yes."

"How could you do..." She shakes her head, blinking rapidly. "What I just saw you do. Do you have no respect for my family? For my dad?"

Brandon shuts his eyes, and I can feel his despair in the air between us. "I love your dad. I don't... I didn't want to hurt anyone."

Sofia laughs humorlessly. "I think you just didn't care. You're just as bad as secular men of the world, Brandon. You're so sex crazed, you don't care who you hurt."

Rage flares suddenly, making my tongue loose. "Sofi, that's ridiculous. You don't have any idea what you're talking about."

Brandon turns to me, lifting a hand. His eyes are so cold and remote, I want to curl into a ball on the floor. Gone is the man who sat in his desk chair and watched me with wicked eyes.

"I'm going to tell Mom and Dad," Sofi says. "I'm going to tell them exactly what I walked in on."

Brandon lifts his chin. "That's your right."

For the first time since Sofia walked in on us, his voice is firm. Of course. He probably wants her to tell my dad.

He wants atonement.

Sofia's eyes meet mine one last time before she turns around and marches away, and a heavy silence settles over the room. I turn to look at Brandon, and his face is taut. His eyes are dark and unreadable.

"Are you okay?" I ask.

He sighs heavily. "I should be asking you that. I'm the one who wronged you."

My teeth clench of their own will, even though I expected this from him. "That's ridiculous."

He whips around to face me, his eyes flashing. "Do you have any idea what just happened here? She walked in on me with my young PA bent over my desk in the middle of my church. Pastors get fired for far less than this."

My throat squeezes tight. Why didn't I think of that? He said getting caught would be a scandal for him. He could lose everything. This church gave him community and meaning, and he could lose it all.

Because of me.

"I won't let that happen," I say firmly. "I'll make sure my family doesn't do anything about this. They probably won't want to anyway, because of *my* reputation."

His eyes grow unfocused. "I almost want to get fired. I deserve it."

I scowl at him. "You deserve it? What about your church? They'll be losing an incredible pastor with a gift for teaching, all because of what?" I gesture at his desk. "A little fun you had with a fully consenting woman?" I shake my head. "Maybe men of God need to give up on black and white thinking. It seems to be pretty self-serving if you ask me."

"Self-serving?" He takes a step in my direction. "This is the first time I haven't thought about myself since this madness began."

"Oh, really? Wanting punishment to make yourself feel better? It sounds pretty self-serving to me. Kinky, even."

He scowls before looking away from me. "I'm unfit to be a pastor. I'm just like—" His lips close. "I'm unfit."

"Oh, you're just like your dad, huh? Is that what you were going to say?"

When he flinches, I want to reach out and touch him, but I must hold my ground. I can let go of his rejection of me—however much it hurts—but I refuse to stand by and watch him throw away everything that brings him meaning just because of some stupid guilt.

He swallows. "I knew I had his tendencies, but I never thought I'd do what he did."

"How is this what he did?" I raise both hands in the air. "Do you have a wife you're hiding?"

"I betrayed people I love."

I let out a groan, unable to help myself. "People who have no business feeling betrayed. My dad doesn't own me. Purity culture has certainly worked hard to make him think he does, but the reality is this has nothing to do with him."

"It doesn't matter what the truth is. It doesn't matter who's right." He's nearly shouting now, and I welcome it. "He's my dearest friend, and he asked me to help his daughter. Help her spiritually. How do you think he'll feel when he finds out I bent her over my desk instead?" He shakes his head. "People of integrity don't willfully hurt the people they love most."

And I'm not one of those people.

"What about me?" I ask, because I can't just pretend it isn't shattering my heart to hear him put my father above me yet again.

His stern expression falters as he looks away. "We may never see each other again."

My head grows a little fuzzy. "I'm sorry, what?"

"Your family will probably hate me after this. The very least I can do for them is stay away from you."

My whole body grows cold, and the world around me grows suddenly darker. I never understood the phrase "rose-colored glasses" until now. I thought it was only a metaphor, but there's a shade to the room that wasn't there a moment ago. It's not rose colored but a hideously dim orange and red, as if the sun were burning out.

I don't think words could work their way out of my throat even if I expended every ounce of my will.

I need to get out of here.

If he senses my turmoil, he doesn't show it. His handsome face is hard and cold. Without a word, I make my way out of the office. I don't bother to gather my things. I just rush down the hallway, and before I know it, I'm sprinting.

As soon as I slam my car door, my phone chimes.

> Sofia: I'm calling a family meeting tonight, and I want you there.

I let out a long breath. Absolutely fucking not. I'm getting the hell out of town.

I pull up my phone and type in the first place that comes to mind. After a few clicks, the voice of my navigation starts talking. I pull up a playlist on Spotify and turn up the volume as loud as my ears can tolerate.

. . .

Brandon

It's been three agonizing days since I last saw her. The memory of her retreating back as she walked away from me plays on loop in my head. Her padding footsteps, their slowly increasing speed will probably echo in my ears for the rest of my life.

Loving her is the worst pain, but didn't I predict it would be? This is my punishment, and I deserve this overwhelming ache in my chest.

I took advantage of her. I wanted her so badly, I threw my morals into the dust and stomped all over them.

I wanted her at all costs.

Even when it meant betraying everyone I hold dear.

"Do you think I should tell my congregation," I ask my bishop.

He leans back into his desk chair. "If you feel like full transparency is necessary—spiritually necessary, that is—then perhaps. Otherwise, I don't see the purpose. You're repentant. You've put an end to your sin."

I let out a long breath. "There needs to be consequences. At the very least, you should formally reprimand me."

He's quiet for a long while because that is his way. He doesn't have the warmest disposition, and yet his silence is more soothing than any words of comfort.

"Bludgeoning yourself won't do you any good. You know that. Why don't you take a few weeks off and spend some time in prayer?"

I shut my eyes, running my hands over my head. "A vacation. Just what I deserve after everything I've done."

"And what about your pain? Is that not a punishment?"

"Not when..." I inhale sharply through my nose, fighting the wave of emotion squeezing my throat. "I don't regret what I've done. Not for a moment. Every time I think back on it all... Every time I imagine going back in time, I know I would do it again. Even after all the people I hurt."

His chair squeaks as he leans forward. "That's probably because you have feelings for the girl. Or woman, I should say."

I scoff. "She is a girl. And I hurt her the most. She might not see it now, but she will someday. She'll remember me as that former friend of her dad's who took advantage of her."

That thought is agony. My memories of her are so precious I wish I could bottle them up and open them whenever the world gets too cold.

"What kind of person doesn't regret something like this?" I ask almost to myself. "I've probably lost my dearest friend."

"Only you can answer that."

"My worthless father never regretted anything either. He's never apologized to my mom. Or Ethan's." I laugh humorlessly. "I don't think I've ever heard an apology from him for anything."

He lets out a long sigh. "It's not about feelings, Brandon. It's about choices. You're already different from your dad just by the fact that you came to me and confessed."

I grunt. "When I got caught, yes."

He sighs heavily. "I don't know what more I can say to you. If you really want punishment, reflect on everything you've lost. Emotional pain is much more powerful than anything I could say or do."

I nod.

"And maybe reconsider if this is all what you really want. You wouldn't be the first pastor to start over with a woman after wrongdoing. Just because you sinned, doesn't mean you've ruined your future with this woman."

Longing wraps around my lungs, squeezing so tightly it's hard to take a breath. I don't even want to imagine a future with her. It's too agonizingly sweet to bear.

She deserves so much more than a broken man like me.

$* * *$

When I step out of my car, I catch sight of a man standing on my porch balcony. Even yards away and with his back to me, I feel his rage like a bonfire.

Hector.

I called him the day after Sofia walked in on me and Mariana, almost certain that she had told him everything by then. His lack of answer or callback only confirmed it. I've texted him several times over the last three days without receiving even an acknowledgement.

Looks like we're about to have our reckoning.

I let out a long breath as I make my way to the porch. I know he hears my footsteps, but he stays where he is, as if enjoying the view of the ocean.

He probably wants to throw me over the cliff.

"I know you want to hit me," I say when I get close. "So go ahead."

Hector whips around, his jaw clenching. For a moment, it seems like he might actually do it. But then he releases a breath and shakes his head. "You must think all men of God sin as carelessly as you."

The rebuke is like needles pricking all over my skin, more insidiously painful than a punch would be. I wasn't careless. I cared a great deal about how he would feel if he found out about me and Mariana.

And I hurt him anyway.

Hector's nostrils flare. "Is your idea of ministry sleeping with my daughter in your office?"

I shut my eyes. "You know it isn't. What I did was despicable."

Hector's face softens for a moment and then hardens again. "She's my little girl, Brandon. You slept with my little girl."

The anguish in his voice fills my stomach with cold sickness even as irritation heats my skin. I hate that I hurt him so deeply, but for fuck's sake, she's not a little girl. It's only now that I hear my own words echoed back to me that their hollowness rings true.

"I know," I say softly. I can't give him any hint of my thoughts. He'd take it as me making an excuse for my reprehensible behavior.

"Why did you do it?" he bites out. "Was it because Sofia wouldn't sleep with you? You probably wish she was faltering in her faith like my Mari, so you could have gotten what you really wanted."

My eyes widen. Somehow in the mire of everything, I'd forgotten that Hector is still unaware of mine and Sofia's agreement. "No," I say quickly. "I never felt that way for Sofia. I never should have courted her to begin with."

He huffs, shaking his head. "I never would have pushed you to do it if I knew this is who you really are."

I wince. His words are like a stab in my chest. What can I say in reply? That I was weak? That I was lonely? The truth is so much more disgusting.

Fucking your daughter was more exquisite than the moment you brought me to Christ.

"You're no longer welcome in my home," he says with a finality that leaves me breathless. "And if you ever come near my little girl again, I won't hit you, but I will get you fired, Brandon. I'll make it my mission. I know you're a big man here in Santa Barbara, but I've built a lot of connections with important people over the years. Don't try it."

I expected this, but holy fuck. The man who in some ways replaced my father has been yanked from me forever because of my own selfishness.

Hector is standing right here, and yet he's gone from my life. The family I came to love is no longer mine.

The woman I love is gone forever.

Fuck, I never thought I could feel a pain like this again. This is like the moment I watched my mom leave the world. Her breathing had been labored for hours—a torture to witness—and then it suddenly went shallow. Each breath tinier than the last. Even though I had been waiting for death, hoping her pain would end soon, I still wanted to scream and beg her to stay for just a little while longer.

But I couldn't. I had to let her go.

Chapter Twenty-Nine

M ariana

"Apparently, my whole family had a meeting behind my back," I tell Livvy over the phone. "It was a whole thing. Even my tias and tios were there. Ridiculous."

"They should be more worried about where you are right now than who you're sleeping with."

Livvy's sweet indignation makes me smile dreamily. I sink deeper into the plush chaise, my head a little hazy from the heat of the sun. Around me, the sounds of water splashing and children's voices filter through the air. My heart is quiet for the first time in three days.

This will have to be a new beginning for me. My relationship with my family imploded because I hurt them, but it was bound to happen eventually. Their slow rejection over the years has been constantly on my mind—Sofia's rejection of me most of all—but I've never spoken a word of it to any of them. I was as full of resentment as an overblown balloon.

This isn't how I wanted to force a confrontation, but at least now we'll all have to talk. To finally have it all out.

When I tell them I'm an atheist, they'll probably blame it all on Brandon. Think that he disillusioned me further about the church. But that's not my problem. I can't control their willful delusions anymore, like my dad's heartfelt belief that he can bring me back to God by sheer will.

I can only control myself.

"They all think I'm with you," I say.

"Yet none of them have called me. Our dads got lunch together the other day, and Ness says all they did was pray for you. It's so annoying, Mari. Why are Christians so stupid sometimes? I can't believe I used to be the same way—giving my 'thoughts and prayers' when I should have been taking action."

Livvy sounds so sweetly outraged I want to laugh. Ever since she deconstructed her own faith, she's given me frequent apologies for the "insensitive things" she used to say to me when she was more fundamentalist. They don't bother me like they bother her. Who cares who she used to be? She's not that way anymore.

Maybe there's hope for my family.

"I'm driving to Anaheim," she says, her voice firm.

I frown. "No way. You have way too much going on. I feel like shit that I'm not there with you a week before your wedding."

"You know I don't care about that." Livvy exhales a long breath. "Are you sure you don't want me to come? Everything is pretty much ready to—"

"Olivia Grace Gallo, soon to be Olivia Grace Walker. Stop."

The sound of her laughter fills my chest with warmth. "I'm probably making you feel worse, huh?"

I smile. "Yes."

A silence follows. The only sound coming through the phone is the distant hum of the ocean. She's probably sitting on her kitchen patio. The thought is comforting, like I'm there with her.

"Alright," she eventually says, "But promise me you'll come

home soon. Getting some space is good, but I don't want you to isolate yourself."

"Don't worry about me. Right now, I'm watching kids play in the pool."

She sighs. "Aww, I wish I was there with you, love."

"I'll come home tomorrow. I promise."

I'll have to face it all then. Including my heartbreak and the reality of moving forward in my life as a stranger to Brandon.

Fuck, why does love have to be so painful?

Brandon

Sofia stares down at her coffee cup, her expression masked. Our conversation for the last ten minutes has been stilted to say the least, but I expected it.

A few hours after Hector left my house yesterday, I got a text from her. She said she wanted to talk and insisted it would be civil. I told her she didn't have to make me any promises. If she wanted to scream at me, I wouldn't mind. I owe that to her.

At first, I couldn't believe that she wanted to meet at our usual Starbucks—the place we spent those first few dates—but after I thought about it, it made perfect sense. This is a safe place for her. She's uncertain about me now after the way I betrayed her family.

She looks up at me, her eyes glassy but determined. "Why did you do it?"

My hands tremble, so I set them firmly on my lap. "I didn't... I didn't think about the consequences. I was incredibly selfish."

She frowns. "Didn't God convict your heart? While it was happening, I mean."

"He did." My voice is hushed. "All the time. But I ignored it."

Her expression grows pensive. We sit in silence, the air heavy between us.

"I guess I need to forgive you." Her voice is quieter than before. "God has already forgiven you. I should too."

I lean forward, setting my elbows on the table. "I don't think he expects it of you. I wronged you, Sofia. I hurt your whole family. You have a right to be angry. Ultimately, forgiving me would be for your heart alone. To free you of the burden of being angry."

"I guess that's true." She smiles sadly to herself. "To be honest, my heart isn't free. It's full of...sin. Maybe it's good this happened. I deserved it."

I frown. "What do you mean?"

Her grimace is so faint and quick, I would have missed it if my gaze weren't fixed on her face. "I've done something bad. Something wrong. Worse than what you and Mariana did, because I violated God's covenant of marriage."

I open my mouth and close it, unable to find the words. I can guess where this conversation is going, but I don't want to push her toward it.

"I can't believe..." She shuts her eyes and takes a breath. "I can't believe I did it. I still feel like... Like it was someone else." Her eyes open suddenly and probe me with a hard stare. "Do you think it's possible that I have a demon inside me?"

The earnestness in the question makes my heart clench, making me want to rage against the church she was raised in, the one that used to be mine. She truly believes garbage like this.

"No," I say firmly.

She frowns. "It never crossed your mind that maybe you do? When you... When you were sleeping with my sister?"

"Never."

It was more like fearing that I'd found heaven and would be cast away from it. Like Moses being forbidden from entering the promised land.

I squeeze her hand. "We all sin, Sofia. We don't need any extra help from the devil to do it."

She nods rapidly, and her chest heaves. A soft little cry

follows, and I sit while she weeps soundlessly. A short while later, she wipes under her eyes with her fingers and lets out a brittle laugh. "Everyone is probably staring at me, huh?"

"No," I say without looking around. "No one even noticed."

She takes a shaky breath through her mouth. "What you said...about being set free. Would you mind... I probably sound unhinged asking this after all that's happened between us, but would you mind praying for me?"

A strange lightness lifts at my limbs. "Not at all."

I take a deep breath before bowing my head. "Dear Lord, I ask that you help Sofia find peace in her heart. Let her know how much you love her. How you can forgive her for anything that she's done. Allow her heart to be set free."

"Yes, Lord," Sofia whispers.

"And remind us, Lord, that we can always turn to you in our darkest hours. That your love is unconditional, your mercy boundless."

"Amen," Sofia whispers, her face serene, the tension eased from her features. "I have a favor to ask. Can we still... I've been dreading Livvy's wedding so much—because of Finn—and now after what I've done..." She shuts her eyes, shaking her head. "I have to go. The Gallos are like family. My parents would never let me miss it, but I don't want to do it alone. Would you mind if we still went together as friends?"

I haven't even let myself think about how I'm officiating Livvy's wedding in a few days, and how I'll be forced to be around all the people I've lost.

I'll be forced to see *her*, possibly for the last time.

I force a smile. "I'm honored that you still want to go with me, but I don't think your dad would allow it."

She rolls her eyes dramatically, looking so like my sweet Mariana that my chest aches. "My dad needs to mind his own business. It's partly his fault I feel like such a failure for being single at twenty-nine. In some ways... I think I had a harder time getting over Finn because he was so devastated by it all. He felt so sorry for me."

I nod, not wanting to speak ill of Hector after all that I've done.

Her eyes grow determined. "Will you help me take charge of my own life by doing this for me?"

I smile. "I will."

Her cheeks darken. "Thank you."

"It's my pleasure."

Her smile fades. "What's going to happen with Mariana? Are you going to keep...dating her?"

Hearing her name makes a rope coil around my lungs. "No, that's over." I frown. "She didn't tell you?"

She averts her gaze. "None of us have talked to her in days. I think she's staying with Livvy."

"You think?"

When she flinches, I realize that must have sounded like an accusation.

"She told us all she needed space," she says, her tone defensive. "My family can be a little intense during a crisis."

"But you don't know where she is?"

She shrugs. "She's very social. She has plenty of friends she could be staying with."

"Have you talked to Livvy?" I clip out.

"No, but Livvy's fiercely loyal to Mari. I think she's mad at all of us..."

Sofia keeps talking, but I hardly hear the words. A cold dread wraps around my heart. Mari might not even be with Livvy for all we know. She could have gone anywhere.

She's adrift, and it's all because of me.

God, keep her safe.

Chapter Thirty

B randon

Mariana is still nowhere to be found.

I've called her sixteen times in the last twenty-four hours and heard nothing but her voicemail.

That sweet melodic lilt of her playful voice and that little giggle at the end. Fuck, I love her laugh.

I'll die if I can never hear it in person again.

Restlessness courses through me like a flock of startled birds. The silence of my house closes in, pressing against my ribcage.

Fuck, I can't live like this.

Here I am prowling through the suitcase I never emptied after the trip to Big Sur, an animalistic desperation driving me. I'm looking for something of hers. I know that's what I'm doing, even though I've felt disembodied from my actions since I heard she was missing. I'm going mad.

Finding something of hers won't make me feel any better. Her things aren't her.

I need to take action. Even when it's not my place to do it.

I frantically pull out my phone. My hand shakes as I press Livvy's name on the screen. Thankfully, she picks up immediately.

Her tone is light as we exchange a bit of small talk about plans for the rehearsal dinner. A prickling sensation begins at the base of my skull, slowly creeping down my spine like a spider. Does she sound this way because she knows where Mari went?

"Oh, and one more thing," I say, unable to wait any longer. "I talked to Sofia yesterday, and she was a little worried about Mariana. She says she hasn't heard from her in days." I swallow. "Is she with you?"

There's a long pause.

Too long.

"Why hasn't Sofia called me if she's worried about Mari?"

The hint of accusation in her tone is a balm. She wouldn't sound indignant if she were worried.

Mariana must be with her.

"I'm not sure," I answer.

"I haven't heard from Mari either," Livvy says, her tone biting.

The breath leaves my lungs.

"I need to go," Livvy says. "Sofia and I need to talk."

I take a deep breath to fight the dizziness descending over me. If Livvy hasn't heard from her, this is dire.

As soon as Livvy hangs up, I pull up Mariana's name in my contact list. My heart thrums in my ears as I press her name for the seventeenth time. It rings once before going to voicemail, and I want to throw my phone against the wall.

Lord, help me find her.

Mariana

· · ·

Rows of vineyards stretch out along the rolling hills. The evening sun casts a golden hue over the narrow highway.

Damn, I love driving. The rumble of the road makes my frazzled brain grow quiet. I could almost forget that I'll be back in Santa Barbara in an hour, and all of my troubles will be in front of me again.

The buzz of my phone interrupts the lulling hum of the road. When I glance at the screen and see the name, my heart seizes.

Brandon.

After taking a deep breath, I set the phone back in the cup holder and tighten my grip on the wheel. This is probably the twentieth time he's tried to call me, but I've somehow been able to stay strong. I haven't even listened to any of his voicemails.

At first, I was impressed with myself for my strength. What if those voicemails are full of regret and longing? What if he's telling me he made the biggest mistake of his life, and he wants to be with me no matter what? Even if it means losing his church.

But what if he's not?

I'd rather hang on to this heavenly hope, even if it makes me feel pathetic. I'll face the reality when I get back to Santa Barbara.

As the voicemail notification chimes, I force myself to take in my surroundings. The ocean stretches out, an endless blue. The house in the distance is as big as a castle, like Brandon's house. What would it be like to live there with him, waking up every morning to a view like this?

I'd scarcely see it because I'd have him. His big body would be wrapped around mine like it was in those magical few nights we had on that trip. Or maybe I'd be sitting at a vanity while he braids my hair. We'd be too consumed with each other to notice the view.

Ugh. Fantasies like that will only slow the healing of my broken heart. I've seen evidence of it in Sofia.

Maybe I shouldn't have been so hard on her for holding on to Finn so tightly.

An hour later, I stretch my arms up high after stepping out of the car. The air is much cooler than it was in Anaheim, and it's refreshing after my long, stuffy car ride.

Everything will be okay.

I'm resilient.

As soon as I open my apartment door, Brandon's huge form looms over me. "Why the fuck did you not return a single one of my calls?"

I take a step back, and my pulse pounds against my throat. "What are you doing here?"

His jaw clenches. "Answer my question."

I blink once, hardly able to process the sight in front of me. What is he even doing here? I glance at his side and see Sofia on the couch. She shoots me an apologetic look. "I told him you were fine."

"Answer my question, Mariana," Brandon repeats.

My head grows fuzzy. This was the very last thing I'd expected to encounter when I came home. Why are they even hanging out?

I swallow. "I was waiting until I got back into town to call you."

He crosses his arms over his chest, his jaw ticking. "You couldn't even give me the courtesy of sending a text and letting me know you're alright?"

"I didn't know you were worried. I thought you were calling about...everything that happened."

His nostrils flare. "I'm supposed to believe you didn't listen to a single one of my voicemails or read a single one of my texts?"

My skin heats at his high-handedness. Why does he think he has the right to behave this way after he told me we could never see each other again?

I grab my phone and shove it in his face. "Here. Take a look."

Brandon snatches it from my hand and starts scrolling through my messages. If I weren't so frazzled, I would laugh. He's back to being my stern boss daddy.

Brandon shoves the phone back into my hand. "Fine. You

didn't listen to them. Still, you should have known we'd all be worried sick."

Rage flares suddenly, compelling me to step closer, nearly grazing his chest with mine. I raise my chin to meet his gaze. "Not after Monday, Brandon. I believe your exact words were, 'we may never see each other again.'"

His eyes soften. "I'm sorry. I thought something happened to you. So did Sofia."

"Really?" I grit my teeth. "Because she doesn't look worried at all."

Sofia winces. "I told him it wasn't unusual for you to go on a trip by yourself."

There's no anger in her voice. There's not even coldness. She sounds almost like the Sofia from my youth.

What is going on with her?

"Where were you?" Brandon asks, his tone deceptively casual.

I shrug. "It's none of your business."

His eye twitches. "Were you safe?"

I snort. "As you can see, I'm fine." I push past him and walk toward Sofia. Her eyes are huge, but she doesn't seem upset.

Something's changed in her. I can't quite pinpoint it, but she's different than she was before I left. And strangely, the change is not anger or pious self-righteousness or anything I'd expect after what she caught me doing.

"I need to talk to my sister," I say. "Please give us some space."

For a moment, Brandon just stares at me, his eyes wide. "Again, I'm sorry." His voice is rough. "I shouldn't have lost my temper."

"That's okay," I say, but I make a pointed glance at the door.

I won't accept half measures from him any longer. If he wants to have a conversation, he needs to admit that I'm a grown woman. He needs to tell me outright that he accepts me as an atheist. Not just as a human being, but as a partner. His partner.

"I'll..." He scratches the back of his head. "I'll talk to you later."

"Sounds good." I keep my tone curt.

His eyes grow determined. "We need to have a conversation. Things ended too abruptly last week."

"We can do that." I smile tightly. "But not now."

Those determined eyes grow hesitant, and exhilaration pumps through my veins. I'm taking control. He doesn't get to boss me around like he used to.

As soon as he leaves, I turn to Sofia. I can't approach her yet. I need to gauge her emotions first. Is she going to lash out at me now that he's gone?

I almost wish she would call me a sinning whore for what I did—if that's what she's really thinking—but she only stares back at me with a placid expression.

I don't get it. It's like she's transformed.

Something happened.

"Can I sit down?"

She frowns. "Are you really asking me if you can sit on your own couch?"

"I'm asking if you're too mad to let me anywhere near you."

She lets out a long sigh. "I'm not mad at you."

I find myself walking over to her cautiously, and I'm not quite sure why. "Why are you acting so weird?" I ask as I sit down.

"What do you mean?"

"You saw something really shocking last week. Why aren't you asking me a million questions?"

She glances down at her lap. "It's none of my business."

I shake my head. "I don't get it. When Dani's sister moved in with her boyfriend, both of you were crying over it. Like she died. Why aren't you crying over what I did?"

She shuts her eyes, licking her lips. "I'm more mature than I was back then."

I scowl at her, unable to help myself. "That was last year."

"A lot can happen in a year."

Her voice is quiet, almost dispassionate. This isn't like her.

Even the old Sofia—the one who adored me—wouldn't be this stoically forgiving if I had done something really bad.

"What happened?" I ask.

She flinches. "Nothing."

"Yes, it did. Something happened, and it made you forget what happened with me."

She grows very still, almost frozen, and I feel something in the air between us.

She's upset about something.

I set my hand on hers. "Sofi, is everything okay?"

Her lips twitch slightly, and then her face scrunches inward. She covers her eyes with her hands and lets out a heaving sob.

"Oh, Sofi." I rub my hand up her arm. "What happened? Who do I need to beat up?"

She shakes her head rapidly, not even giving me a crying smile. "It's all me. I did something really, really bad."

Suddenly, it all clicks into place. The emerald dress. Showing up at Brandon's office that day.

She didn't forget about Finn after what she saw. She probably went straight to her little meetup with him.

And she would have been emotional and vulnerable from the scene she had just witnessed...

I run my hand up her shoulder and give it a squeeze. "Did you have sex with Finn?"

Her head jerks up, her eyes popping open. "How did you know?"

I smile sadly as I play with the hair hanging over her shoulder. "It was bound to happen."

She scowls, gritting her teeth. "Bound to happen? You think that little of me?"

I repress a smile. She's too fragile right now for me to point out that she actually did the thing that she's outraged at me for predicting.

"I don't think little of you at all. I just think given your history with Finn, and how much he hurt y—"

"It's still disgusting, Mari. Finn has a wife. I violated the covenant of marriage. I gave my purity..." Her lips quiver. "I gave up my purity to a married man. I had an affair. I'm a sinner."

I squeeze her hand. "Aren't we all sinners?"

She lets out a groan, collapsing back onto the couch and covering her face with her hands. "You don't get it," she mumbles into her palms. "You could never get it because sex means nothing to you. I gave up everything. I hate myself."

I reach out and gently pull her hands away from her face, leaning in to catch her gaze. "I don't buy that purity bullshit. You didn't give him anything other than sex."

"I don't know how I'll ever forgive myself," she whispers as if she didn't hear me, her eyes filling with tears again.

"You will," I say firmly. "You made a mistake because you're human, but you won't beat yourself up forever, because you know it won't do any good. What's done is done. The best thing you can do for Finn's wife is leave him behind."

She sniffs, wiping her eyes. "Do you think I need to tell her what happened?"

I squeeze her hand. "That's up to you. I don't think you need to make any decisions right away though. Let yourself heal first."

She nods slowly, her eyes dazed. "You really don't think less of me?"

I snort. "Four days ago, I was bent over a pastor's desk with my ass in the air."

She slams her palm over her mouth and bursts into laughter, and I laugh with her. God, it feels so good to laugh after the misery of the past few days.

Sofia shoots me a watery smile. "Thanks for traumatizing me, by the way. I think that image is burned into my memory forever. That and Brandon's..." She lowers her voice. "Penis."

My laughter turns into a shrieking cackle. "He has a nice one, huh?"

She wrinkles her nose. "Gross. I don't think penises can

possibly look nice. I didn't even see Finn's, thankfully. It was too dark."

I suck in my lips. "Am I allowed to ask you how it was? Your first time, I mean?"

Her expression grows stern. "No, Mariana Isabel, you're not. I'm not going to compound my sin by adding lust and gossip to it. I need you to give me the space to repent."

"I can do that."

She stares at me for a long while, mischief alighting her eyes. "It was good though," she says quickly. "Really good."

My eyes grow huge, and she smiles slyly back at me.

Lightness fills my body. My God, this is what I've longed for since we've grown apart. I've wanted to sit and talk about boys together like we did years ago.

All isn't lost. I can pick up the pieces and move on. Even if I'll never have the man I love, my family will always be here for me. My imperfect family who loves me fiercely.

Chapter Thirty-One

B randon

It's now been six days. Six days of hearing almost nothing from her. I've been texting daily asking when we can get together, and she's been putting me off. She finally gave me more than a few words yesterday when she told me we needed to wait until after Livvy and Cole's wedding to have our talk, that she's too busy to talk now.

Why am I so desperate to talk to her? It's not like it will change anything. The best way to show her how much I love her is to remove myself from her life. She deserves so much more than a self-indulgent, broken man.

I run my finger over the worn-out leather on the couch. The whole room smells like beer, and I've never felt older in my life. Here I am, sitting in the living room of a frat house, seeking comfort from my baby brother who's now all I have left in the world.

"Do you think Hector really means it?" Ethan asks.

"Yes," I say immediately. "He's a man of firm principles. I admired him for it even before I became a Christian. After the way you and I grew up..." I shake my head. "I need people in my life who remind me that not all men are capricious and selfish."

Ethan scowls. "You're not capricious or selfish."

I raise a hand in the air. "Obviously, I am. Look what I did."

"Yeah, but you did that because you fell in love with Mari."

I shake my head. "I behaved recklessly before I fell in love with her. I hate to put it so crassly, but I was thinking with my dick."

"I just can't believe that. It was so clear to me from the beginning that you had real feelings for her."

I shut my eyes and take a deep breath. "If my heart had been in the right place, I would have done it all differently. I would have told Hector right away that I couldn't in good conscience court Sofia, that the person I really wanted was Mariana. The truth is that I'm just as driven by lust as Dad. It's a generational curse."

Ethan scoffs as he pushes up from the couch and walks toward the kitchen. "I'm going to get you a beer."

I can't help but smile at my non-drinking brother wanting to dull my pain with alcohol. I must really look like a mess.

When he comes back, he's holding a small glass with amber liquid inside. I frown in question, and he lifts a brow. "I figured you needed something stronger than beer."

"I appreciate it," I say as I take the drink from his hand and throw down a burning sip.

Ethan plops back down on the couch. "I don't think I'm as fucked up from Dad as you are."

I'm startled by his use of the word "fuck." Ethan rarely swears. "Why do you say that?" I ask.

He shrugs. "I hate what he did to my mom. And even more that he's never really apologized for it—to me or to her—but I don't feel like it has anything to do with who I am. I'm not going to be a cheater just because my dad is."

I groan. "I take after him more than you do."

"But you don't, though. You're nothing like him. I love Dad, but I can only handle him in small doses. I usually screen his calls and return them, like, a month later."

I laugh humorlessly. "Me too."

Ethan's eyes fix on my face. "You're nothing like him. You're the most dependable person in my life. As much as I love my mom, she's...distant sometimes. But not you. Not ever. I'd be lost without you."

His words squeeze my chest, making my vision cloud over. I clear my throat, fighting back tears. "Well, I am old enough to be your dad. I have to live up to it."

He shakes his head sharply. "Don't minimize it. You've been there for me, and I was dad's love child, but you never took it out on me. You were never jealous, even back when he was still married to my mom. If you were, you certainly never showed it."

I scowl. "How could I take it out on you? You were a baby. My only brother."

Ethan leans forward, resting his elbows on his knees. "And I think you always knew that I needed you. You're there for the people who need you. That means something. That's someone who has principles. You're not like Dad."

I swallow to fight the sob threatening to work its way out. I never thought twice about my love for Ethan and its effect on him. It was always a given.

If only my love for Mariana could be the same. Enough to wipe away the misery I caused her and her family.

But it's so much deeper than that. My love for her borders on obsession. Ethan is wrong that I'm not like our dad. I'm so like him. I just happen to be more loyal.

I'll never stop wanting Mariana, but my need for her will suffocate her boundless spirit. A few years of my love—maybe even months—and she'd resent me for it. She'd resent me for trying to hoard her away, steal the most unencumbered years of her life.

Loving her means letting her be free.

Even when the thought alone is like death.

. . .

Mariana

My dad's expression is grim. He's barely looked at me since he let me inside the house. My mom has been a little better—asking me about when she needs to buy my grad school textbooks and if I need any "school clothes"—trying to pretend like nothing has changed these past few weeks.

Sofia is my rock. She's sitting on the couch beside me, but she doesn't know why I called this little family meeting. Even though I know she might be as hurt as they are when she hears what I have to say, at least she now has a bit of empathy after what she sees as her fall from grace.

"I have to say something that is going to probably hurt." My voice is surprisingly firm. "But I just have to say it."

My dad's expression doesn't change, but both my mom and Sofia frown.

It's now or never. "I'm an atheist."

The words linger in the air. My mom and Sofia's eyes grow impossibly huge.

"What?" My mom's mouth is hanging open.

"Are you being serious right now?" Sofia asks.

My dad doesn't look up, but his jaw ticks. He was probably expecting this. He, more than anyone else, seemed to read the warning signs from the beginning.

Which is why he tried so hard to steer me in a different direction.

I sigh. "It's not like I'm a murderer. I'm just an atheist. I have been for a while."

Mom's eyes well with tears, her fingers clenching the fabric of the couch armrest. Fuck. I knew this was coming. I knew she would cry.

This is okay. This is fine.

This is me accepting myself.

"But...you've been going to church." Sofia blinks rapidly, as if trying to make sense of my confession.

I sigh, looking down at my hands. "Yes. I had reasons for that. Partly, I was trying to please you all. And partly..." I huff out a nervous laugh. "I was horny for Brandon."

"Mari," my mom scolds.

Dad's nostrils flare as he meets my eyes for the first time. "It's because of him, isn't it? He drove you away from God." He shakes his head. "I never should've trusted him."

I scowl. "He's a damn pastor, Dad. How could he drive me away from God?"

"Through his sin." He raises his voice. "He was supposed to be an example for you."

I let out a long sigh. "Dad, I don't believe in sin."

His eyes widen, but it doesn't deter me.

I raise my chin. "You can't blame Brandon for something you've seen coming since I was a little girl. You know you have."

He looks away. "You're just passionate. It's part of your journey. God's going to use you to do wonderful—"

"No, Dad." I shake my head sharply. "I can't be *used* by a God who doesn't exist. I know he exists for you. For all of you—" I gesture to Mom and Sofia "—but he doesn't exist for me. I've tried my entire life to believe, but I can't. I wish I could. It would make my life so much easier..." My throat grows tight. "But I can't."

A whimper draws my attention to my mom, but I can't look her way. It's hard enough to say all of this without having to provide comfort for her grieving my lost soul.

"Why didn't you say anything before?" Sofia asks, her tone full of indignation.

I take a moment to collect my thoughts. "I was afraid you wouldn't see me the same way. That you wouldn't love me the same way."

She inhales sharply. "That's crap, Mari. Don't put that on us.

We never said you had to be a Christian for us to love you. I mean, I am worried about you because atheism…" She shakes her head. "It's a total rejection of God. I hope you take some time to really think about the consequences."

I fight the urge to roll my eyes. "Thanks, sis. I'll keep that in mind."

"Don't get sarcastic, Mariana Isabel," my mom says.

I can't help but smile at the way she trills my name.

"This is a really big deal," Sofia says.

I sigh. "I know."

"Yes, it is," my dad says, his voice biting. "And yet she never said anything about it until Brandon took advantage of her."

I whip my head in his direction. Rage makes that spirit of rebellion rise like a geyser within me. "Brandon didn't take advantage of me, Dad, because I'm not a fucking child. I love him. I love him with all my heart—" my voice cracks "—and I think he loves me too. But he's too stubbornly set in his antiquated ways, just like you. I'm the one who's hurt by it. That's what you being like this—" I wave a hand at him "—does. It hurts people like me."

His expression falters. "Did…" He licks his lips. "Did I hurt you?"

I strain my mouth to keep my lips from quivering. "Yes. You hurt me by interfering in my life. By making me feel like I'm not good enough if I don't follow God."

He takes an unsteady breath. "I love my children no matter what. You know that."

"Do I?" My voice cracks.

His eyes grow glassy. "Mari—" He gulps back a sob. "I don't want you to think… I love you. I love you more than my own life."

My mom nods jerkily. "We love you, Mari. You can be an atheist. You can be anything you—" Her voice breaks.

My dad sets his hand on my mom's thigh. "What your mom means is that our love is not conditional. It never was. I'm heartbroken to hear—"

When he gulps back a sob again, a warm trickle falls down my cheek. I can't stand it when my dad cries. I've only ever seen it a handful of times in my entire life.

"I'll always pray for you," he chokes out. "Because I love my Lord, and I want all my children to experience the miracle that I have. But it doesn't mean I don't love you."

I nod jerkily. "That's okay. It's your relationship with God, not mine."

"Can we still go to church together?" Sofia asks.

I manage a smile. "Sure. We can go to church. Not Brandon's church anymore, of course. But if we found another pastor who's really educated on Bible history, I'd love to go with you."

"And I won't pressure you anymore," my dad says. "I don't want you to feel..." He shuts his eyes. "You can believe whatever you want."

I reach out and take his hand, and he squeezes mine so tightly it almost hurts.

Chapter Thirty-Two

B randon

The day of the rehearsal dinner is here.

I'll finally get to see her precious face. It's been agony counting the minutes until now because I know what my restlessness means. When my mind was constantly on this night even as I tried to focus on other things, I knew.

I'll never have peace. I'll always be waiting to see her.

Waiting for something I'll never have.

In my darkest moments, I wanted to rage at God for putting me in heaven only to take it away. I can't in good conscience pursue Mariana after everything I've done.

Forcing a talk with her would be an excuse to be close to her, and I can't do it. It's selfish, and I'm doing everything in my power to show her how much I love her by letting her go.

Letting her go.

Fuck.

It feels like death.

After walking into the restaurant, I immediately spot her. Her hair is styled in loose waves. Her pale-pink dress makes her brown skin glow.

After taking a deep breath, I stride over to her, clutching my hands behind my back to hide the way they shake.

"Mariana," I say, my voice steadier than I feel. She looks up, her brown eyes meeting mine. "I just want you to know that you don't have to listen to my apology if you don't want to hear it. This isn't about me, and I'm sorry for pestering you with my texts."

There, I said it. I brace myself for her reaction, something that indicates this moment means as much to her as it does to me. But what I get instead knocks the breath out of me.

"Okay," she says, a neutral expression on her face. With that, she turns away from me.

"Okay?" I mutter, unable to help myself.

She smiles tightly before walking away, and a pang of loss grips my chest so tightly it's hard to take a breath. How could the most beautiful relationship of my life end with a little "okay?"

A tap on my shoulder pulls me out of my head. I turn and find Sofia standing there, a soft smile on her face. The sight of her is bittersweet, a stark reminder of the moment my life imploded.

"You look handsome in your suit."

I smile, shaking my head. "I'm overdressed. I had no idea it would be this casual."

She shrugs one shoulder. "You're the pastor. In this crowd, you're a celebrity. You should be more dressed up than everyone else." Her smile fades. "Can we...sit together at dinner tonight? I'd be more comfortable." She twirls a finger around a strand of her long hair. "And I promise my dad won't make it weird."

Warmth spreads through me. It's comforting to have a friend in the Hernandez family.

"Of course." I smile. "I understand."

A loud peal of laughter sends a rolling shiver down my spine. Mariana.

Fuck, I love that sound. She laughs with so much abandon when she's with people who let her be her bold self. She laughed like that with me sometimes.

Now, she's laughing that way with Zac.

Oh Christ, am I going to have to watch them like this all night? Will I be sitting impotently with Sofia watching him fondle Mariana?

This is what it really means to be unselfish. This is what it means to show her that I love her enough to put her needs above my own.

I still want to rage against God. I want to throw her over my shoulder and take her somewhere far away from here.

I want to keep her there. Forever.

But I can't.

I have to let her roam free.

Mariana

My heart is light, and my skin is warm and tingly. The champagne has been flowing all night, I've been a bit of a lush.

Oops.

It makes it so much easier to be around Brandon. I love Livvy too much to let my heartbreak ruin her wedding weekend. If I have to be a lush to get through tonight, so be it. Livvy doesn't mind.

Beside me, Zac is laughing at something Cole just said. He's been hanging all over me all night, which he tends to do when he's buzzed. I usually nip it in the bud, but not tonight.

I'm making progress. I'm actually having fun tonight. My shattered heart is somehow as light as a million dandelion seeds drifting through the air, and I refuse to let Brandon bring me back to reality.

That'll happen tomorrow when my buzz wears off.

"Alright," Zac says. "We're going downtown after this. Bar crawl." He turns to me, leaning in close. "You up for it?"

From the corner of my eye, I see Brandon clench his jaw, but I avert my gaze. "I can't stay out too long. I have to get up early for wedding stuff."

He wrinkles his nose. "Bridesmaids have to do all the worst shit. All I have to do is put a suit on and I'm done. Alright—" he turns to the group "—we'll be going to a few bars that remind us of Livvy and Cole. In fact, we'll only go to the bars Cole wouldn't let Livvy drink at that first night she went downtown."

I snort at the memory. "That was the night before they finally hooked up."

Livvy shushes me. "My aunt is right there."

I wince. Maybe I'm a little tipsier than I thought I was. "Sorry."

Across the room, Brandon's eyes are still locked on us, a shadow cast over his handsome features.

Let him look. If he wanted things to change between us, he would have told me by now. He wouldn't be sorry for "pestering" me with texts.

"Bathroom break?" Livvy smiles at me from across the table.

I shoot her a questioning look. She just came back from the bathroom. She must want to talk to me about something. I push my chair back and follow her through the crowded restaurant.

Inside the bathroom, it's quiet and cool. Livvy pulls me into the big stall and locks the door.

"What's up?" I ask.

She giggles, leaning against the wall. "Brandon looks like he's about to throw hands at Zac."

I snort, rolling my eyes. "He does seem to be in a pretty bad mood."

Livvy's giggles subside. "I mean it. He's been watching you two all night. Glaring." She shakes her head. "He's acting like a jealous ex-boyfriend."

I shrug. "He's a jealous ex-fling."

Livvy grabs my shoulders—a sign that she is, in fact, quite tipsy. My Liv is touchy and affectionate, but she's not usually this forceful. "You deserve someone who's all in. Not someone who wants to keep you from every other guy even though he won't commit to you himself. Someone who's letting his daddy issues stop him from giving you his whole heart."

I let out a nervous laugh. "He's your pastor. It's a bummer that this is how you see him now because of everything I've told you."

She scowls. "Don't you dare blame yourself. You didn't force him to sleep with you on a pastor retreat. You didn't force him to bend you over his desk right in front of your sister in his church office."

An almost hysterical giggle bubbles out of me. Ah, the absurdity of it all.

I never thought I would live a life like this.

Livvy's big brown eyes are full of concern. "Maybe you should talk to him."

"No." I hate myself for the prickle of tears behind my eyes. Fuck champagne. "I'm not going to initiate anything. He already told me we don't need to meet up and talk. That he's sorry for pestering me."

She scowls. "He said that?"

I nod jerkily.

She sighs, wrapping me in a hug. "He's going to regret it. No one could pass up on you and not regret it."

I giggle a little hysterically. "I love you."

When Livvy and I walk out of the bathroom, Zac is standing at the bar right outside, a shot glass in each hand. The lights from the chandeliers reflect off the liquid, making it shimmer.

"Just in time!" Zac grins. "I want you guys to sneak these while the grownups aren't looking. My treat in honor of the bride."

Livvy glances at me, then at Zac. "I can't. If I drink any more, I'm going to look like a zombie on my wedding day."

"She's not taking one." I grab both glasses from Zac before Livvy gets a chance to change her mind. "*I'll* drink in honor of the bride."

I knock back the first shot, the burn searing my throat, then the second. The room spins a little as I slam the glasses on the counter. Livvy squeals, and Zac throws his arm around me and pulls me into a rough hug. I giggle, a warm glow spreading through me.

Then my eyes lock with Brandon's. He's walking toward the bathroom, his face rigid, eyes dark. His stare is so intense, it feels like a physical touch. He looks ready to explode.

Good. He needs to see the reality of his decision.

When we make it back to the table, I slump down in my seat, the world spinning a bit. I grab my napkin and discreetly wipe the drops of the shot that dripped down my dress. My cheeks burn when I see Brandon making his way back to his seat, his gaze fixed on me. The energy between us is electrifying and uncomfortable.

He has no right to act like a jealous boyfriend. This is Livvy's night, and he's making it all about me.

"Well," I say loud enough for half the table to hear. "I'm feeling a little tipsy, so I should probably head home."

Brandon's gaze shifts to his glass of wine.

"We'll be wrapping up soon," Livvy says, her eyes full of concern. "Cole and I can take you home if you can wait ten minutes."

"No, that's okay." I smile slowly, the alcohol fizzing in my veins making me bold. "I just texted a friend, and he's already headed here to pick me up."

Brandon's head jerks up, his eyes narrowing on my face.

Fuck, why did I do that? There's no reason to make him jealous when it won't do either of us any good. Alcohol must be making me impulsive.

As soon as I make it to the concrete outside, I pull up the Uber app. I'm just about to order a car when a voice halts me.

"I know what you're doing," a deep voice resonates behind me.

I flip around, letting my skirt dance around my thighs. "What am I doing?"

He walks in my direction, his gaze hardening with each step. "You're punishing me. Using this opportunity to show me how much I'm losing."

His slight emphasis on "much" makes my heart flutter, but I manage a scoff. I cross my arms over my chest. "I'm not punishing you. I'm just trying to move on."

Something flickers behind those dark eyes... Something that looks almost frantic. He looks away and takes a deep breath. "With Zac? Are you... Is it serious?"

The words are so faint. I can barely hear them. But the pain behind them is unmistakable. How could he be so silly? How could he think I want Zac when I love him with all my heart?

Probably because Zac is my age.

"No, of course not." My voice is just above a whisper. "It'll be a long time before I can..." I swallow. "Feel this way for someone else."

He flinches as if I hit him. When his eyes meet mine again, they're filled with agony.

"I'll never feel this way for anyone else." The words are hushed. "I'm so sorry, Mariana. I'm so sorry I did this to you."

A small flicker of anger sparks within me, and my skin begins to vibrate. "Stop making this all about you. Everything that we did was my choice. The only thing that's stopping me from being with you now is that you obviously don't want an atheist. Which I understand. I honestly do. It would be hard—"

"Is that what you think?" he nearly shouts, his incredulity as clear as glass.

My anger is doused as if by a bucket of ice water. "How could I think anything else? You said it was about losing my family, but you've already lost them. What's stopping you now from being with me?"

"Mari..." He shakes his head, stepping back. He's quiet for a moment, as if collecting his thoughts. "How could you think... You have to understand that I'm doing this for you." He huffs out a humorless laugh. "I must have some vestige of integrity left that I'm not taking you into my arms right now."

I grunt, coldness clamping around my heart. "For once, I wish you'd choose me over your precious integrity. What does integrity even mean if it makes you hurt someone as much as you're hurting me now?"

He doesn't speak, and I find myself wishing I could huddle into a ball. Hide away from him like a child who feels like she's disappeared when her eyes are shut.

"This right here." He raises a hand. "This is why you terrify me."

I frown, a strange emotion rising in my chest. "What are you talking about?"

He stares at me for a long moment, his eyes strange and remote. "I could worship you. I could give up the God I love. For you."

I swallow. "I'd never ask you to do that."

His lips tighten into a twisted smile. "I know you wouldn't. That's why you're so remarkable, my Mariana. You called to my heart the same way God did four years ago. Except I wasn't afraid of him. I'm afraid of you."

"What are you afraid of?"

His eyes drift from the top of my head to my toes, then back up again. "I already threw my principles into the wind because I coveted you. I'm afraid of becoming so greedy for you that I'll suffocate you. I have this wicked impulse to bind you and keep you all to myself." His voice grows hushed. "Forever."

When I smile and take a step in his direction, his expression grows almost fearful. Is he worried he's not going to be able to stop himself from touching me?

Good.

"That doesn't scare me," I say. "No man could bind me if I

didn't want him to. If you're able to keep me with you forever, it's because I want to be there."

He swallows. "You say that now. But who knows how you'd feel years from now. After graduate school. After giving your youth away to be with an old—"

"Brandon, if you call yourself an old man one more time, I might hit you."

His lips quirk slightly, but that somber expression remains.

I let out a long breath, feeling like my spirit is drifting away with it. "You should go back inside before anyone notices you're gone. And I think we should try not to interact at all at the wedding tomorrow."

His dark eyes fill with pain, but he doesn't say any more.

Chapter Thirty-Three

B randon

The salt-laced breeze brushes against my skin as I stand in front of the gathered crowd. Livvy and Cole have been beaming at each other since the moment they took their positions at the altar, but my gaze keeps drifting to my left.

Mariana.

Her lilac dress dances in the wind. She'd probably wear something like that to her own wedding—something light and bright just like her.

Our wedding.

It would be just the two of us, because my willful Mariana would probably decide to do it on a passionate impulse, like the night I baptized her. Maybe we'd do it at that very spot on the beach. At sunset of course, just like that magical night that changed my life forever.

"You're going to have to officiate your own wedding, Pastor," she'd say in that playful voice.

When mist rises to my eyes, I take a deep breath, pulling my attention back to the wedding. Longing won't do me any good, and there's a job to do, after all.

"I don't know about you, but I'm pretty happy about this breeze." My voice carries over the rhythmic pulse of the ocean. "If I sweat any more in this suit, this could become a really uncomfortable ceremony. For all of us."

A few people chuckle, probably out of relief that I'm not going to deliver a fire and brimstone sermon at a wedding.

"We've come together on this beautiful day to celebrate something so special, so profoundly human. Love."

Don't look her way. Don't do it.

I keep my eyes fixed on Livvy as she smiles up at Cole. He looks at her with heavy-lidded eyes, his smile faint. His hands tremble slightly at his sides. He looks like he can't even believe his good fortune at getting to marry this woman.

I know exactly what he's feeling.

I'd feel the same way if I were standing across from Livvy's best friend.

"Love. Such a small word for something that carries so much weight, isn't it? It isn't just about heart-fluttering, knees-weak, rom-com moments." My voice catches. "It's about understanding, standing by each other when life gets messy. It's about celebrating differences and cherishing commonalities."

Both Cole and Livvy's eyes grow misty. It's their love story I'm here to honor.

I must keep my mind off Mariana.

"In a world that often feels like a tough place, we're here celebrating love—this amazing, divine thing that brings us together. Love, in its purest, truest form, connects us on a deep, human level, yet it also points us toward the divine."

My voice falters, and I take a steadying breath. My gaze once again finds Mariana. Her eyes meet mine, shining brightly.

Is this as hard for her as it is for me?

"And today, right here on this beautiful beach, we're here to bless Livvy and Cole, to honor their journey of love."

As I turn my attention back to Livvy and Cole, ready for their vows, my gaze lingers on Mariana one last time.

Love. It can be as vast as the ocean behind me and as piercing as the sun above.

And it can be painful.

Oh God, it can be painful.

* * *

She's sitting at the bridal table, and her head is thrown back. She has such a wonderful laugh. So bright and ardent, just like her. She laughs with every part of that pretty heart-shaped face. Her eyes alight, and her huge grin shows all her teeth. I can't stop myself from drinking in the sight.

I'm so absorbed in watching her that Sofia's arrival startles me. She's out of breath. "My dad wants to talk to you."

I inhale a sharp breath. "What?"

Her brow furrows. "He promises he won't be too intense. I guess the wedding made him a little emotional, and whatever he has to say can't wait." She smiles faintly. "You know how he is."

Dizziness descends over me, making my pulse beat against my neck. "I never thought he'd want to talk to me at all. He said as much when he confronted me."

She sets her hand on mine. "He was angry. I think he's starting to cool down. To see Mariana's perspective."

My heart lurches. "Mariana talked to him?"

She nods. "She met with me and my parents a little bit after everything went down."

I wish I could unravel every single detail of that conversation from Sofia's mind, but I need to focus on the here and now. Hector wants to talk. That's better than I ever could have hoped for.

"Send him over."

She grins, giving my hand a squeeze before walking back to the other end of the tent. I watch her go before shifting my gaze to Mariana. She's still glowing, smiling at her best friend.

My chest squeezes so tight it's hard to take a breath. I knew this wedding would be difficult, but I didn't think beyond the fact that I'd be close to the woman I love but can't have. It somehow never occurred to me that my own wedding would be constantly on my mind.

The wedding that will never happen.

There's no one for me but her.

I'm thankful to be pulled out of my head when Hector approaches my table. His body language is stiff but not angry. If anything, he seems a little nervous. I've never seen him nervous before.

The sight of it fills my heart with tenderness. If this really came about because he listened to Mariana, he's made real progress in his relationship with her. In the four years I've known him, he's never listened to her on serious topics. Not *really* listened. She's his baby.

Maybe he's starting to see her as a grown woman.

Maybe I should, too.

"You did well today," he says as he sits across from me. "Always a charmer."

I huff. "I don't know about that."

He's quiet for a moment. "I want to talk to you about Mari."

My pulse begins to pound. "Yeah?"

His dark eyes grow intense. "I want to apologize."

"You do?"

"I overreacted. I've always been too protective of my girls." A sheepish smile tugs at his mouth. "It's misogynistic, as Mari tells me. She's twenty-four years old. She can make decisions for herself." He shuts his eyes for a moment. "She loves you. I'd be a terrible father to get in the way of that."

The lightheadedness that descends over me makes me momentarily insensible. Mariana *loves* me? She's never said so.

Did I ever let her? I've been so consumed with guilt, I'm not sure I would have believed her even if she did.

I swallow. "She said that to you?"

"She did. She said she loves you with all her heart."

My own heart soars into the sky. Holy fuck.

This is a woman who speaks the truth. The one I adore for her strong opinions. If she told Hector she loves me with all her heart, she really meant it.

"She said a lot of things." Hector laughs softly. "I'm still processing most of it, but that girl knows her own mind. She always has. Ever since she was little. I don't know why I tried so hard to change her. I should have known it was futile. She's a powerhouse."

An aching warmth fills my chest. He's always been right about that. She's the most remarkable person I've ever known. A bright light.

I could have learned from her from the very beginning, but somehow, I was too stubborn to acknowledge it.

I've been so like Hector in that regard, but he came around sooner than me.

He sets a firm hand on my shoulder. "There was more to your relationship than I thought, but even if there wasn't, I shouldn't have interfered. Brandon..." He shuts his eyes for a moment, and when he opens them again, they're bright and shining. "You have my blessing. I'd be lucky to have you as a member of my family."

I stare at him, my jaw slack. The world around me is buzzing with electricity.

"Thank you," I manage to say, my voice hoarse with emotion. "I love you. I love your daughter. There's nothing I want more than..." I avert my gaze to collect myself.

"I know." He squeezes my shoulder before standing up. "I'll stop blabbering. No need to make a scene at Livvy's wedding." He gives me an intense look. "I think maybe you need to talk to Mari."

I nod, inhaling what feels like the first breath in these two weeks of misery. I want to go to her now. I want to beg her forgiveness for treating her like a child.

But would doing that really be for her or would it be for me? I want nothing more than a reason to take everything I want. To steal her away from her young world and make her mine. Is that desire clouding my judgment?

A moment after Hector leaves the table, Sofia joins me again. "I take it your talk went well?"

I swallow. "It did."

She grins. "He's really trying."

"I can tell. He seems like a changed man."

Her eyes grow unfocused as she stares down at her champagne glass. "Mari surprised us all. I think we're all starting to see her in a different light. Especially me. She's been so helpful since..." Sofia glances around the area as if looking for someone.

Ah, Finn.

She wants to make sure he isn't listening.

"I told her everything that happened," she continues. "And she's given me so much wisdom. I never expected it, but that was probably stupid of me. She's an old spirit."

A chill ripples over my skin.

An old spirit.

Why did I never see it before? Sofia is absolutely right. My Mariana saw the measure of things from the very beginning. She knew that I was so in awe of her dad I was afraid to form my own opinions of her. I saw her as a baby because he did, too. But she taught us both a lesson.

She saw my struggles from the very beginning, all my human frailties. And she gently tried to coax me out of them.

I'm not my father. Interpreting my desire for Mariana—the most precious human being I've ever known—as lust inherited from him was foolishness.

Foolishness that came from terror. I saw the destruction my dad wrought on my mom's life. How depressed and fragile he left her. It was agony to see her so unhappy. There was nothing I could do. Instead, I had to watch her slowly fade away. My precious mother withered like flower petals under the callous sun.

I never wanted to inflict the kind of pain my father did. Not on someone so precious to me.

But I did it anyway. Mariana loves me. Holy fuck, she loves me. And I tried to push her away.

Never again.

I inhale an unsteady breath. "Would it be inappropriate for me to talk to Mariana tonight?"

Sofia's eyes grow wide. "You mean...about your relationship?"

I lift my hand and run my fingers through the hair at the crown of my head, now damp from sweat. "I've been an idiot. A selfish idiot when I thought I was being honorable. I thought I was doing what was best for her."

Sofia's smile grows cheeky, reminding me of my sweet Mariana. "From what I know about my sister, she's the only person she'd ever let decide what's best for her."

The breathless laugh that escapes my chest is almost hysterical. Of course my Mariana would never let me make that decision, but I tried to force it on her anyway.

I've been a fool, and it's time to make it right.

Chapter Thirty-Four

M ariana

Brandon is headed my way with an urgency that sends my heart pounding. His eyes are wild, his brow furrowed.

What is this about?

"Mariana." His voice is choked. "Can I... Can I speak with you for a moment?"

Warmth radiates within me. There's no mistaking the look of longing in his eyes. I nod and stand up from my chair in a daze, the whole world around me growing fuzzy and bright. He leads me away from the crowd, down to the beach. The sand beneath our feet muffles our steps.

Finally, when we've reached a spot away from the noise of the party, he stops. He turns to me, swallowing hard. "I've been a fool." His voice shakes.

I wait for him to say more, but he seems too full of emotion to speak. I stand with him in delicious silence. The setting sun bathes his face in blinding golden light, his thick lashes casting shadows down his cheek. He's so damn beautiful.

I'll remember this moment forever. It will be burned in my memory, like the light of a distant star.

"I didn't listen to you. It was... I hate myself for not seeing..." He shuts his eyes, shaking his head. "Sorry. I'm just overwhelmed."

Lightness lifts at my limbs, making me feel like I could float away. This is the man who delivers sermons with the fluidity of a watercolor brush on a canvas. Now, he's struggling to form basic sentences.

When he opens his eyes, they're dark and intense. "I love you so much it scares me. I was so afraid that I..." He swallows. "I was so afraid that you'd resent me for stealing your youth..."

When his voice shakes, I set my hand on his arm. "It wouldn't be stealing when I'm giving it to you freely. I love you, Brandon. I want you to have my youth and my old age. I want you to have all of it."

His eyes grow misty, sparkling under the setting sun. "I understand what the Bible says about marriage. About two people becoming one flesh. This past week and a half..." He sniffles and wipes under his eyes. "It was like I lost a limb." He shakes his head. "Even more than that. It was like I was disembodied, walking the earth like a revenant. It's only now that I'm with you that I... That I feel human again."

My heart squeezes inside my chest. "Brandon..."

"Mariana." His voice cracks, and tears trail down his cheeks. "Please forgive me. Be with me. Be with me forever."

His words hit me like a wave, making me momentarily dizzy. I sway toward him, and he takes me into his arms. His lips find mine, and he kisses me gently. Sweetly. He reaches up to cup my face, his fingers threading through my hair as his mouth moves against mine.

"I could have given it all up for you, my sweet Mariana. I could have given up everything. Even the church."

LUST

I melt into him, wrapping my arms around his neck. "You'd never have to. You can have everything."

He lets out a low groan. "And I want it all, Mari. I'm a greedy man. It's my greatest sin. And I've never been as greedy for anything as I am for you."

I kiss his neck. "I've wanted you to be greedy for me since the first time you touched me."

He kisses me hard, and heat ignites between us, a blaze of longing engulfing my senses. Every touch, every sigh is a silent pledge.

As we break apart, both of our chests are rising and falling rapidly.

"You're mine after this," he says. "You're coming home with me and never leaving." His eyes grow hesitant. "Is that okay?"

A hysterical giggle bubbles from my chest. "There's nothing I want more than to go home with you. And stay."

We stand without speaking, the sound of the waves crashing in the distance. Brandon's fingers trail down my arm. "Forever?"

I nod, warm trickles running down my face. "Forever."

* * *

Brandon is so giddy he seems drunk, but I know he didn't have a drop of alcohol after he confessed his love. He just stared at me with a tender expression that made my heart squeeze in my chest until the reception ended. After Livvy and Cole made their grand exit in a helicopter, he nearly dragged me to his car, determined to take me home.

Home.

That's what this house feels like now.

"I want you living in this house." He kisses the tip of my nose. "I want to put babies in you." He yanks the hem of my dress up, exposing my lower half. "Right here."

His warm palm touches my belly, and I giggle. "Is that where babies go?"

He smiles ruefully, though his eyes are still wild and dazed. "I think so." He lowers his palm to my naval. "Here?"

I lift his hand from my skin and bring it to my mouth, kissing his palm. "I think you're getting a little ahead of yourself, Pastor."

His smile fades. "Do you want kids? Someday, I mean."

Something wicked rises within me. "Would it change your mind about me if I said no?"

He scowls. "Of course it wouldn't. How dare you even ask me that?"

I shriek when he lifts me into the air and cradles me to his chest. "I want *you*, Mariana Isabel Hernandez. I do want kids, but I don't need them if I have you."

My head is fuzzy as he carries me into his bedroom. My God, I feel like I could die of happiness.

I never thought we'd be here.

"I do want kids," I say dreamily as he sets me onto the bed.

Brandon's eyes alight. "Really?"

I smile at the joy in his expression. "I've always wanted a family, even more so now." I reach up and place my hands on his shoulders. "Now that I've found you."

He leans down and kisses me, his hands roaming over my body. "Fuck, Mari, I can't believe I was so stupid. How could I have ever lived without this?"

A moan escapes my lips as his hands find their way under my shirt, his fingers exploring every inch of my skin.

I arch my back, pressing my body closer to his as his lips trail down my neck, leaving a trail of hot kisses in their wake.

He wastes no time, yanking down his pants and pressing himself inside me. "Fuck!" he nearly shouts after burying himself to the hilt. "I've missed this."

I moan. "Me too."

"I'm not letting you leave this bed for days. I hope you're ready for it."

I hum in response, lost in the pleasure of his hard body covering mine and his big cock stretching my insides.

The next few minutes are fevered and frantic. The room is filled with the sounds of our gasps and moans. Brandon is relentless, but I match him thrust for thrust.

My fingers dig into his skin as I feel my release building, the pressure in my core becoming almost too much to bear. But Brandon doesn't let up, his movements becoming faster and more frenzied as he drives me closer and closer to the edge.

"That's it, my girl," he says, his wild eyes fixed on my face. "Let go. Show me you're mine. Cry out for me."

His words send me over the edge, and I release a shriek, my body convulsing as I ride out the waves of ecstasy. Brandon follows soon after, his own release filling me with a warmth that spreads through my body.

We lie there for a while, our bodies still entwined, our breaths slowly returning to normal. I look up at him, his face soft and gentle, and I know that I've never been happier than I am right now.

Just a few weeks ago, he gave me a similar dreamy look, except that one was edged with guilt.

Letting go of it all is heaven. Here I am, lying in bed with the man I love, and he never wants me to leave.

His smile is sleepy as he strokes my cheek. "I want to make you my wife soon. Does that scare you?"

Warmth washes over my whole body like a gentle tropical wave. Did I fantasize about this moment?

No, my fantasies were much more modest than this. I would have been overjoyed if he'd simply held my hand in front of my family.

"No," I say, and his smile grows. He brushes his mouth lightly against my shoulder.

"I don't want to suffocate you, because I know you have so much life to explore, but I'm impatient to make you mine."

Mine. The word pulls a soft groan from my chest.

"I want to explore with you," he says. "I don't want you to miss out on anything. If you want to travel the world, we'll do it together." He smiles softly. "We'll start by hiking Machu Picchu. If you want to get your PhD after you finish your masters, I'll follow you wherever you need to go to get it. I don't want to cage you, my darling Mariana. I want to fly with you."

His words hit me like a meteor. My God, have I ever been loved like this before?

"I love you, Brandon." My voice quivers.

He grabs my face and kisses my mouth hard. "I love you too, my beautiful, fierce, perfect Mariana."

Epilogue

B randon

She smiles at me as she climbs out of the pool, water gliding over her sun-kissed skin. The sunshine warms my whole body, and fuck if I'm not the happiest man alive.

How is it possible that this is my wife?

She makes her way over to me, smiling brightly. After wrapping her arms around my neck, we're a whirl of lips and skin. Her laugh vibrates against my mouth. "Ethan is right next to us. We're grossing him out."

I smile against her mouth. "He can handle it."

"No, I can't," Ethan says.

Hector laughs from the edge of the yard, standing in front of the barbecue. "That's newlyweds for you, Ethan. We've got another year of this, at least."

"Oh, much longer than that." I kiss Mari's neck. "I'll be nauseating all of you for years to come."

Mari giggles when I nuzzle her soft-as-a-flower-petal neck with my nose. Fuck, I love her laugh.

And I love that it's all mine. *She's* mine. I can kiss her and nuzzle her whenever the fuck I want, even in front of the family I used to fear I would lose.

My wife shoots a saucy smile at Ethan. "Are you sure you aren't jealous? I know you wish you were kissing Lily right now."

Ethan's cheeks grow pink as he rolls his eyes at her, clearly trying to seem nonchalant.

I don't know what happened between him and Lily recently, because for some reason, he hasn't wanted to open up to me. But I'm almost certain they had some kind of confrontation.

Maybe even a sexual one.

About two weeks ago, he started getting flustered and pink in the cheeks anytime I mention her. And my playful little wife loves to take the opportunity to tease him for it.

A smile tugs at my lips as I pull her wet form against my chest and lower my mouth to her ear. "Wicked girl. You just earned yourself a punishment when we get home."

She hums a sweet little sound that makes my dick twitch. "Why do we have to wait until we get home? My parents value the sanctity of marriage. It wouldn't be a sin to have a bathroom quickie."

I let out a low groan. "You're a minx, wife. I need to take you in hand."

She giggles. "Minx. I love the old man words you use."

I lift my palm in the air and bring it down hard on the delicious crease between her plump ass and thigh.

"Oh my God," Ethan groans. "Please stop. You're traumatizing all of us."

A peal of laughter sounds from across the pool. "My mother is watching, Brandon," Ana says.

I wince as I lift my gaze to where Mariana's abuela sits quietly on a lounge chair. Fuck.

"I'm sorry, Luisa," I say. "I didn't realize you were there."

Luisa waves a hand. "No need to apologize, Brandon. Hector was much worse with Ana." She chuckles and takes a sip of her drink.

"I was," Hector says almost proudly as he sets the skirt steak on the grill. "Let's let the newlyweds be and keep our eyes to ourselves. My daughter needs to cleave to her husband."

I can't help but smile at his word choice. Hector is constantly quoting the Bible. So frequently in fact that I've often teased him that I need a damn break from my day job. But in this case, he couldn't have chosen a more perfect word to describe my devotion to this little woman who is now my wife. Cleave means to cling or adhere too. We are bound together as a single unit.

She's my flesh, and I am hers.

"I take that as my dad's permission," my wife says with a twinkle in her eyes. She lowers her voice. "How about that bathroom quickie, husband?"

I grab her shoulders as I stare down at her, trying to keep my lips from twitching. "Meet me in five minutes."

She laughs as she presses up to her tiptoes and brings her lips to my ear. "The bathroom by the guest room. No one will hear us there."

I smile darkly. "Good. They won't hear me paddling your ass for being such a naughty little minx."

My wife's eyes sparkle with mischief as she pulls away and walks inside the house, and as I glance down at my watch, waiting for the time to pass, my heart is so full it could explode.

Love and lust, I've come to understand, aren't so much opposing forces as they are two points on the same spectrum. Like the lightest hues on a color wheel, one has the potential to deepen the other.

That first spark of lust for my perfect Mariana ignited within me on a day just like this one. At a family barbecue that now feels like an eternity ago. And fuck, I'm so grateful that it pulled me in against my will.

She's my life. She's my future. She's my everything.

. . .

Thank you for reading! Want more Mariana and Brandon right now? Sign up for my newsletter by using the link below, and you'll get a FREE second epilogue AND spicy scene!
www.skylermason.com/lust

Next in the Purity series...

Sin: An Enemies-to-Lovers College Romance

This is Ethan and Lily's love story.

Tropes: Virgin hero, sassy sunshine heroine, jealous/possessive hero, and MUCH more!

PRE-ORDER SIN NOW

Author Note

How soon after the epilogue of Lust do you think Brandon put a baby in Mariana like he said he would? Go to my Facebook group and tell me your guess. I'm very active in this group and will respond to your comment as soon as I can.

Mason's Minxes on Facebook

Acknowledgments

My darling Gabrielle Sands, I grow more grateful for you with each passing day. You are the best work wife a girl could ask for and an incredible friend.

My sensitivity reader Sylvia, I could not have written this book without you. Thank you for giving me such thorough feedback.

My editor Heidi Shoham, thank you for making me a better writer with each book.

To my readers, I adore you. Thank you for loving romance as much as I do, and for making it possible for me to write the series of my heart.

Printed in the USA
CPSIA information can be obtained
at www.ICGtesting.com
LVHW041230091123
763265LV00076B/2728

9 781088 073810